# Arielle Immortal
## Seduction

### *The Immortal Rapture Series*
Volume 2

## Lilian Roberts

Cover Design by Shari Ryan
Edited by Jacy Mackin

Previously published as *Arielle Immortal Seduction*,
Self-published, 2013

*This is a work of fiction. Names, characters, places, brands, media, and incidents are either the product of the author's imagination or are used fictitiously. Any resemblance to similarly named places or to persons living or deceased is unintentional.*

ISBN 978-1-945415-09-8

Library of Congress Control Number: 2014904120

*For my Sister*
*I miss our chats. I miss your laughter.*
*I miss you! The void you left is vast*

# Chapter 1

SEBASTIAN HAD BEEN IN NEW ZEALAND for almost two weeks and Arielle hadn't spoken to him once. She hadn't been able to call him because his number was on her mobile phone, and she couldn't find the phone anywhere. She was sure that it would turn up sooner or later. She spent her days in class, shopping with Gabby and Eva, and studying for exams. She managed to keep her mind on the books, but she ached for Sebastian's touch every moment of every day.

She went out with Paul a few times, sometimes to nightclubs for drinks. He was an attentive friend, but she could feel that something was different between them now. She didn't want to ask him about it, though, and encourage any heart-to-heart conversations about their friendship. At times, the temptation to clear the air was dangerously strong, but her instinct to leave it alone was stronger.

Paul called her house to tell her that he had found her phone under the back seat of his car and that Sebastian had been trying to reach her. There was an undercurrent of jealousy in the tone of his voice.

Arielle frowned and stifled an oath. *How stupid of me,* she thought to herself as a flare of guilt spread across her mind. She had promised Sebastian she would have her phone with her at all times. Anxiety spread through her, partly because of Paul's jealous tone but mostly because she knew Sebastian would be furious with her about Paul answering her phone.

"Please bring the phone to school tomorrow," she said.

"I will," Paul replied, his voice short.

*What's wrong with him?* Arielle thought, but she chose not to ask. "Thank you, Paul, I'll see you tomorrow in class," she said quickly and ended the call.

When she got the phone back, the battery was dead, and it wasn't until later that afternoon that she retrieved nine missed calls, four voice messages, and several text messages, all with the same question, "Where are you? I've been trying to contact you." His voice on the first message, was warm and eager, but by the third and fourth voice message his voice was clipped, filled with frustration.

Arielle scowled at the tone of his voice, but she understood why he was disappointed with her. She wasn't very happy with herself right now, either. She regretted missing a bunch of his calls, but there was nothing she could do about that now. When they finally spoke, she tried to explain to him what had happened. She emphasized how much she had missed him, but Sebastian was not happy about the amount of time she was spending with Paul. She felt vaguely dissatisfied with the way their conversation had ended.

The third Friday Sebastian was gone, Arielle and her friends decided to go out. They were at their regular pub, laughing and talking, having a lot of fun. The conversation was stimulating and before long it was after midnight. Arielle was tired, her eyes were watering, and her throat ached. She began to feel like she might be coming down with a cold.

She was busy talking to Frances, a new girl, and was engaged in their conversation when she heard someone making a lot of ruckus sitting in the seat next to her. She looked over and noticed a tall, blond, and extremely good-looking guy gazing at her and Frances. There was an arrogance about him; he had that kind of expression that proclaims, "There is no female on earth that would reject me."

Arielle turned away from him and continued her conversation with Frances, but he leaned closer and rudely interrupted, "Hi. I'm

Matt, and you are?"

"My name is Frances," her friend said excitedly.

Arielle glanced at her, surprised that anyone would fall for that kind of guy.

"Are you here with anyone in particular?" he continued, looking directly at Arielle.

"No," Frances replied. She was either clueless or determined to take advantage of what she thought was an opportunity.

Arielle was a little uneasy and slightly startled. She couldn't tell what this man was thinking; he didn't belong to that special group of people in her head. He was looking at her like he was getting ready to start some superficial game playing. She was sure that he was directing his questions at her, but she got up and let Frances pick up the game since she was clearly interested.

She walked over to the bar to tell Eva and Ian that she was leaving.

"Is something wrong?" Eva asked.

"No, I'm just tired. It's almost one, and I'd like to get to bed. I think I may be getting a cold." They both hugged her, and she started to walk toward the bar exit.

"Where are you going?" It was that rude man again, his voice right next to her ear. Arielle turned and looked at him startled, but she didn't stop walking and didn't answer.

"I think you're very beautiful, and I'd love to get to know you better," he said as she increased her pace.

"I'm not interested," she said.

"Aren't you interested to know anything about me?"

"No, not at all."

"You don't look to me like you're not interested," he said with an insidious grin on his face.

His words took her by surprise. She was close to the exit now. She stopped and turned to face him, an annoyed look on her face. She hesitated for only a short second, "What would ever give you that impression?" she snapped.

He closed the distance quickly and pulled her close forcefully. He leaned forward and kissed her on the lips.

Shocked, she drew back and slapped him. He put his hand on

his cheek and just smiled.

"I can't understand why you're so mad," he said. "I just want to be friends and have some fun together."

"I have plenty of friends," Arielle said. "I don't need your friendship, and I'm not interested in anything you have to say, so please go away."

She started to walk towards the door again, but he grabbed her wrist and pulled her back. Arielle's jaw nearly dropped. She whirled around to face him and tried to snatch her hand back, nearly losing her balance.

"Let me go, you idiot," she hissed.

He kept smiling, totally unaffected by her outburst. "Don't go," he said. His voice was hard. His eyes conveyed that he had drank too much. "I think you like me, but you don't want to say it," he said. His voice had taken on a luring overtone.

"I think you see things that aren't there. You need to let go of me because if you don't, I'll scream." Arielle's heart raced, but her voice was surprisingly composed.

"I find you very exciting, and if you have a drink with me, I promise I'll behave."

"I'm involved with someone, and I don't want to give you the wrong impression. Please let go of my hand. I hate to make a scene, but I will if I have to."

He finally let go of her arm but said, "I don't see any ring on your fingers, so I know you are neither engaged nor married. I'm not giving up."

"You can do whatever you want to do, but I'm telling you one more time I'm not interested. I have a serious boyfriend. You're wasting your time."

"Oh, but you don't know me," he said, chuckling in a distasteful way. "I never waste my time on anything I don't think I can have."

Arielle suspected his attitude was related to his drinking, but she wasn't interested in analyzing him. She wanted to get home and go to bed.

"Hey, Arielle, are you leaving?"

She turned and saw Paul walking in. Her face lit with pleasure, and she grinned wide. A delightful feeling of relief overwhelmed her. He came close to her, wrapped his arms around her, and gave her a kiss on the cheek. He was warm and cheery. There was no hint of the jealous disposition she had detected in him during their last awkward conversation about Sebastian.

"Did you just get here?" she asked.

"Yes, I had to go back home to get my wallet. Nothing is free," he laughed, and Arielle joined in. She was so relieved to see him and grateful that he had gotten her out of a difficult situation.

"Are you okay? You look a bit pale."

"Oh, I think I'm getting a cold, and I'm tired," she said, and looked down at her shoes, trying to hide her anxiety. Something in her voice made him look at her quizzically. Reaching out, he hugged her again, and she returned his hug affectionately. Paul was one of her best friends. She liked spending time with him and hoped that Sebastian would get over his jealousy. She got distracted when out of the corner of her eye she saw Matt watching them intently. His gaze was creepier than his appearance. At least he wasn't coming closer. Arielle relived the distress she felt when he had grabbed her wrist. She quivered and pressed her eyes shut for a long moment. She shoved the weird feeling out of her mind, and when she opened her eyes, she found Paul watching her carefully.

"What is it?" he asked. Looking past her, his gaze fell on Matt. "Is there a problem?" he asked again, without taking his eyes off Matt.

"No, I just don't feel very well," she replied quietly.

Paul sensed her uneasiness and arched an eyebrow. "It doesn't seem like nothing to me," he said and rolled his eyes. "Are you all right?"

She hesitated to speak but then chose to remain silent. She glanced quickly toward Matt. He was still there staring at them.

"Do you want me to take you home?" Paul interrupted her thoughts. "It's no trouble at all."

"Oh, please, that'd be great," Arielle said, trying not to be overly enthusiastic. But she didn't want another encounter with Matt. She felt much safer going home with an escort.

Paul put his arm around Arielle, and they walked out. As they drove home, a tense silence filled the car.

"What happened back there?" Paul finally broke the quiet.

"Oh, there was a guy trying to pick me up. He was drunk, and he made me nervous," she muttered.

"You should've told me," he said protectively. "I would have taken care of the creep right then and there."

"I didn't want to create any problems for you," she said.

"That wouldn't have created a problem for me, sweetheart," Paul snorted. "But it would have created a huge a problem for the creep," he added, laughing quietly.

Arielle chuckled at the smug tone in Paul's voice and pressed his hand gratefully with her own. A long silence followed as they both fell deep into thought. Arielle got the feeling that something else was bothering Paul. She didn't want to ask but felt a caring urge rise inside of her from wanting to be there for him.

When Paul pulled up to the flat, Arielle cleared her throat and decided to ask the unspoken question that had been lingering between them. "Paul, I've noticed there is something strange about you lately. What's going on? Can you tell me?" Arielle asked, gently.

"Do you mean what's wrong with me besides that fact that I'm in love with you and you are in love with someone else?" A dash of sadness was in Paul's voice.

Arielle turned to face him, stunned. She closed her eyes for a long moment and took a deep breath. "For the love of God, Paul, I thought we had cleared the air about that a while back."

He shrugged, and a smile brushed his lips but swiftly disappeared. "Please forgive me, I didn't mean to say that," he said apologetically.

She watched him carefully and remained quiet, giving him time to say what was on his mind.

He drew in a deep breath and seemed lost in thought. She smiled dimly and snapped him out of his trance. "Paul, what else is wrong? Please talk to me."

He shifted slightly and gave a nervous laugh. "I think there is something going on between my parents. They're hardly talking to each other, they are arguing a lot. And they're not sharing the same bedroom any longer."

She looked stunned. "Have you tried to talk to them about it?"

Paul's face paled. "No, they seem to quiet down whenever I go home, and they never say a word. But I know things are not right. I have a feeling that my father may be cheating on my mum."

"I'm so sorry, Paul," Arielle said. "They are in a very challenging business and around a lot of beautiful people. I'm sure they have to deal with enormous temptations."

"I understand all that. But he doesn't have to be submissive to every shallow bimbo he encounters just because she's beautiful."

Arielle was quiet. She knew that she didn't have any good solution for Paul's problem. Nothing anyone could say would make him feel better about a situation like this.

"I'm so sorry, Paul," she said again. "I hate to see you hurting." She reached over and gave him a kiss on the cheek. He smiled and gave her a grateful look.

"Thanks, Arielle," he said. "I feel better just being next to you."

"Well then stay *next* to me," she said. "Because I like to see you happy. I've been worried about you the last couple of weeks. I wish you had said something to me about this. I thought maybe you were mad at me."

"I love you, Arielle," Paul said, shaking his head. "Even though I know how you feel about Sebastian, and I do respect your decision, I can't stop loving you. Anyway, I hope you can forgive me."

"I feel privileged to know that you love me," Arielle said. "I'm just sorry that I can't return your love in the same way. But I'll love you as my friend forever. I'll be here for you anytime you need me. You can count on me for that."

He leaned over and kissed her softly on the lips, and she didn't pull back. He needed her; she could see the tears in his eyes. His kiss felt like a call for love and understanding, not a sexual thing, and she was glad to kiss him back, as a friend.

"Are you all right?" she asked gently after he pulled away.

"Yes, I'll be okay, don't worry about me," he said as he stepped out of the car. He walked around and helped her out. After a warm hug, Paul made sure she got in the door safely, and she waved as he drove away. She went to bed and fell asleep immediately.


The next day, Sebastian called to tell Arielle that he was going to be away for a much longer time. "I just can't wait that long," she said, sighing deeply. She could hear him chuckle with pleasure at her longing for him.

"Do you miss me?" he said.

"Just a little," she lied.

"Well, then, I may have to stay away a little longer, to make sure you miss me a lot," he teased.

"I miss you more than life itself," she replied. "Will that make you come back tomorrow?"

"I miss you too, baby, but I need to finish up here. Don't worry, I'll be home as soon as I possibly can," he said, laughing quietly.

"I'm glad you are amused while I'm dying here."

"Arielle, your face is in my mind constantly. I'm having difficulty getting my thoughts together. All I seem to be able to do is to think about you. You are in for big trouble when I get home," he said, laughing again.

"I can't wait to see you!"

"Arielle, just one more thing. Please don't worry if there are lapses of time between my calls. I'm facing some serious issues. However, I'll try to text you every chance I get."

Arielle groaned. "What do you mean by 'lapses of time'?" she asked glumly, unease sweeping through her.

"It may be a couple of days between calls, and maybe sometimes even longer. I don't want you to worry; it just means that I can't break away to talk. But like I said before, I'll text you." A long, awkward silence followed.

"Arielle, are you there?" he prompted.

"Yes, I'm here," Arielle mumbled.

"What's wrong?" he asked anxiously.

*What kind of a ridiculous question was that?* She thought. "I hate being away from you," she whimpered.

"I love you more than life," he reassured her, but she remained deliberately silent. "Arielle, did you hear me? I love you," he whispered, his voice filled with emotion.

"I love you, too." She spoke lightly; her voice overwhelmed with disappointment.

"Arielle!"

"What?"

"What's wrong, baby?"

"Oh, for God's sake, Sebastian, I miss you. I want you to come home; I want you here with me!"

Sebastian smiled, his heart filled with joy knowing she wanted him home. "I love you," he murmured. "Try to understand, I'm doing this for both of us. This is all about the security of our company. Yours and mine."

Arielle knew he was right. "Okay," she replied. "Anyway, it's not like I have a choice."

"I'm sorry," he said and chuckled again. Arielle was a constant heavenly thought in his head, and one he couldn't simply set aside, even if the issues he was facing were quite complicated.

"Don't feel sorry for me, I'll survive," she said petulantly.

She heard his soft chuckle. "I'll call you soon, I promise. Miss me!" And he was gone.

 *Chapter 2*

**IT WAS AN EASY DAY AT SCHOOL.** Arielle had only two classes that day. As she walked to the car alone, her mind was thousands of miles away. She was thinking of her gorgeous boyfriend when a voice made her jump.

"Hey, there."

She spun around and saw that Matt, the rude jerk from the night before, was gaining on her, a wide smile on his smug face.

"Hi," she said reluctantly. Her expression was impassive, the tone of her voice cold.

"How are you?" he asked.

"Oh, I'm okay," she said, looking around to see who was nearby. Matt made her very nervous.

"I wanted to apologize for my behavior last night," he said. "I had too much to drink, and I'm not sure what I said. But whatever it was, I'm sorry about it."

"Thanks," she said, walking quickly as if she were in a bigger hurry than she was.

"Is Paul your boyfriend?"

"No, he's one of my best friends," she replied.

"So, where is your boyfriend?"

"What is it that you want from me, Matt?" She braced for an

argument.

"I'm only trying to be friendly. I moved here at the beginning of the year, but I don't think I've ever seen you before."

"Where did you move from?" she asked, curious in spite of herself.

"Frankfurt."

"Frankfurt? Are you German?" she asked, surprised.

"Yes, I am."

"You have absolutely no accent."

"My parents are English, but I was born in Germany. After my father had retired we stayed there, but we spoke English in the house."

"Oh," was all she said. She picked up her pace. *Why in bloody hell, did I bother to ask anything about him?* She thought. She was in the car now, and it seemed like he didn't want to go.

"Is there something I can do for you?" she asked frostily, desperately wanting to get away.

"No, not really I just wanted to talk to you. You are very beautiful, you know that, right?"

She kept looking for her keys silently. She hoped she could get rid of his undesirable presence.

"Arielle, I would love to take you out to dinner or a film. I know you have a boyfriend, but he isn't here right now, and I just think you are very nice, and I would love to get the chance to know you."

"Thanks, I appreciate the offer, but I don't think so." There was something about Matt that turned Arielle off. She wasn't sure what it was that bothered her about him, but she didn't want him anywhere near her.

"Okay then, I'll see you later," he said, walking away and looking a bit pissed off. Arielle was relieved he was gone, and she instinctively shuddered, as if trying to shake off the bad vibes that emanated from him.

Her phone rang as she got into the car. "Hey, do you want to catch a film?" It was Paul.

"I've got a few things I have to do first, but I'll call you when I'm done and if there is a film that works out for us, then sure, I'm game."

"Okay, I'll wait for your call."

Arielle smiled happily. She loved spending time with Paul. She stopped at the dry cleaners and the store to pick up a couple of things for the flat and then headed home.

She took a quick shower, changed, and then called Paul. "You can come and pick me up," she said. "What shall we see?"

"*Inception*," said Paul. "I heard it's really good."

Arielle agreed, but when they got to the theater, she wished she hadn't. Matt was there with a friend of his.

"Hello," he said. Arielle inwardly frowned and looked at him only briefly. Matt didn't belong to that special group of people in her head, but his friend did, and she didn't like what she saw in his thoughts.

Matt and his friend went into the same screening room as Arielle and Paul. They didn't sit very close to them, but Arielle could see Matt staring at her with a look that made her uncomfortable. She wished she could hear his thoughts, but since she couldn't, she was aware only of a vague feeling of menace.

As Paul came back with popcorn and the lights went out, she clearly heard Matt saying to his chum that he was going to teach her a lesson by the end of the month. She was shocked to realize that she heard Matt's words through his friend's mind. *I knew it!* She thought. *He's a weasel, just like I thought.*

Clearly he was a liar, and his motives were less than honorable. Everything about this bothered her. She was unable to pay attention to the film. She caught little parts here and there, but she knew she was going to have to see it all over again if she wanted to understand the story.

As she and Paul left the cinema, Arielle's mind was clearly somewhere else. Paul, always sensitive to her moods, put his arm around her and looked at her inquiringly.

"What's going on in there?" he asked, pointing to her head.

She leaned close to him and whispered, "Paul, I don't trust that guy, Matt. He is pursuing me and making me uncomfortable. I want you to keep an eye on me when we are out. I have a terrible feeling about him, but I'm not very clear what the feeling is about."

"Do you want me to have a talk with him?"

"No, please do it my way, just in case I'm wrong."

"Okay, I'll keep an eye on him," he said. He smiled and gave her a kiss on the cheek. She hugged him fondly, and they walked to the car.

The next evening Gabrielle and Eva were going out with their dates. Before leaving, Eva looked at Arielle with that mysterious look of hers. "I don't feel good about you staying here alone, Arielle," she said. "I have a bad feeling about it."

"Did you have a vision again?" Arielle asked.

"No, not a vision. It's just a very strong feeling about you being hurt. I wish you would come with us."

"Eva, I'm going to lock the door and stay home. I need some time alone. Nothing is going to happen. Go now and have fun." She kissed them goodbye, and they left, still looking worried. But Arielle was looking forward to the chance to relax, read a book, and wait for Sebastian's call. She smiled at the thought of him. She took a long leisurely shower, changed into her pajamas, and picked up a book to read.

Around seven-thirty the doorbell rang. Arielle opened the door and realized instantly she shouldn't have done so. *Bloody hell!* She thought.

Matt stood at the door, wearing his usual arrogant smile. "Hello, Arielle, can I come in?"

"What do you want?" she asked. She tried to keep her voice even and light, but it was hard to do.

"I want to talk to you."

"I'm sorry, but I'm busy."

"You're not busy, and you're alone," he said. "Your roommates are gone, there is nothing to keep you busy. Not too busy for me, anyway."

Her mouth fell open. "Have you been following me?" she asked.

"Mmmm, you could say that," he said with a disgusting smile.

"I think you'd better leave," she said, her voice angry and firm.

"I'll leave when I'm good and ready," he said, and pushed Arielle inside, closing the door behind them.

"Matt, what is it that you want from me?" she said exasperatedly.

"You. I. Want. You," he muttered, each word clipped. "And I'm going to have you. You're not the Miss Goody Two Shoes you think you are, and I'm here to teach you a lesson."

Fear shot through Arielle's body as she reached up to her neck and realized that she had taken her necklace off when she took a shower. She panicked and tried to run to the door, but he blocked her way and grabbed her arms.

"Let go," she said with a firm, tense voice. "Let go of me now or I'll scream!"

He snaked his arm around her waist and pulled her hard against his chest. He clasped one of his hands over her mouth, and for a startled moment his penetrating gaze made her wonder if he could read her mind. "If you scream, I'll hurt you, I'll hurt you bad," he hissed. His lips brushed against the side of her face. "Try to go along with this, Arielle, and enjoy yourself, because it's going to happen," he said sharply.

*Oh, my God! I can't believe this is happening,* Arielle thought, her brain frozen with fear. *Why didn't I listen to Sebastian and keep that bloody necklace on me at all times? What am I going to do?*

Seeing no way out, and with no one to help her, she knew she would have to fight. It was her only choice.

With his free hand, he ripped her pajama top open. His eyes widened, and a nauseating smile painted his face. "No bra. Excellent!" he exclaimed. "So, you were waiting for me," he added and laughed out loud. His eyes were red and wild with a mad, ugly desire. As he pulled her closer and started to rub himself against her body, she felt the floor shift beneath her feet, and vomit climbed her throat. She pushed him away as hard as she could and tried to get away, but he grabbed her hips and pulled her against his groin. He groaned.

She tried to scream, but he covered her mouth with his, and she could smell the alcohol on his breath. He grabbed her arms and held them together with one hand as the other grabbed her breasts and squeezed them so tight that tears run down her face from the pain. He ran his tongue down the column of her throat. She started to sob.

"Please, Matt, don't do this, you don't want to do this. God, please stop."

"I asked you nicely, but you didn't want to play nice. I told you that I always eventually have what I want, and you are what I want."

He crushed her lips under his one more time as if he was trying to devour her whole mouth. Tears ran down her face as he pushed her down. She hit the floor so hard it felt as if every bone in her body shattered. The pain was unbelievable. He pulled her pajama bottoms down, straddled her, and started to stroke her. Anger and frustration turned his body to steel ready to crush her.

Arielle fought back with all the strength she had. She cried and pleaded with him, but he wouldn't stop. He was like a wild animal, and she was losing the fight. She felt completely exhausted. *Please God*, she prayed silently. *Please help me.*

She tried to get out from under him, but he had her pinned down with his weight. She was crying so hard she couldn't stop her body from trembling. Fear had taken over her.

He tried to force her thighs apart, and she kneed him in the groin. He let out a groan, cursed out loud, and slapped her so hard she thought her jaw had dislocated. She nearly passed out.

"You will pay for that, bitch!" he said, spitting the words out. He was squeezing her so tightly the pain was unbearable. He was all over her, and now he was excited, wild, and angry. He pulled his pants down, and she closed her eyes as she slipped into unconsciousness.

The next thing she knew, Gabby and Eva were staring at her in horror. She looked at them with terror-filled eyes.

"What in bloody hell happened here?" Gabrielle cried out.

Arielle tried to speak, but no words came out. She began crying uncontrollably, looking around the room, terror covering her face.

"Don't worry," Eva said. "Troy got Matt away from you. He's holding him outside until the police get here."

Eva put her arms around Arielle and hugged her tightly. Tears were still running down her face, but they were tears of joy now.

"My God, Arielle, you are bruised all over," Gabrielle said.

"Gabby did… did he… did he…" She couldn't finish her sentence. "I can't feel my body at all," she whimpered, covering her face with her hands.

"No, he didn't," Gabrielle answered, with a tone of grim satisfaction, adding, "We got here just in time. Eva made us come back. She knew something was wrong."

"Oh, thank you, Eva, I love you so much!" Arielle cried, lying back down again and closing her eyes. She didn't let go of her friends' hands, and they didn't try to pull away from her. They just held their arms around her, and she felt safe.

A short time later, a policewoman came into the room and motioned to both Gabrielle and Eva to approach. Eva made sure the blanket they had draped over Arielle was still protecting her naked body before she stood up. She gave her friend a reassuring smile, and turning, she followed Gabrielle to talk with the policewoman at the entrance of the flat. Arielle lay trembling on the floor, unable to move and closed her eyes. It wasn't long before a warm hand touched her forehead. She opened her eyes and regarded the kind face of the policewoman apprehensively.

"How are you feeling, dear?" she asked Arielle.

"Not so good," she murmured, voice full of agony and tears in her eyes. She could feel excruciating pain traveling throughout her body.

"Can I ask you a few questions? Do you think you feel up to it?" the policewoman asked kindly. "If not, I'll wait until we get to the hospital."

"Yes, I can," Arielle said softly. With both hands she clasped the end of the blanket and pulled it tight all the way up to her chin. Her move didn't escape the policewoman, but she was familiar with that type of reaction from traumatized victims. Suddenly, the unmistakable sound of angry voices came from outside. Arielle lifted her head and stared wildly toward the door.

"It's okay, dear," the policewoman said, placing her hand over Arielle's hands. "You are safe now, there is nothing to worry about."

Arielle averted her gaze to the officer and saw her calm expression. Relieved, she forced a smile, apparently convinced she was now safe.

"Can you tell me what happened?"

Arielle sucked in an agonizing breath and told her all she could remember. She was almost done giving her a preliminary report when a couple of paramedics came in carrying a gurney. They smiled soothingly as they checked to make sure she wasn't bleeding. They lifted her aching body, set her gently on the gurney, and moved her into the ambulance. The pain, as she was moved, was agonizing. Arielle feared she was going to pass out again. They covered her with a warm blanket and transported her, along with Gabrielle and Eva, to the hospital in minutes. Troy and Ian followed in their car.

Arielle had been in the examining room a short time when her mother burst into the room, a terrified look on her face. "Arielle! My God, what happened?"

Arielle tried to smile but couldn't; her lip were swollen, and her eyes were black and blue. "Don't worry, Mummy," she said. "I'll be all right." She could hear the doctor assuring her mother that except for the bruising she was fine.

"There was no penetration, but she'll need some counseling following an incident like this," the doctor added, speaking softly so as not to disturb Arielle, who of course was tuned into every word.

"Darling, will you ever stop getting hurt?" her mother said, folding Arielle in her arms. "You're coming home with me," she added. Arielle just nodded and smiled softly.

Gabrielle and Eva were waiting in the waiting room with Ian and Troy. When Arielle and her mum walked out of the examining room, her friends approached them, and they all hugged warmly.

"Thank you for your help, all of you. I love you so much," Arielle murmured, tears in her eyes.

"Arielle, we are going home, but we'll come and visit as soon as you feel like having company," Gabrielle said. The stress in her voice was palpable. She was hurting for her best friend.

Arielle nodded. "All I want to do is to get into the shower and wash his hands off of me," she murmured.

And indeed, as soon as she got home she headed straight for the shower where she used a whole bar of soap and scraped her skin raw. She let the hot water run over her skin for a long time. The heat lessened the pain, and she felt a little better as she came out of the shower. But her jaw dropped when she looked at her naked body in the full-length mirror. There were dark bruises all over her face and body. She looked as if she had been run over by a bus.

Completely exhausted, she fell into bed, but every time she closed her eyes she would see Matt's wild face and his filthy smile.

Lying there in the dark, she started to cry again, her head full of terrible thoughts.

 *Chapter 3*

IN THE DAYS THAT FOLLOWED, Arielle had a hard time accepting that her body was just as clean and pure as it had been before the attack, even though she had not been raped. She was glad that Sebastian hadn't called during this time. There would have been no way that she could have hidden the torment she was going through from him. She knew he would be able to sense her anguish. He did text her several times, and she was able to reply to his texts carefully, hiding her sadness.

A few days after the attack, Gabrielle and Eva called to ask if she needed some company, and Arielle was happy to have them come over. She needed to talk and they were the perfect listeners. They were her sisters. They sat together in her bedroom and Arielle started to talk slowly, expressing the way she felt. This would be the first time she would talk, to her friends about her commitment to abstinence.

"I'm still a virgin," she muttered. Looking down, she clasped her hands on her lap. Silence followed that felt endless. Arielle searched for the right words to continue with her story. She finally stood up and started to pace uncomfortably. Then, she stopped and turned to face her two best friends, regarding them warmly. "You see, I've been waiting for true love and fireworks," she said. "Somehow, even though there was no penetration from that filthy jerk, I feel so dirty. I feel like I'm spoiled. I still feel his disgusting hands and body touching me, and it makes me sick all over again."

Gabrielle and Eva listened sympathetically, but there was nothing they, or anyone else, could do to make Arielle feel better. She would have to work this out on her own, and they knew that she didn't lack courage. She would emerge out of this terrible mishap, stronger and more secure.

It was late in the afternoon when Arielle's friends left. They were consumed by gloom, knowing how their best friend was suffering.

In the first few days after the attack, she cried for hours at a time and slept nearly the rest of the time. She knew she was tormented from shock, but her friends and her parents feared she was falling into a deep depression. She didn't want to go anywhere or visit anyone, and she was pleased to know her friends didn't expect anything from her. Her parents found a therapist for her, and she went each day for a one-hour session. Still, Matt had become a ghastly nightmare that wouldn't go away. He haunted her dreams every night, often with flashbacks of the attack, and she would wake up crying in a cold sweat. She stopped going to classes because she didn't want to face anyone, and she didn't want to discuss the details of the incident.

Her mother was wonderful during this time. She took tender care of Arielle and never brought up the incident unless her daughter did.


One Saturday morning three weeks after the attack, she woke up tired. Her mum came into her room with a smile on her face.

"Can I make you something to eat, darling?" she asked, as she pulled the drapes back and let the sun pour into the room. Arielle smiled and reached out for a hug.

"Thanks, Mum, but I'm not hungry right now. Maybe a little later." She got out of bed and into the shower while her mother picked up around the room.

The water felt invigorating as it flowed over her aching body. Stepping out of the shower, she took a towel and wrapped it around her hair. She grabbed another towel and quickly dried herself.

Turning toward the full-length mirror, she frowned at the girl looking back at her. She could still see the bruises, the cuts on her lips, and bags under her eyes from lack of sleep. She closed her eyes and grimaced as a gradual shudder surged through her body. Sebastian's face filled her thoughts, and her heart thudded uncomfortably. How would he react to this episode? Would he go looking for Matt? She searched for an answer, but there was none. Her shoulders slumped. She squeezed her eyes tight against the sting that was growing behind her eyelids.

"Arielle, are you finished?" Her mother's voice startled her. "Do you need help?"

Glumly she stifled her anguish and feigned calm, masking the misery that cloaked her existence. "No, thank you, Mummy, I'll be out shortly."

She picked up the hairdryer and switching it on; she proceeded to dry her hair. Tears pooled in her eyes and she swallowed hard. Oh, how she wished Sebastian had been here, and that all this was nothing but a bad dream. Touching the corner of the towel to her eyes, she wiped a few runaway tears.

"Where's Daddy?" she asked, emerging out of the bathroom.

"He's in the family room. He didn't want to bother you. He came in several times while you were sleeping to make sure you were all right. He is really worried about you and very angry about the whole thing. Arielle, this is the second time you have been seriously hurt within a month. You can't imagine how that grieves us."

"I'm sorry, Mother. The last thing I want to do is worry you and Daddy."

Her mother gave her a quick hug and left the room. Arielle lay in bed and closed her eyes. How was she going to tell Sebastian what had happened? What if he went after Matt? He would kill him. She didn't care if Matt was dead or alive, but she didn't want Sebastian involved in any trouble. There was less than a month left before he would be home. What if her bruises didn't go away before he returned? How would she ever explain them to him? What if he didn't want her after this? What if he thought that she had brought it on herself?

She sighed, longing for reassurance that Sebastian still loved her, and laughed ruefully at the irony of her saving herself for marriage and then almost losing her virginity to a rapist. *I'm going to have to rethink my decision to abstain from sex with Sebastian pretty seriously*, she thought. *I mean what's the point of it? Don't we truly love each other?*

She was engulfed with intense anger and anxiety, something she had never felt before. It was like everything was her fault. She could have and should have just walked away from Matt, never even spoken to him at all. Maybe that would have kept him away from her. Hadn't she sensed from the beginning that he was nothing but trouble? What had she been thinking?

She sighed. This would never have happened if Sebastian had been here. She needed to hear his beautiful voice. She didn't want him to know about what had happened to her, but she was dying to see him.

Every day, she checked her bruises and counted the days until he would return. Time was passing slowly, and the bruises were getting lighter, but they were still visible. Arielle's pain was much better, but she still didn't want to get out of bed, or go anywhere or see anyone anytime soon.

Her friends came over to visit often, and she was happy to see each of them. She asked Eva to bring her the necklace from her jewelry box.

"Is there a special meaning to that necklace?"

"I know it'll sound silly, but Sebastian says it's a good luck charm that protects the wearer from evil," she said and chuckled. She knew that Eva believed in that sort of thing and inwardly smiled to see Eva look relieved when she put it back on.

"Why did you ever take this off then," Eva chided her gently, "if Sebastian told you to keep it on at all times?"

"I know, I know, I took it off just to take a shower. I never imagined anything like this was going to happen to me in our flat. I'm just so thankful you came back when you did," she said smiling and gave Eva a big hug. "And thank you, Troy, too, for all you did for me."

"It was nothing," he whispered in her ear.

"This is the second time you saved me," she said. "I owe you big time!"

"Don't worry about that. I'll collect," he chuckled. Arielle knew exactly what he meant. Troy was going to need her help when it was time to tell Gabrielle about his immortality.

Arielle asked her friends not to talk about what happened, and they promised to keep her secret. She didn't want everyone at school to know what she had gone through.

Matt's parents posted bail for him, but campus police advised the faculty and campus security that he wasn't permitted back on school grounds. There was a court order for him to stay away from Arielle, but she felt certain that this part of her life would not be over until after Matt's court appearance, which was set for the following month, and where she would have to testify.

She was dreading the day, horrified that Sebastian would learn the details of the attack. She was sure he would be there in the courtroom, and she didn't want to think of what he might do. *How am I going to explain this to him?* She thought, her heart filled with agony.

When she finally returned to school, it was difficult to concentrate on routine activities. She continued to stay at home with her parents, and she couldn't go back to the flat after what had happened there, at least not yet. Her friends understood, and nothing more was said about that.

One day, Sebastian called to let her know there had been some additional complications that would further delay his return.

"I'll try to call as soon as I can. I love you, baby."

"I love you, too," she replied, this time without any complaints.

"Miss me, Arielle," he said, and the line went dead. It was the first time she hadn't tried to keep him on the phone.

She didn't like the idea of being away from him for this long, but she was glad that the additional delay would give her more time to recover from the attack. She knew the next few weeks would go quickly and that her studies would consume a lot of her time. She had no desire to go out, and she didn't want to be around people at all. She feared she might not be able to trust even people that she had known for a long time anymore.

One afternoon, she decided to take a book and sit in her favorite spot in the garden. She had read *Rebecca* before, but it was one of her favorite books, so she decided to read it again. She felt sympathy for the second Mrs. De Winter and the passionate love she had for Maximilian. As she walked under the trees and down the walkway into the garden, she could smell the freesia. Its fragrance made her smile.

The air was clean, the birds were singing, and there was not a single cloud in the sky. She loved this garden so much. It was her private paradise. As she turned a corner, she was surprised to find her father sleeping on one of the chairs, the newspaper open on his chest. He looked tired, and his face was a bit pale.

She went close to him, and his breathing was soft and normal, so she let him sleep. She sat down close to him and opened her book. When it began to grow dark, she woke him up.

"How long have you been here?" he asked, startled.

"I'm not sure," she smiled. "But it has been a while, and you have been sleeping peacefully."

"How are you, Arielle? Your eyes look red and swollen, have you been crying again?"

"Yes, I have. I can't help it, Daddy."

"I'm worried about you, but I know you are strong. You'll come out of this soon," he encouraged her.

"I wish Sebastian were here," she sighed. "I know I would feel better if he were here. On the other hand, I don't want him to know what happened."

"If you love him you'll have to tell him," her father said with a sympathetic look.

"No! No, Daddy, he may do something, and I don't want him to get into any trouble for me. Anyway, everything turned out fine. Except for my ego being bruised," she added with a rueful smile.

"Arielle, this goes beyond damage to your ego. Think about it, think about what you have been through. This guy is a criminal, and he has to pay for his crime."

"Well, he's been expelled from school, and he has been indicted for attempted rape. He's out on bail because of his parents, but he'll pay for what he did. He's a crazy person, and I just want to forget about the whole thing. I want Sebastian to stay out of it. Please,

Daddy, don't say anything to him."

"All right, I won't. However, if he ever finds out what happened, he'll wonder why you kept it a secret from him. I'm just playing devil's advocate," he said, looking at her sympathetically and then adding, "I know you'll do the right thing."

It was getting dark now, and she got up and helped him get out of his chair. He looked a little weak to her, and he was walking slowly. She couldn't remember her father ever looking so weak before. When they got to the house, he gave her a kiss and whispered, "I love you, Arielle. You are my little girl, and I'm so proud that you are my daughter."

Arielle held him tight, and her eyes welled up with tears. She was so happy this wonderful man was her father. She smiled as she helped him go upstairs. Then, she went into the kitchen to talk to her mother.

"Mum, is Daddy all right?"

"I think so, darling, why do you ask?"

"He just looks a little bit pale, and he seems really tired."

"He is on a new medication the doctor gave him for not sleeping very well. I'm afraid it makes him sleepy all the time," she sighed.

"Well, I'll keep an eye on him while I'm here, but I want you to promise me to keep an eye on him when I go back to the flat," she said.

"All right, Arielle," she said with a smile. "Don't worry about your dad. I'll watch out for him."


Three weeks had gone by since the attack, and Arielle started to feel a little more comfortable with herself, her surroundings, and her friends. She was ready now to move back to the flat, and her friends spent a lot of time there with her.

She got text messages from Sebastian almost every day now, and she replied from wherever she was. Some of his text messages were pretty sexy, and they made her smile with excitement. She knew he couldn't wait to see her and she felt the same way.

Paul persuaded her to go to the cinema with him several times and helped her regain her old self. She had tried very hard to put bad thoughts behind her, and move on with her life, the life that she loved and the life she was determined to embrace.

One evening about a month and a half following the attack, Arielle, and her friends were all in the flat watching the telly. Suddenly, Matt's name was all over the screen. Stony silence fell in the room, and she felt a chill move down her backbone as the anchorwoman's words filled the room.

"A young man's lifeless body was found behind an apartment building at Brighton University, following the rape of a college student. His name was Matt Winston, and he had a court case coming up next month for the attempted rape of another college student. The cause of death was strangulation, but the police couldn't find any clues or fingerprints at the location."

The silence was deafening. Arielle's friends were not surprised when she finally said, "Yes! That's justice. He's never going to hurt anyone ever again," and was overcome by a nervous, wrenching sob. She looked around at her friends through the hands that were covering her face, and could see satisfaction in their faces as well, but it seemed to her that there was something beyond satisfaction showing in Troy's face.


With this news, Arielle felt her worries wash away. She didn't have to worry about the trial anymore. She smiled with contentment as multiple feelings swirled in her head. She felt deep sympathy for Matt's last victim, who hadn't been able to escape his vicious attack, and renewed gratitude and relief that her friends had been able to prevent her own rape.

She knew Troy and Sebastian often talked on the phone, so she had asked Troy to promise her he wouldn't say a word to Sebastian about Matt. She wanted to tell him when she was ready to talk about it and not before. Troy promised her he wouldn't say a word.

*I do love Troy,* she thought. *He's such a great guy, and he has been there for me in two very difficult situations. He's like my knight in shiny armor,* she thought, chuckling to herself.


One night, about a week after the news about Matt had broken, the three flatmates decided to spend some time together just talking. They opened a couple of bottles of wine and sat in the living room to discuss their love lives. They hadn't had the chance to be alone and just talk since the beginning of the last term. Eva went first.

"Ian has changed my life. My whole world revolves around him," she gushed. "I never want to be apart from him, ever." Then she chuckled happily. "He's the perfect boyfriend! He loves me, he takes care of me, and he makes me happy. What else is there to ask for?" she concluded, exuberance in her voice.

"So, what's next?" Arielle asked.

"I don't know, but I sure would like a ring," Eva laughed, and they all laughed with her.

Next, it was Gabrielle's turn.

"Troy is perfect," she said, her face filled with excitement. Then with a serious voice, she added, "All I want to do is tear his clothes off every time I'm near him." She looked at her friends and burst out laughing. It was a funny statement coming from Gabby, who normally never talked about her sexual cravings.

"I know what you mean," Eva added with an arch smile and a giggle.

Arielle looked at both of them. "I'm sure Ian and Troy feel pretty much the same way about you," she smiled.

"What about you, Arielle?" Gabrielle asked.

"Well, I've already told both of you how I feel about Sebastian," Arielle said. "He's an amazing boyfriend. He's thoughtful, warm, generous, and pretty incredible in every way. I know I've been waiting for him all my life, and from what he tells me, he seems to feel pretty much the same way about me. I don't think I could be any happier than I am right now."

Arielle knew that both of her friends had been intimate with their boyfriends, and she had told them that she was still a virgin, but she didn't want to discuss her feelings about this particular issue at that time.

As she listened to them talking, she wondered why she had been so afraid to give herself to someone she loved with all her heart, someone she knew she would be spending the rest of her life with.

After a while, silence fell in the room, each of the girls lost in their own thoughts. They had gone through two bottles of wine and were now lying back on the sofa, spilling out various details about their boyfriends. Arielle didn't remember how or when she fell asleep, but when she woke up, she and Gabrielle were on the floor. So sore she could hardly move, she looked around and was astonished to hear Gabrielle moaning in pain as she too tried to get off the floor.

"You guys look pitiful," Eva laughed.

Arielle and Gabrielle looked at each other and saw that Eva was right; there was nothing else to do but laugh. For the first time since the ugly encounter with Matt, Arielle felt truly happy and so fortunate to have such wonderful friends in her life.

 *Chapter 4*

**IT WAS A TYPICAL GLOOMY, RAINY MORNING** in Brighton. Arielle got up to get a cup of tea, picked up a book, and jumped back into bed. It was during that first cup of tea when she had a strong intuition that she needed to go home. She felt strange,, without knowing why, that the most important thing she needed to accomplish for the day was to spend time with her parents. Her father hadn't seemed to be doing that well, and she was worried about how her mother had told her that he had stopped taking his morning walks in the garden for a couple of weeks now.

Arielle could see her mother was hiding the stress she was feeling, and that she was putting too much energy into pretending Arielle's father was doing fine. Something was telling her she needed to be there that day, a vague intuition of some sort. She finished her tea and before long was on her way home.

Everything seemed normal when she arrived, except that her mother was preparing breakfast alone. Usually, her father was part of this activity on the weekends.

"Where's Daddy?" she asked as she came in the door and gave her mum a kiss.

"He wanted to read the paper in the living room today," her mum replied.

Arielle proceeded to the living room. She saw that her father was sitting in his chair, looking like he was reading the paper. The first thing she noticed was his face. He looked pale, and there was moisture dripping off the side of his temples. There were dark circles under his eyes, and his body was sluggish. She felt a cold shiver run down her spine. Arielle ran to her father's side.

"Daddy, what's wrong?"

"I'm not sure," he whispered. His voice was barely audible.

"Are you in pain?"

"My chest feels heavy, and I can't move my arm. I feel weak and a little disoriented," he replied. His speech was uneven, unsure.

"Don't try to move. I'll be right back," Arielle said, and she ran to the kitchen.

"Mummy, please call an ambulance. There is something terribly wrong with Daddy."

Arielle's mum dropped the plate she was holding. It shattered on the kitchen floor. Instead of picking up the phone, she ran to her husband's side. Arielle picked up the phone instead and asked the operator for an ambulance. She quickly provided all the information they needed to get there. A sick feeling took over Arielle as she hung up the phone. This was her father, one of the most important people in her life. "Please God," she prayed. "Please don't take Daddy."


The ambulance was there in a matter of minutes. They put an oxygen mask on her father to help him breathe and administered an IV while they monitored his situation. Arielle held his hand, tears rolling down her face. Her heart was breaking, and she was praying as hard as she could.

"What's wrong with him?" she asked one of the paramedics just before they climbed into the ambulance.

"It looks like he's had a stroke," the paramedic said. "We'll be at the hospital shortly, and they'll be able to evaluate the damage." Then, Arielle's father was on the way to the hospital before she could even comprehend what was going on.

*The damage? What damage?* She couldn't even imagine anything bad happening to her father. Her mother had accompanied her father in the ambulance. Arielle drove to the hospital alone, her heart overflowing with concern. She arrived just as they were taking her dad into the emergency room.

Arielle held her mother in her arms, trying to calm her down as her own heart was breaking. They both sat in the waiting room, tears in their eyes. After a while, the doctor came out and told them he'd had a mild stroke.

"We're going to keep him here overnight to make sure he does all right," he said. "If everything's okay, we can send him home tomorrow."

"Is there any damage?" Arielle asked with a shaky voice.

"We won't know for sure until tomorrow," the doctor replied. "We need twenty-four hours before we can tell if there has been any brain damage. Let's hope that everything will be all right." He smiled and told them not to worry, that they were doing everything they could to make sure he came out of this experience unscathed. Then, he walked away.

Arielle's heart sank as she looked at her mother's face, which had lost its color. She was pale, trembling, and her eyes were full of tears. When they brought her father to his room, he looked as if he had aged several years in a matter of hours. Arielle's mother sat next to him while he slept, holding his hand. Arielle bent down and kissed him on the forehead, tears saturating her face.

"I love you, Daddy," she whispered, hoping he could hear her, but doubting that he could. "I'm going to go for a walk, Mum," she said. "I need to think." She knew she had to face it sooner or later, so she might as well deal with it head on.

Outside she pulled out her mobile phone and pressed Sebastian's number. She had no idea what time it was, where he was, or what he was doing, all she knew was that she needed to talk to him. She needed to hear his voice reassuring her that everything was going to be all right. He picked up on the first ring.

"Hello," he said. "How's the love of my life?"

"Hi," she said, her voice barely audible and clearly distressed.

"Arielle, what's wrong, baby? Where are you?"

"I'm at the hospital."

"The hospital! Are you hurt?"

"No, it's my dad, he's had a stroke."

"Oh, I'm sorry, baby, how is he doing?"

"We won't know until tomorrow. They need twenty-four hours until they can tell if he has any brain damage." There was silence on the other end for a moment, and then he spoke, his voice calm and supportive.

"I'm sure he will be fine," he said. "How's your mum holding up?"

"She is devastated, and I feel so bad. I don't think I have the strength to be optimistic for both of us. How I wish you were here!" she said, and she started to sob.

"Arielle, please stop crying. I'm sure he will be okay. I wish I were there too, but it's hard for me to do that right now."

"I understand. I just wanted to hear your voice."

"I'll be back as soon as I can. I'm in a meeting right now, but I'll try to call you later today."

"Oh, I'm sorry for interrupting your meeting."

"It's okay. You can call me whenever you need to. Don't worry about the time or what I am doing. If I can pick up the phone, I will. If not, leave me a message and I'll call you right back. I love you, and don't worry, your dad will be fine."

"I miss you," Arielle said softly.

"That's all I want you to do when I'm not there. I love you so much and miss you more than you'll ever know. *Miss me*," he said softly, and the phone went dead.


Feeling better, Arielle went back to the room and sat with her father until it was late. He was still sleeping, but his breathing was much better than it had been earlier in the afternoon. She held his hand and bent down to kiss him as she thought how fragile this wonderful man looked right at that moment. A mixture of emotions flooded her. Her heart was breaking, and she was unable to accept the situation he was in. Finally, the nurse asked Arielle and her mother to get some rest and come back in the morning. "I'm sure he's going to be fine," she assured them.

They left the room reluctantly and went home without saying a word to each other. That night, Arielle lay down in her mum's bed with her and held her until she went to sleep. She stayed awake for a long time afterward. She didn't think she would be able to sleep at all, but the next thing she knew sunlight was slipping through the window shades and her mum was up and ready to go. Before long they were on their way back to the hospital.

By the time they arrived, Arielle's dad had already been through all the tests required for the day. He was awake and alert.

"Good morning, Daddy," she said, ecstatic to see him looking so much better. Her mum moved close to him and hugged him, exuding sheer bliss.

"How are you feeling this morning, dear?" she asked, her voice both warm and shaky. Arielle kissed him on the forehead, filled with joy to see her number one man alert and with a smile on his sweet face.

"I feel good," he said. His voice was steady and strong.

"Did you talk to the doctor?" her mum asked.

"Yes, I did. He said he would be coming around again in a few minutes."

Arielle and her mother sat next to the bed and talked quietly, trying not to exhaust Arielle's father. He didn't seem to have any problem with his speech, and his face looked perfectly fine. Arielle felt happy and relaxed as the doctor walked in smiling. *Well,* she thought, *that's a good sign.*

"Good morning," the doctor said cheerfully.

"The good news is he's going to be fine. There is no danger. He hasn't lost the use of any limbs, and he's in good shape for now. We will put him on medication and with a good diet, and a little rest, he'll be just fine. It was a mild stroke. He can go home today." Arielle and her mother let out simultaneous sighs of relief. They each laughed.

"Thank you so much!" her mother exclaimed, wiping her eyes, which were filled with tears of joy.

For the next couple of days, Arielle stayed at home, reading to her father and taking care of him as her mum made his meals and sat quietly with him, holding his hand.

By the third day, he was feeling pretty good. She was happy to see him get up and walk slowly with her mother in the garden. By the end of the following week, everything was back to normal. He was on a new medication, and he was back at work. Arielle was so happy to see him well, with no lasting effects from the stroke. She knew it could have been much worse.

 *Chapter 5*

**IT WAS THE FIRST OF DECEMBER** and nearing the time when Sebastian would be back. The holidays were approaching, and everyone was getting ready to start decorating and shopping. Arielle's mother had already decorated the whole house. She hung beautiful Christmas wreaths with large red bows on every window and door. She had placed Christmas decorations in every room. The halls were decked with branches of holly and mistletoe.

Christmas was a time Arielle always looked forward to. Her mother would decorate two Christmas trees, a very tall one in the family room with its high ceilings, and an even bigger one in the foyer. The stockings hung by the fireplace, and the atmosphere was exuberant.

Exams were coming up the second week of December. Arielle knew she would have to buckle down to get through them. She was happy Sebastian wasn't coming before her exams, so she didn't have to worry about studying while he was there.

It was a Wednesday morning and a typically rainy day. Arielle had a class late in the afternoon, and afterward, she decided to go shopping for a new outfit. The rain had picked up, but she was determined to get out of the flat, and since Gabrielle and Eva were in class, she went alone.

She was searching for a new pair of jeans when suddenly her phone rang. To her surprise, Sebastian's name popped up on the screen. Arielle smiled, and an exhilarating feeling washed over her. Quickly, she pressed the answer button and looked around for a quiet corner so she could hear him better.

"Hello," she said quietly, walking away from the crowd.

"You don't sound very excited, baby." The musical voice that made Arielle's heart beat a million miles an hour was coming from the other end. She could hardly speak from pleasure.

"Sebastian, I'm in a store full of people, that's why I'm talking quietly," she explained.

"Why don't you walk outside?" he replied chuckling.

"I can't, it's pouring rain," she said ecstatically, unable to keep her excitement at bay. "So, are you coming home?" she asked breathlessly.

"Yes, I'll be home tomorrow night," he said. Arielle gasped out loud, and her knees gave in. She could hardly believe the moment she had waited for so long was finally here.

"I can't wait to see you!" she said, and the decision she had made sent a flashing, scorching sensation through her veins.

"I was hoping you would say that," he murmured. "I thought after all this time maybe you had forgotten about me."

"Have you forgotten about me?" she countered, snorting.

She heard his soft chuckle through his next statement. "Forgetting about you would be like forgetting to breathe."

She chuckled with joy. "What's your flight number?"

"Have you missed me?" he asked, ignoring her question.

"Yes, of course, I have, I can hardly wait to see you."

"I'm so happy to hear that," he said.

"I have your face imprinted in my mind, and it's the only thing that keeps me going," she added.

"That sounds pretty serious," he said with a soft titter.

"Yes, it is for me."

"I'll be there tomorrow afternoon. I love you," he said, his voice passionate.

"Not as much as I love you," she countered quickly.

"That depends on what you consider as much."

"You are my whole world, Sebastian. I don't think I can convey the enormity of my love for you with words."

"Arielle, I can't breathe if you are not next to me, you are the focal point of my existence," he whispered, longing in his voice. She was so blissful hearing his words she could hardly speak. He took advantage of her speechlessness to tease her, saying, "So you see? I do love you more." She could feel his grin, and almost feel his sensuous lips on hers. Her body shivered with excitement at the thought of being in his arms.

"Please hurry home," she breathed.

"I can't wait to get my hands on you," he said in a deep sensual tone, making her shudder. He gave her his flight information and she heard him say almost in a murmur, "Miss me." And the line went dead.

Arielle was so overcome with longing her throat felt dry, and her heart beat faster. She picked up her packages and jumped into the car, barely missing the downpour. His amazing face filled her mind, and she smiled as she turned the radio up, letting the music take over.

It was now raining hard, and the sound of the water thrashing the windshield seemed to balance the beat of the music on the radio. She turned her windshield wipers on, and her thoughts drifted to the weekend ahead. She felt completely mixed up and anxious. His last statement had sent ripples of fire across her veins. "I can't wait to get my hands on you," he had said, sending a scorching sensation through her body. "Well, I can't wait for him to get his hands on me either," she said and broke out into a hearty laugh. She had been going back and forth in her mind concerning her feelings about her virtue, and she was at a crossroads. Sebastian would never know how many hours she had spent pondering this issue and wondering why she should abstain from sex after her attempted rape. She was happy that he wouldn't be able to read her thoughts and discover the reasons she was drastically altering her commitment to virginity. What had happened to her was a secret she was determined to take to her grave. Now that she wouldn't have to testify in court, she couldn't think of a good reason that Sebastian should find out what had happened. She had asked all her friends to keep it quiet and never bring it up, and they had promised to do so.

By now, Arielle was sure that nothing could make her continue resisting what she knew she and Sebastian both desired. She wanted him more than she had ever wanted anyone on the planet. The desire ripped through her like a tornado. She focused on the unshakable craving to surrender her body and soul and plunge into the astonishing passion called Sebastian. He was the man of her dreams, the man she wanted to be with, to spend every waking moment with, just fulfilling his every sensual desire. She was longing for him, and she felt thrilled just knowing that he would be home soon. She loved to press her lips at the hollow of his throat and taste the sweet scent of his mouth. She loved to hear him moan with exhilaration and to know that she was his absolute benediction.

Tomorrow night she would be in his arms. She just couldn't wait. She was going to skip classes on Friday because she wasn't planning to leave him alone, not even for a single moment.

*His presence rejuvenates me,* she thought. *I need him more than anything I've needed before. I want to gaze into his beautiful emerald eyes, wrap my arms around his gorgeous body, and kiss those sumptuous lips of his.* Her thoughts ran wild. The excitement made her body ache, and she stifled a groan. It was almost unbearable. She went home to drop off her packages and picked up her books for her afternoon class. Then she sat in the auditorium, buried in her own thoughts, and never heard a word of the lecture. She was nearly suffocating from excitement and could hardly wait for the next day to come.

After class, as she and Paul walked to their cars, she looked lost in thought.

"Are you going out tonight?" he asked.

"No, I'm sorry, Paul, I have a lot of things I need to do tonight because Sebastian is coming home tomorrow!"

"Oh, all right then," he said. "See you later."

She smiled a happy smile and gave him a hug, then slipped into her car. All she wanted to do now was get home, read, and then go to bed. As if maybe that might move the clock faster. She chuckled at the thought and squeezed herself in disbelief, delighted that the day she had waited for so long was finally almost here.

Sebastian's plane took off on time. It was a short flight from Madrid to London. When they landed, he picked up his bags and walked out the sliding doors of the airport. Arielle's car was parked in front. She had a sensual smile on her face. She jumped out of the car and fell into his arms. His arms closed tightly around her as she stretched up to meet his lips, locking them into a scorching kiss that seared their minds in a suggestive promise of pleasure. She pressed even closer and, parting her lips, she let his tongue savor the softness of her mouth. He groaned, and she moaned suggestively.

Sebastian pulled back and sucked in a tight breath. His eyes roamed her face, and he savored the sight. She looked even more stunning than he had remembered her. "Mmmm," he murmured against her lips. "You did miss me," he said and chuckled.

They both seemed to have forgotten about the crowds at the airport. She was exciting and extremely sexy. She had an almost transparent, light blue shirt on and a pair of tight jeans. He remembered her saying on the phone that she had made an important decision, and there had been something slightly different in the tone of her voice.

He didn't want to interpret this the wrong way, but the possibility of her decision having to do something with her commitment to chastity made his throat dry. He wasn't prepared to hope that, that was what she had in mind. He knew she wanted to wait for marriage, and he was determined not to make her feel uncomfortable. He could give her the ring he had bought for her only a few days after he met her, but he didn't want to force her into making a commitment she wasn't ready for.

The thought of her being a virgin was blistering enough to send hot waves of desire throughout his body. He had a feeling Arielle might be afraid that making love with him might be the end of their relationship. He thought he remembered her saying something like that a long time ago, but he couldn't remember her exact words.

*How can I make her understand my love for her is like a volcano that has erupted and will remain, burning and smoldering forever?* He thought. *She'll be my wife and my lover for eternity.* How he wished she could see the clear picture of his feelings for her. He wanted her to feel his heartbeat, but alas, that was never going to happen. His heart had been dead for centuries and would remain silent for centuries to come. But his love for her was alive and very real.

He looked at her beautiful face and knew she was not going anywhere tonight but home with him. He was not going to let her out of his sight. For tonight, he was a completely selfish man, and he wanted her all to himself.

The night before, as Arielle had prepared for Sebastian's arrival, she realized that her mind was made up. Sebastian was the man of her dreams, the man she was planning to spend the rest of her life with, and she was not going to make him wait anymore. She wondered if her decision would surprise him enough that he would want to know what had made her change her mind. She couldn't allow him to take her necklace off and find out what had happened with Matt. The thought of that made her feel so terrible, she bit her lip so hard that only the pain made her realize she needed to relax.

She drove to the airport, parked in front of the baggage claim exit, and turned the radio on. The soft music made her heart feel peaceful as a smile broke across her face. *This must be what they mean by bliss,* she thought, and her face lit up with anticipation. She closed her eyes, knowing it was about fifteen minutes before the plane would land. She was overwhelmed just thinking of him.

"It feels like I've been waiting for centuries," she murmured, chuckling at the irony of her words. Suddenly she saw him walking out through the sliding doors, and the sight of him took her breath away. How could a person who had spent so much time flying around the world and living out of a suitcase walk out and look like an airbrushed painting, not a real person? Every head turned to look at him as he strode toward the car. Arielle was not surprised.

He was so beautiful. Arielle beamed just knowing he was hers. He was aware of people's reactions everywhere he went, but he paid no attention, he just zeroed in on her face. His amazing lips were curved up into the familiar smile that filled her with joy. She flew out of the car and fell into his arms. She wrapped her arms around his neck and plastered her body to his. Their lips met in a scorching kiss that made her body quiver and his senses leap to unimaginable heights. She could feel his excitement pressing firmly against her stomach, and her breathing hitched.

"I missed you so much," he whispered in her ear. Then he pushed her back gently and stared at her from head to toe, smiling with anticipation.

"You look very sexy," he murmured.

"I do?" she said sheepishly, feeling suddenly shy.

"Have you missed me?" he asked as he released her and, taking her hand in his, led her to the car.

"Oh, just a little," she said softly.

"Maybe you want me to leave for a little while longer?"

In answer, she stopped, her hand twined about his neck and pulled him down toward her forcefully. Her kiss was hard, passionate, and her lips parted beneath his. He kissed her back with equal passion. Sebastian felt their lips fuse and burn. He was now sure that she had a plan, and there was no doubt she would reveal it soon enough.

"Get into the car, you are testing my patience," she breathed against his lips.

"Mmmm," he moaned, looking a little surprised. He opened the passenger door, and she slipped inside.

He walked gracefully around the car without taking his eyes off of her and slipped into the driver's seat. "Is there something I should know? You're acting a bit strange," he said. She felt his burning gaze on her. Turning to face him, she noticed that his face showed barely suppressed delight.

"I love you, Sebastian, and I've been a fool," she said.

"Oh? Did something happen while I was gone?"

That special smile was showing up again. He pressed the start button, and the engine roared to life. He pushed on the gas and reached over to take her hand. They drove for a couple of kilometers without any conversation at all. Suddenly, a look of concern stretched across his beautiful face, and his expression turned anxious.

"So… What's on your mind? You are awfully quiet," he remarked, with a sidelong glance toward her.

Arielle didn't hear his question; she was too busy figuring out how to seduce him. This was a new platform for her, one in which she had absolutely no experience. She startled him a bit when she leaned over, wrapped her arms around his neck, and searched for his lips. His scent was like a remedy, his mouth was hot on hers, and his tongue tasted like honey. She kissed him hungrily. When she stopped to take a breath, she could hear his voice coming out in gasps.

"What is going on with you?" he purred, breaking away for a moment and stopping the car on the side of the road. "You are getting me very excited. Have I missed something? Talk to me, Arielle." His voice was breathless.

"I missed you, Sebastian, and...well, I don't want to wait any longer. I'm deeply in love with you and was very affected by your absence. My body aches when you're not near me, and all I want to do is find myself in your arms. There is nothing and nobody out there if you are not with me. I'm through waiting, Mr. Darcy," she added with a soft chuckle.

Surprise spread across Sebastian's face as Arielle's overt craving left no doubt about her intentions. Her statement inflamed him; his eyes never left her face as his hands let go of hers and moved gently around her back and under her shirt. He gathered her closer and kissed her hungrily. He stroked her skin gently with his fingers as she breathed heavily and moaned with pleasure. He ran his warm palms down her lower back and softly tugged her even closer as the kiss turned predatory.

Arielle's senses soared, making her shudder. She reached over and pressed her hand over the length of his excitement, and he groaned deeply with desire. His mouth was hot, and his breathing was elevated. She stroked him softly and his lungs locked. She could feel him rigid and tremble under her hand. His eyes were on fire, and his breath was sweet against her face. He was breathless.

"Arielle! Stop!" he exclaimed anxiously, feeling his passion growing, causing him to nearly lose control of his senses. His mouth felt dry, and his mind roamed uncontrollably, trying to understand her motives. Their eyes met again, and he held her gaze with clear wonder. "You'll be the death of me," he whispered.

She laughed with delight at seeing how flustered he was and

drew herself away from him. He pulled the car back onto the road and drove up to the entrance of the hotel, where they were expecting him. He came around to her side of the car and took her hand. She could see the burning desire in his eyes as he pulled her through the doors of the hotel entrance without speaking.

When the elevator door closed, he wrapped his arms around her waist and pressed her against the paneling. His tongue touched her lips and probed into her honey-tasting mouth with a wild hunger. The fragrance of freesia in her hair was mind blowing. Arielle closed her eyes and inhaled deeply to enjoy his sweet immortal scent. She felt like she could stay in his strong embrace forever.

The door to the penthouse opened, and he pulled her inside, their lips still locked in a wild, possessive kiss. He locked the door behind them and started to unbutton her blouse. He wrapped his arms around her and unclipped her bra, sending a burning sensation through her body. He lifted her and carried her to his bed with a huge smile on his face.

"Are you sure you want to do this?" he asked again gently. He tried to suppress his longing, remembering her previous desire to remain a virgin. He waited patiently for her answer, but she urged him on with anticipation. Slowly, he moved his hands over her waist and pulled her jeans off. His eyes were full of craving at the sight of her naked body. Arielle's heartbeat sped up as he moved faster and pulled the rest of her clothes off. He stopped for a long moment to relish the glorious sight of her naked body.

"You are so beautiful," he murmured. He started to undress watching her reaction carefully. She was looking at him with temptation in her eyes.

He stood in front of her naked with a wild look in his eyes, looking like Michelangelo's statue of David. He was magnificent, and she was speechless. She reached up with hungry anticipation and pulled him toward her. Waves of wild desire rippled across every muscle and every vein when their bare bodies touched. She was soft, sensual, and indulgent. He was all hard muscle, body full of alluring appeal. He was panting hard, and his pulse was pounding painfully. His arms slipped around her and enclosed her body tightly against his.

She stopped breathing. Dragging in a deep breath, he pulled back and looked deep into those deep blue eyes that were filled with passionate desire. He wanted her with an intensity that startled him.

"Are you sure you want to do this?" he asked again, gasping hard. He wanted to make sure she was ready, that he wasn't forcing her to do anything against her will. She reached around his neck, placed her hand on the nape of his neck, and pulled herself up to meet his lips in a ravenous kiss. Her skin burned, and her body trembled with longing. She didn't bother to answer his question. All she could think of was how much she wanted to make love with him. She held herself tightly against his body, and her hands stroked the planes of his back. His mouth circled hers with a wild hunger, his lips moving methodically from her lips to the side of her face, across her jaw line, down her neck, gasping hard. He stopped when he reached her breasts, and she moaned, pulling herself even closer. His lips encircled her nipples, and his tongue stroked them gently. This was the most exquisite, most intoxicating feeling she had ever known. He tugged softly on the tender, sensitive buds and he groaned. The euphoric sensation filled her eyes with tears of delight. His hands moved down from her waist to her hips, around her thigh, making her body quiver. She ached from eagerness as he took his time. She was sure now that he was doing it on purpose. He wanted to make sure she didn't have any regrets if they moved on. He suddenly stopped again and pulled back.

"Arielle, baby, why do you want to do this now?" he asked breathlessly. "I know how strongly you want to hold onto your abstinence." His voice was still coming out in gasps.

Arielle cupped his amazing face and gazed into the emerald ocean of his eyes. She whispered breathlessly against his lips, "I've finally realized there's never going to be another man for me. I want to be with you for the rest of my life." Her lips pressed softly on his, and his lungs seized. He hesitated, and she pleaded, burning with anticipation.

"Sebastian, *please*," she whispered with a trembling voice. She heard him groan with pleasure, and he tried to hide a soft chuckle as she wrapped her arms around him and stroked his back, as she arched her body towards his.

Once more he tried to stop, but his pulse was leaping, and he knew he was not strong enough to refuse her. He found her mouth again, and she stopped breathing. She could feel him, aroused and hard against her skin, and she felt a hot sensation infuse her body from her head to her toes. His movements were slow and calculated, making her beg for him to take her. He had a sensational smile on his face, but she could feel his hands trembling as he tried to hold her tight against him.

"Arielle, Arielle..." She could hear him whispering her name over and over again as he panted and gasped for air. His hands traveled slowly down to her hips and held her tightly against his body. With a frantic move, he pushed deep inside of her through the sensitive thin line of her virginity. Arielle froze as a sharp pain shot through her veins. She cried out. Then, the pain faded just as fast as it had come and bliss took over, setting her on fire. She took a sharp breath and he groaned in ecstasy. His muscles were locked, and his body shuddered with frantic passion. He remained still, astounded by the shocking sensation and sensitivity of the moment.

Arielle too was stunned and enthralled with the amazing sensation. She had never expected anything so powerful. As soon as the pain subsided, the sweetness of the moment enveloped her.

Sebastian was watching her as she shifted slowly and he saw the tranquil reaction in her beautiful eyes. When he felt her relaxing again, his movements started again, soft and slow, and she anxiously joined in. Gradually, they became faster and more intoxicating. For as long as Arielle has known him, he had always been in total control of every situation, but he didn't seem to have any control right now. He was amazing, and she didn't want him to stop. Their lips were locked in a frantic, wild kiss, making both of them moan with exhilaration. If there were such a thing as paradise, it would have to be right where they were at this very moment. He moved slowly, methodically, and with every move, she gasped with pleasure at the extraordinary sensation. He muted her sounds by setting his lips at the hollow of her throat, and she was lost as their souls fused together and their bodies joined in a triumphant bliss. She wrapped her legs around his waist, pulling him even deeper into her as she dug her fingers into his back and he let out a growl of fulfillment.

"Oh, Arielle!" he cried.

The taste of his scent gave her the most amazing joy, and she wanted him to know that she wanted to give him as much pleasure as he was giving her. She pulled his head toward her until his lips met hers again and she kissed him, hard and demanding, as a thunderous climax shattered both of them.

When it was over, a tremor of elation shook her very soul. She wanted him to stay right where he was forever, in pure and utter satisfaction. There was a long, happy silence for a good while. Then, she heard his voice coming out of the silence as a soft murmur.

"I've been roaming this earth for almost five centuries, and I've never felt anything like this before," he said. "This is the most amazing sensation, the most incredible feeling, that I have ever known." He moaned again, and then added, "Arielle, you are magnificent, and I am absolutely and utterly in love with you. There is nothing in my world that compares to the feelings you arouse in me. I'm at a loss when it comes to keeping myself in check around you. I'm incapable of making any sound decisions when I have you in my arms. I feel totally bewitched by you, Miss Lizzy, and I promise to love you forever."

He rolled over onto his side and took a deep breath. She lay on her back in the dark and smiled, completely content. Time seemed to stand still, and she closed her eyes, totally relaxed, thinking of the pleasure of his touch. She was startled when his hands encircled her again and pulled her with a rapid move on top of him. He was smiling, and his eyes looked happy, thrilled.

As for Arielle, she was completely and irrevocably in love with Sebastian. She didn't have any prior experience in lovemaking, but he was the most amazing lover. He made her very essence quiver, and her body burned as if she were literally on fire. Nothing she had ever experienced in her life had ever felt as good as making love to him did.

"Arielle, I love you," he whispered. She lay sprawled on top of him, with her head on his chest and her eyes closed, thinking about how happy she was to be loved by this man. They lay there for a while holding each other, unable to move, looking relaxed and contented. His arm was still wrapped around her waist, and he was holding her tightly.

"What are you thinking?" she heard him whisper. He nuzzled her hair.

"I am thinking about how completely and utterly happy I am," she said with a deep sigh of contentment.

"I love you," he whispered once again. *Will he ever be tired of saying that?* she thought, savoring the moment.

They fell asleep in each other's arms. When Arielle opened her eyes, it was dark. His arms were still wrapped tightly around her, and the thought of what had happened earlier made her smile.

He was awake and looking at her with a warm smile.

"Are you happy, baby?"

"Oh, Sebastian, I'm ecstatic! This is where I want to be for the rest of my life."

"Your wish is my command," he said with a big smile. "Are you hungry? Do you want me to order something for you?"

"I'm hungry only for you," she said.

"Mmmm," he purred. "I love the way you think." She squirmed in his embrace, and he moaned.

"So, how do you feel about spending eternity with me?" he whispered as his lips brushed against her ear, making her shiver.

"I am deeply committed to you. I can't think of anything else I would like better," she said. She let her lips press against the corner of his mouth, making him moan.

"Can I ask you a question? And I want you to be honest with me," he said, watching her with a piercing look.

"What?"

"What made you change your mind?"

Arielle knew this would come up, and she knew she had to make whatever she said sound good. She didn't want him to remove her necklace and find out about Matt.

"Do you want to know?"

"Absolutely," he said. "You had me convinced you were going to abstain from making love until we were married, no matter how tormenting it became for both of us."

"It's very simple," she said, carefully choosing her words. "I pondered that question in my mind for more than a couple of months while you were gone." She paused as if thinking it over again, and then added, "I'm in love with you, Darcy, and there is never going to be another man for me. I want to spend the rest of my life with you. I couldn't think of a single good reason to keep my commitment."

"Well, you are the most exciting woman I have ever met," he said. "And I'm certainly glad you changed your mind." He rolled over on top of her again and crushed her lips beneath his as his arms encircled her again and held her tight. His body was warm and exciting, and it took him but a minute to send her once again into complete rapture.

# Chapter 6

**FOR TWO DAYS, THEY DIDN'T LEAVE** the room. It was the most pleasurable weekend Arielle had ever had, and she knew Sebastian felt the same way. Sunday morning, he ordered room service and after eating they decided to take a walk along the beach. It was a beautiful day. They walked on the warm sand together as they had before, arms around each other. Arielle talked nonstop about everything and anything, often making him laugh out loud with delight.

"You make me so happy!" he said. "I just want to spend my life doing nothing else but making sure you are incredibly happy with me."

Arielle smiled and stood up on her toes to kiss him. Her lips were sore from their wild lovemaking the night before, but that didn't stop her from kissing him again.

"Can I ask you something?" she asked as they strolled along hand in hand.

"Sure, anything," he smiled.

"You said earlier that I was the most sexual woman you have ever known. How many women are we talking about?" It bothered her a bit, thinking about all the women that had been in his arms before her.

"I'm not going to discuss this with you now," he said gently. "That was a very long time ago, actually centuries ago, and there is no particular person that I would care to chat about."

"But there must be a number in your head. Give me an approximate number."

He was quiet, and she couldn't read his face. "Are you angry with me?" she asked when she still didn't get an answer.

"No, but I don't want to talk about something that is absolutely of no importance to me. All I care about is you—from now until eternity."

He put his arm around her and stopped her from protesting by pressing his lips to hers. "Please stop," he said. "Let's not discuss this anymore. I love you and only you."

Arielle dropped the subject even though she was not satisfied with his response. Her curiosity was entirely based on jealousy. The thought that Sebastian had touched another woman the same way he had touched her was driving her absolutely crazy. She refused to believe that he had provided that same amazing sexual experience to any another woman on this earth but her. How many girls had he fallen in love with? How many of them had been serious relationships? And why had they ended? Would some of the women be coming back to claim him, as Arnabel and Savanna had done?

He *was* an amazing lover, a man who knew exactly what to do to make a girl writhe in his hands. If she had been one of those girls he had left behind, she was sure she would be looking for him for centuries to come. How many of them would she have to face up to? She was getting very stressed and, pressing her lips together, she tried to force herself to relax.

She was so completely lost in her thoughts that when he spoke again, his voice startled her. His breath was warm against her ear, sending ripples of excitement through her.

"Where are you, Arielle? Do I need to take that necklace off?"

She reached up, kissed him gently, and sighed deeply. "I'm just so jealous," she murmured.

He pulled her around to face him; his hands slipped under her shirt and moved over her skin softly, raising goose bumps in their path. He bent down and kissed her hard, as his hands explored her body. She indulged in the heat and in her enjoyment of the sensuous planes of his beautiful body.

"Arielle," he whispered. "We are destined to be together for eternity. I have looked for you for over five centuries, and now that I've found you, I'll never let you go. I can't breathe without you, baby." His voice was throaty, and he was gasping again. "I can't imagine a future without you. I'm yours and you're mine for eternity. If you love me, please trust me, and just love me."

She looked into his amazing emerald eyes and held his gaze. Lifting her hands she cupped his face, and rising onto her tippy toes; she pressed her lips on his hungrily. "I do love you, Sebastian, I will love you forever," she breathed against his lips.

"That's all I'm asking from you," he said, and the kiss deepened. His arms snaked around her once again, and he pulled her even closer. They stood there holding each other, lost in each other's thoughts, as their breaths fused and the rest of the world faded away.

She finally pulled back, and taking a deep breath, she took a step back. Reaching over she placed her hand in his and they started to walk again. Arielle continued talking about all the trivial things regarding school, her roommates, and everything she had done in the weeks he was gone. The attempted rape was lingering somewhere in the back of her mind, but she didn't bring it up and she was glad he couldn't read her thoughts. He was smiling again, pleased with their conversation. Late in the afternoon they got back to the hotel, giving him enough time to pack again and make the drive to the airport.

The drive to the airport was hard, and so familiar by now. She was depressed beyond comforting, and no matter how hard he tried to lift her mood he didn't succeed. She cried, asking him to stay.

"Leaving you, this time, is harder than ever," he said. Please don't make it any harder for me. I need to see your smiling face before I get on that plane."

He reached over, pulled her close, and kissed her with a burning desire. The salt from her tears made him crazy. "I'm not sure I'll be able to make it without you, but I have to try," he said. "I need to get back to work. There are still a lot of outstanding issues from my trip to New Zealand to resolve. And you have school."

She gazed into his gorgeous eyes with love and kissed him with longing. "Please hurry back," she said.

"We'll talk on the phone every day, and I'll be back before you know it. I can't stay away from you," he said with a smile.

She watched him walk through the doors with his familiar, seamless stride. Before disappearing from sight, he turned around and winked at her, giving her the smile he knew she loved more than anything. She could see his lips move, saying, "Miss me!" He was her dream, her eternal love. and now he was gone again in the blink of an eye. It was almost like a bad scene from a movie being played over and over again, where she was stuck in the same place at the airport. She watched the plane take off, turned around, and walked towards her car with a broken heart. *God, I already miss him so much!* she thought. *How will I bear being away from him?*

She'd promised her parents she would stop by the house after she had dropped Sebastian at the airport and have dinner with them. Her father was in good spirits, and they talked for a little while before dinner.

"How did Sebastian do with the emergency?" he asked.

"We didn't talk about that, so I'm not sure what happened," she said. "He might tell you next time he's here."

"Did you have a good time together?"

"Yes, we spent a lot of time with our friends, going out to dinner and the cinema," she said. She didn't think she would ever be ready to talk about their intimate weekend with her father.

"Dinner's ready," her Mum called. They had a great time discussing school and her upcoming exams. Following dinner, Arielle went up to her room to get a few things she needed to take back to the flat. Then she thanked her parents for a great dinner and headed out.


Sebastian's thoughts were somewhat more peaceful than Arielle's. He got on the plane and sat quietly staring out the window until the clouds made the city disappear from his eyes. He closed his eyes and recalled the days he had spent with Arielle, as if by telling himself the story again he could relive every moment, up until their sweet farewell. He vividly recalled holding her close against him, lifting her face to his, and piercing through her sapphire eyes. He wanted to feel the warmth of her body and the softness of her skin one more time before boarding the plane. He ached from the pain of leaving her behind. He thought about how he had kissed the tears on her face and tasted the salt that gave him a true feeling of her emotions. He had told her how much he loved her and how much he would miss her as he sealed her luscious lips with his.

He pushed his seat back and tried to remember the details of her beautiful face in his mind. *God*, he thought, *I love her with every part of my existence, every thought that occupies my very soul.*

Making love to her was an experience that had shaken him to his very core. In the last five centuries, following the experiences he had shared with countless women, he had never felt such excitement, fulfillment, and pleasure. He was startled by the ecstasy of the moment when they had fused together. It had been everything he'd dreamed of and longed for and more, much more.

She had been so soft, so warm, and so pure! He moaned quietly, reliving the moment. He felt hot all over again, and he wanted her— now! Making love to her was an unbelievable and completely new experience for him, experienced as he was.

*I used to be so in control before I met her,* he thought. Never had he felt so out of control, but also so blissful. He broke into a smile that made him feel warm all over. *She has put a spell on me,* he thought. *This attraction, this desire, is beyond anything I've ever felt before. All I want to do is to love her, protect her, and spend every waking moment of my existence next to her.*

He wanted to give her a ring, to make her his wife, his partner for eternity. He wanted to take her to exotic places and make love to her day and night. He remembered her sleeping in his arms and he shivered with excitement. It had given him enormous pleasure just to look at her beautiful face as she slept, unaware that he was watching her. Every time he touched her it felt like the first time, with that sweet excitement, pounding heat, and throbbing loins. That had never happened to him before. He wanted to lie down next to her for hours and talk about anything and everything. He loved the sound of her voice, and every time she touched him, he was consumed with an intense feeling that was remarkable, pain and pleasure rolled into one.

He sat there, replaying the scenes from their days together over and over—the softness of her skin, the warmth of her body. God! He longed for her with an unbelievable hunger. Finally he shook his head, afraid he would go out of his mind if he couldn't stop the barrage of erotic thoughts.

He was shocked when he heard the flight attendant announce they were getting ready to land at Biarritz airport. Walking off the plane he felt lonely and miserable, and he couldn't wait to get into the car. He fished his phone out of his pocket and hit the send button. Arielle answered on the first ring.

"Hi!"

He melted hearing her soft, sexy voice. This was the voice he could hear in his ears day and night, no matter where he was.

"Hi, baby," he said, trying to hide his excitement.

"Are you home already?"

"No, I just got off the plane."

"Is something wrong? You sound a bit down."

"I am."

"Why is that?"

"I ache for you, Arielle, I'm lonely and unhappy. I have to have you near me, especially after our last encounter." His voice was quiet and sad.

"I love you too, Sebastian, and I miss you more than anything in this world."

"I don't think I can make it, Arielle. I hurt! This is a new feeling for me. This ache is like nothing I have ever felt before. I'm now jealous even of the air you breathe without my being there."

"You have no idea how much I need you," she replied, her voice soft and inviting, accompanied with a low chuckle.

"Tell me how much you need me," he begged, wishing he could be kissing her sensuous lips.

"I want your strong arms around me, your lips on mine, and your gorgeous body in my bed. How is that for needing you?" she asked.

He sat in the car with his eyes closed, listening to her voice, not wanting the conversation to end. Her face filled his mind and made him smile. He exhaled dizzily, just thinking of their time together. If he could cry, he would be crying from loneliness—that is how deep the pain was.

"Arielle, do you love me?"

"As I've told you before, more than life itself," she murmured. "Sebastian, this was the most unbelievable experience, the most astonishing sensation I have ever encountered in my life. I knew that you had turned my world upside down, but never did I imagine anything like this. Making love with you is all I want to do for the rest of my life," she said, ending with a deep sigh.

Sebastian was elated as he listened to her talk. He was feeling the same way. He was at a loss for words, enveloped in the new and exciting world she had provided for him.

*I'm not thinking straight at all,* he thought. *What the hell is wrong with me? I need to get my emotions in check. I won't make it another day in this condition.*

"Sebastian, are you there?" he heard her asking.

"I'm sorry, baby, I was distracted by your vision," he said and sighed, then softly chuckled. "What did you say?"

"I said that I want you here with me. Every day I watch Gabrielle and Eva getting closer with Ian and Troy, and I'm missing you terribly. I'm missing you every moment of every hour, and it hurts." Her voice quivered with emotion.

"Arielle, there is nothing in this world that compares to the feelings I hold for you," he said. "I want to be there, I want to hold you in my arms forever. I miss you so much I can hardly breathe. I need to hear your voice. So, please talk to me about anything you like, just talk."

"Well, I have to hit the books awfully hard starting tomorrow to get through my exams for the next two weeks. There'll be no time for play at all," she said. "Gabby, Eva, and I have completely different schedules so we'll not be studying together. I'm a little nervous about the exams, but I'll get through them, I'm sure."

"You are very smart, and I know you'll do well."

"If I were as smart as you are I wouldn't have to study so hard," she said. "You're the one who is smart and magnificent. I'm so happy that you love me!" She laughed aloud, and her beautiful laughter filled his heart with pleasure.

"I want you to text me after each exam and let me know how you did. I want you to text me before you go to bed and when you get up. I want to feel like I'm there with you."

"I will," she promised.

*"Miss me,"* he whispered and ended the call.

# Chapter 7

ARIELLE FELT MISERABLE AS SHE DROVE to the flat alone. She hadn't wanted this weekend to end, and she had no regrets about what she had done. Sebastian was the most exciting man she had ever known—and he was all hers. The thought of him sent waves of ecstasy through her body. He had made love to her with such unbelievable passion. Just thinking about it sent shivers dancing down her spine and shattered her senses.

Refraining from sex was a decision she had made, and he had respected that decision until the last moment. She was the one who had initiated the encounter, and she'd even had to encourage him to step over the line. She sighed happily remembering.

It was late when she arrived at the flat. Gabby and Eva were awake, but Arielle didn't feel like sharing any details of her weekend with them just then. They were busy talking. They both looked up and smiled when she walked in.

"Hey, did you have a good time?" Gabrielle asked with an insinuating smile on her face.

"Yes, it was great! How about you two?"

"It wasn't long enough for me," Eva giggled.

"I have to agree with you," Arielle said and laughed softly.

"What's so funny?" Eva asked.

"Oh, I was just thinking about the same time last year. Do you all remember our conversations? About which one of us would be coming back from holidays with an earthshaking new adventure? Well, look at us now! We're all in love with such great guys, and our lives have changed completely."

"For the best, don't you think?" Gabby said a blissful smile on her face.

"Absolutely," Arielle said. "Well, I think I'll be off to bed. I'll see you all tomorrow." She smiled at them and walked to her bedroom, shutting the door behind her. She felt so lonely, and her need for Sebastian was becoming stronger by the minute. She climbed into bed, clenching her journal, eager to capture on paper the incredible experience that was still scorching her very existence. She closed her eyes. *How would I get along without him?* she thought. Their last encounter had changed everything about their relationship. She needed him, and she knew his absence would be a big obstruction while she was trying to study for her exams.

She was startled out of her reverie by the sound of her phone and was surprised to see Sebastian's name on the screen again. Even though they had just finished a very long conversation, she was elated to hear his voice again.

"Hello," she said breathlessly.

"Hi, baby," he said gloomily.

"What's wrong?"

"Nothing, I just needed to hear your voice again. I'm not sure I can do this much longer. I've got to be with you, or I'm miserable."

"I love you so much, Sebastian. I can't stand being away from you either," she murmured.

"This isn't going to work."

"What do you mean?"

"This long distance relationship is going to be the death of me." She heard him sigh. Rueful laughter followed.

"What were you doing?" he asked.

"I was laying in bed wishing you were here and tried to figure out how I'm going to study. And how I'm going to regain the ability to think clearly about school."

"Hmm," he laughed sympathetically.

"Well, I just wanted to hear your voice one more time before I go to bed," his velvety voice murmured. He sounded in need for a tête-à-tête and Arielle was happy to stay on the phone for as long as he wanted to talk. What could be more important?

They talked for a long time, perhaps the longest conversation they had ever had on the phone. Finally, he said, "Miss me." They were words she was sorry to hear because that was always the end of their telephone conversations.

Putting her phone down, she closed her eyes and brought Sebastian's fascinating face back into her mind's eye and smiled.

For a split second, the thought of Annabel came into her mind. She wondered how long it would take for Annabel to find out how much she and Sebastian loved each other, and where Arielle lived now. The thought made her shiver with fear, but she tried to put the thought behind her.

The amazing experience she'd had making love with Sebastian was something that had now changed her life forever. She opened her journal. A smile spread across her face, and her pen began to glide across the blank page.

*December 3*

*There are no words that could describe the amazing sensation of our encounter. And I don't regret a single moment of the whole experience, an experience that fractured my senses and took me to a place that is made of dreams and passion. Sebastian is an astonishing lover. I'm not sure why I waited so long when I know he is the one I'm going to be with for the rest of my life. He is my future, my lover, my Darcy. His body is extraordinary, made out of solid, hard muscle. He is filled with passion and desire for me. His lips are soft and sensuous, and all I want to do is sink into his intoxicating heat and merge into him, one body and one soul. I don't think I can be away from him. I want him with me every moment of the day. I'm thrilled to find out that he feels the same way. I'll hold dear the moment that I gazed into his emerald eyes and saw the battle he was fighting, wanting to honor my commitment to abstinence. I wouldn't let him. My want and my implausible need for him were stronger than anything I had ever experienced in my entire life. My expectations leaped over and above the sharp pain that left me winded for a short moment, but vanished as quickly as it came and was replaced by a swirling exhilaration. I threw myself into that whirling feeling wanting to give him as much pleasure as he was giving me. The final moment of our lovemaking was spectacular. There is nothing that could measure even close to the magnificent sensation. The thudding of my heart that was filled with that extraordinary awareness came crashing down and melted every muscle and every vein in my body. Wow! That is what I call a sizzling volcanic eruption. I can still hear his blissful moans and I can feel his touch that sent scorching waves of longing across my skin.*

*What happened today is a firm commitment that I'm linked to Sebastian forever. Sebastian knows that I'm irrevocably in love with him because he's read my thoughts. I can only hope he loves me with the same passion that I love him because I'd never be able to live without him.*

A perfect smile spread across her face as she closed her journal and pressed it tightly against her heart. She slipped under the covers, closed her eyes and slowly drifted off to sleep.

The next two weeks were the end of term exams. Arielle had planned to hit the books the next day. She knew that if she did, she would be fine. But morning came too soon. She awoke feeling sluggish and not wanting to do anything, especially study. Gabby and Eva were making tea in the kitchen and they didn't seem to feel any more like studying than Arielle did.

"Good morning, Darcy, I love you, and I am ready to hit the books," she texted. She smiled as she pressed the send button. A second later, she received his text, and it made her laugh out loud.

"Good morning, Lizzy, you'll be the death of me."

She loved to hear those words as much as she loved his amazing smile.

"It's such a beautiful day outside," said Eva, stretching in a leisurely way. "I don't feel like studying," she added.

"How about taking a walk at the beach instead?" Gabby asked, chuckling.

"I find it difficult to believe that we'll be able to do any studying at the beach," Arielle said. "I also find it difficult to believe that all the people at the beach have a chemistry test tomorrow."

"Arielle, all I want to do is walk on the beach and listen to my music. All I can think about is that glorious day outside that I'll be missing by sitting inside and trying to study," Eva said, letting out a soft sigh. Gabby looked intrigued by the thought of taking a walk on the beach. She had a look on her face that made Arielle laugh out loud.

"Well, there's no getting around it," Arielle said. "We might as well just get to work."

They all agreed and worked diligently until dinnertime. By the time they got back from eating out, it was too late to do any more studying.

"I am getting ready for bed, I wish you were here," Arielle texted.

Sebastian texted back, "I'm closing my eyes and bringing you into my bed. I can almost feel you! Our bodies merged in pure passion, ecstasy rushing over us like ocean waves in a storm..." He put a smile next to the last word. Arielle gasped at his words, which sent hot waves of passion throughout her body.

The next two weeks were dedicated to exams only. There were no classes to attend, so there was ample time to study. Arielle called Sebastian often during those two weeks, and he was always eager to talk. Every morning and every night she sent him text messages. The sexual content of the messages always made her smile and left her longing for him.

Everything Arielle ever wanted she had found in Sebastian, and she was determined to have it all. She had fallen deeply and irrevocably in love with him and she could barely cope with the thought of being apart even for a short time. She was hoping he would be able to be her date for the annual Christmas party at her parents' house. Oh, how she hoped he would say yes. She missed him so much and couldn't wait to be in his arms again.

Two days before her last exam he called, and she was thrilled to hear his voice. She immediately asked him to come for the Christmas party.

"Sebastian... um... I know you were just here, but would you consider being my date for my parents' Christmas party? I do so want you to be here with me."

"There is nothing in this world that I would like better than being with you," he replied without hesitation.

Arielle let out a breath of relief. "I wasn't sure if you would want to come back here this soon," she said, accidentally releasing a spontaneous moan.

"What are you thinking, Arielle?" he asked bemused.

"I need you!" She sighed as their last encounter flashed again before her eyes and she felt a swirling exhilaration, complete joy, and incredible delight.

"I miss you, Arielle, every time I think of you. And this past weekend I have become even more convinced that you will be the death of me. I can't do a single thing except think of you."

"I would never want to be the death of you," she chuckled. "But I know what you mean. I feel the same. It hasn't been easy concentrating on my classes."

"You can't help the fact that you are so enviable."

"Sebastian, the party is the weekend before Christmas. Can you come?"

"Yes, don't worry, that'll be fine," he said. "Now, what are you going to do tomorrow?"

"I'll be here with Gabrielle and Eva, studying, as usual. My last exam is chemistry. I'm almost ready, but I do need to refresh."

"Good luck, baby, I know you'll do well. Go to sleep now and think of me loving you."

"That's all I ever do now," she said.

"Well, I'm happy to hear that. Miss me!"

 *Chapter 8*

THAT NIGHT, GABBY, EVA, AND ARIELLE DECIDED to stay in and study. The thought of finishing her junior year excited Arielle. It was almost morning when they finally went to bed. Still, Arielle woke up in a great mood and got ready slowly. Her test wasn't until 11:00 a.m., Gabby's was at 12:00 p.m. and Eva was already gone. She had a leisurely breakfast and then went to school.

The test was a little harder than she thought it would be, but she made it through just fine. She felt like a new person when she came out of class. She met Eva at the parking lot. Gabrielle was still taking her test, so they decided to wait for her and go home together.

"Eva, I'm so happy I have you, my own private protector, with your incredible visions," Arielle told her as they walked back toward the building where Gabrielle was taking her exam. Eva looked deep in thought. Arielle wondered what she was thinking about.

"I'm not sure I like the look in your eyes," she said. "What are you thinking?"

"Well, it's the aura you project every time I look at you."

"What do you mean? I don't understand."

"I always feel anxious when I'm around you as if there is something out there waiting to hurt you," Eva confessed. "I know about Annabel, and at first, I thought she may be the one creating all these visions, but the more I see you, the more I feel there are others out there too. I don't know if they are acting on her behalf or if they have their own issues." She looked at her friend unhappily, dismayed to deliver such a gloomy thought. But it was the truth.

"Well, we know that Savanna was sent by Annabel to my birthday party, so I suppose it's possible that she may have other friends she's using too," Arielle said. "I know what she looks like, so maybe that's why she doesn't show up here herself."

"Well, I hope things change, because I can't stop worrying about you," Eva said a bit petulantly.

"Look, Eva," Arielle said, pulling her necklace out of her shirt and holding it up to show her. "You know that Sebastian gave me this necklace. He said it would keep me safe from anyone who wants to harm me. I didn't have it on the night of my birthday, and I didn't have it on when Matt attacked me, and that is why I was hurt."

Eva examined the necklace, and her eyes narrowed with extreme interest. "You told me about this necklace before, but I never looked at it carefully," she said. "Where did Sebastian get it?"

"From his mother."

"Wow, that's big! I wonder how she got her hands on something like this. I have read about similar necklaces, but the last owners I know of were men of royal status, like pharaohs. The Scarab beetle goes back to B.C."

Everything Eva said was true. Her observations sparked Arielle's curiosity. *How much more could Eva uncover just by looking at a necklace? I'll have to give her more credit from now on*, Arielle thought.

They dropped the conversation as soon as they saw Gabrielle walking out of the building with a big smile on her face. The sun felt warmer, and the sky seemed bluer than on any other day. They were done with their exams, and it looked like they had all done well. They smiled happily at each other.

"Let's party!" Gabrielle said as she approached her two friends, raising her arms skyward in celebration. As they drove home, they made plans for the next two days. Sebastian would be arriving on Friday, and that alone made Arielle feel exuberant. She was just walking into her room when her phone rang. Glancing down, she was surprised to see Ian's name on the screen.

"Hi, Ian," she said warmly.

"Hi, Arielle."

"What's up?"

"I need your help," he said pleadingly.

Arielle paused for a short moment. "What can I do for you?"

"I want you to make plans with Gabrielle to bring Eva to Bria's restaurant before we go to that celebration party at the pub tonight. Can you do that for me?"

"Um, sure," she replied, a bit confused. She still didn't know exactly what her role was, but she agreed.

"I've already talked to the restaurant manager, and they'll accommodate us," Ian added.

"What's the occasion?" she asked, utterly baffled.

"I'm going to propose to Eva," he said, his voice filled with excitement.

Arielle was stunned by the revelation. "Oh, my God!" she exclaimed. "That's just great! What time do you want us there?"

"Come around six-thirty. That will give us plenty of time to eat and celebrate the occasion with the party."

"All right. I'll talk to Gabrielle about this in a few minutes," she said, and added, "Ian, I think Eva will die. She loves you so much!"

"I love her too. She is everything I've ever wanted in a girl."

"I'm so happy for both of you."

"Thank you, Arielle. I'll see you at six-thirty."

Slipping the phone into her jeans pocket, she stood awkwardly in the middle of her bedroom. She had a peculiar impulse to laugh or to cry, she wasn't sure. She did not know how to handle all the sweeping emotions that were surging through her thoughts. She finally turned around and walked out of the bedroom.

Gabrielle was sitting in the living room alone, flipping through the pages of a rubbishy magazine.

"Where is Eva?" Arielle asked.

"She went in to take a shower, something wrong? You look strange," Gabrielle said, watching her unblinkingly.

Arielle ran and flopped herself down next to Gabrielle. She gave her hand a quick squeeze.

"Guess what." Arielle's voice was filled with enthusiasm.

"What?"

"Ian is going to propose to Eva this evening."

"Oh, my God!" Gabrielle cried out.

"Shh," Arielle said, quickly putting her index finger to her lips. "We have to make sure she doesn't suspect anything at all," she whispered conspiratorially. "Ian wants it to be a total surprise."

"Oh, Arielle, I'm so excited for her."

It was a bit later when Eva emerged from her bedroom and walked into the kitchen to get a bottle of water out of the fridge. When her phone rang, both Gabrielle and Arielle eavesdropped without being obvious.

"Hi, baby," Eva said. She listened for a short while and then they heard her saying, "Oh, okay, I'll miss you, but I'll see you at the party. I love you, too," she added, letting out a deep sigh.

Both Arielle and Gabrielle turned to look at her. "What's wrong?" they asked simultaneously.

"Ian will not be coming to dinner with us, he has some errands to run," Eva said, a little disappointed. "He's going to meet us later at the party."

"Why don't we call Troy and Paul, and the five of us can go to Bria's together around six-thirty?" Arielle suggested.


Gabrielle and Arielle were so excited for Eva, but they knew they had to keep Ian's secret. The restaurant was beautiful, and they were all very happy to have their junior year behind them. As they were involved in an animated, cheerful celebration, Ian arrived. Eva's jaw dropped.

"How did you know where to find us?" she asked.

"I talked to Troy while they were on the way to your place and he told me where I could find you. I tried to call you, but you didn't answer your phone," Ian replied. He bent his head, and putting his finger under her chin, he tipped up her face to meet his lips in a deep, passionate kiss. It looked like ending the kiss required extra effort on Ian's part.

They had a wonderful meal together. Towards the end, Ian got down on one knee and asked Eva to marry him, holding a small open box with a gorgeous engagement ring glittering inside. Eva gulped and paused to take a few unsteady breaths. She cleared her throat a couple of times, and they saw tears welling up in her eyes. She was staring at the ring with startled eyes and couldn't even move her lips to speak. She looked at Ian with a beautiful smile on her face, then threw her arms around his neck as she kept saying "Yes, yes, yes!" They locked themselves in a passionate kiss once again, while their friends all wished them happiness.

The ring looked amazing on Eva's finger. Ian held her close, and she rested her face on his chest. There was a lot of hugging and kissing following the proposal, and then it was time to leave for the party.

They arrived a little after eight-thirty. There were people everywhere, laughing, drinking, and having a great time. They pushed their way through the crowd and found a table inside. It was turning out to be a wonderful night.

When everyone was out on the dance floor or engaged in deep conversations, Troy pulled Arielle off toward the balcony, looking for some privacy.

"What is it, Troy?" she asked. "You look so worried, is there something wrong?"

"Arielle, I'm going to tell Gabrielle about me tonight, about, you know…" he said. "I know I have to do it, but I'm scared to death that she'll reject me when she finds out."

Arielle reached out and took Troy's hands in hers. "Gabrielle loves you more than her own life, Troy," she said softly. "You don't need to worry, it'll be okay."

"Are you sure?"

"She'll be scared just like I was when Sebastian told me. But I know how Gabrielle feels, and there's nothing you could say to change that." She smiled, drew a deep breath, then added, "Go ahead. Ask me how I know."

Troy looked at her with a quizzical look in his eyes. "How do you know?"

"Because I'm a freak," Arielle giggled. "I can read some people's minds, and Gabrielle's is one of the ones I can read." She laughed as

Troy's jaw dropped. He was looking at her as if she had two heads.

Troy raised his brows. "What?" he muttered, his gaze frozen on her face.

"I can read minds." Arielle repeated and chuckled nervously. Troy looked as if he didn't know whether to believe her or not.

"Can you read my thoughts?" he asked uneasily.

"No, no, you can relax. I can't read immortal minds, and I'm not sure why I can read some people's minds and not others, but that's the way it is."

Troy laughed softly, clearly relieved.

"Gabrielle doesn't know this," Arielle added. "And I would appreciate it very much if you didn't say anything about it to her until I'm ready to tell her."

Troy promised not to say anything to Gabrielle.

"Can you read minds?"

"No, I can't," he said. "I know that a lot of immortals have that ability, but I'm not one of them."

"Go ahead and tell her the truth," Arielle said. "I'll be there if you need me. She needs to accept you for who you are."

"Thanks, Arielle." He gave her a warm hug. He hesitated for a moment, and then he whispered conspiratorially, "I wanted to tell you that I've bought an engagement ring for her. But I'll wait until her birthday to propose."

"Oh, my God, she'll be so happy!" Arielle raised her hand and covered her mouth to mute a squeal. Troy smiled gratefully and hugged her warmly.

"Well, I guess we'd better get back to the others before someone wonders what we're up to," Troy said. They went back inside, got a couple of beers, and rejoined the others.

Late in the evening, their conversation took an interesting turn toward archeology and Cairo. Paul was just getting ready to make a point when the whole place fell into a stony silence. Everyone looked up and looked at the pub entrance. Two couples were standing at the door. The guys were average looking, but the girls on their arms were stunning. One was tall with beautiful red hair and green eyes. The other was just a little shorter, with long black hair and dark eyes.

Their features were flawless, their bodies elegant and graceful. They were both beautiful beyond belief.

Arielle felt a rush of panic. Her body shivered with fear, and her hand reached instinctively for her necklace. She was by now familiar with the immortal look, and these girls were unquestionably immortals. An icy feeling washed over her, and her mouth went dry. Turning slowly, she looked at Troy and saw the same guarded look in his eyes.

Eva reached over and grabbed Arielle's hand protectively. Leaning closer, she whispered, "I have the same feeling I had with Savanna. There is evil in here, and I think they are here for you."

Arielle looked back at her and nodded, managing a calm impression. "I'll be all right," she murmured, as she clasped her necklace. Eva followed her move and smiled.

*What in the world could they be doing here?* Arielle thought. Everything about them told her they were up to no good and that she was in for an unpleasant experience.

*It's Annabel,* she thought. The very thought made her sick to her stomach. She felt like she couldn't breathe and began to feel faint. Arielle watched them out of the corner of her eye as they walked in and stood only about two meters away. She put her head down, trying to breathe normally. Normal conversations resumed.

"Get a load of that," Arielle heard Paul whisper to Ian and Troy.

"Yeah. You don't see that kind of beauty every day," Ian said.

"They are something else," Paul said again. Arielle did her best to remain calm, but she knew the two girls were staring in her direction, and it made her very nervous.

"Eva, I would like to get some fresh air," she said. "Can you come with me?"

"Sure." They stood up and walked together out to the patio.

"You'll be okay, Arielle, have faith," Eva said. "That necklace has amazing powers. I know."

"Um, thanks," Arielle muttered, trying to smile but not quite succeeding.

"They may not even be here for you," Eva said. "Let's just wait and see what happens."

"I just don't like the look of them," Arielle said. "And I hate confrontation. I have a bad feeling about them."

"Well, let's wait and see what happens before we make a mountain out of a mole hill," Eva said, squeezing Arielle's hand.

Arielle took a deep breath and filled her lungs with fresh air. She was sure the women were looking for her. But why was Annabel sending all these women to hurt her? Why didn't she show up herself? She felt that she had entered upon on a long journey through a mysterious world, full of unknown situations and dangerous people. *I'll just have to face them one at a time,* she thought. *It's a little scary, never knowing what looms around the next corner.*

She took another deep breath, and then she walked back into the pub with Eva by her side. Immediately, her eyes found the two women. Both of them were looking at her, there was no mistake about that. As her eyes narrowed, she saw sarcastic smiles flit across their faces, making her feel very uncomfortable.

Eva and Arielle walked back to their table, where their friends were engulfed in conversation. She tried to push the thoughts that were crowding her head into a special place so she could regain control of her own mind, but it was hard to do. Troy looked at her inquiringly. *I must look bewildered,* she thought. *I've got to get a hold of myself.*

Eva reached over and took her hand, squeezing it gently. This gesture made Arielle think that the women must have approached her. Before she could complete this thought, she heard a voice that was soft like velvet.

"You must be Arielle," the tall girl with the red hair said. There was something vaguely familiar about the tone of her voice. Arielle turned around to face her.

"Yes, I am," she replied in a voice sturdier than the way she felt. "And you are?"

"My name is Julia Vanhouser, and this is my friend, Paola Gordioli. We are visiting from New Zealand, and we were told that we might be able to find Sebastian here."

Arielle's body went rigid. Annabel seemed to know that Sebastian wasn't in Brighton and that Arielle was going to be alone with her human friends.

"Do I know you?" Arielle asked. She kept her voice low, as she was trying to keep this conversation private.

"No, I'm sure you don't," Julia said with an unpleasant smile. "But I thought that Sebastian might have talked to you about me. I have been told that you are his latest victim," she added, casting a meaningful look at the other woman.

"Victim? I'm sure you must be mistaken."

"Oh? Do you even know who I am?"

"I assure you I have no idea."

"Well, let me enlighten you, my dear," she continued venomously. Her voice was low but loud enough for Arielle's friends to hear every word. She could see Troy from out of the corner of her eye moving toward her, but the woman didn't seem to be paying any attention to anyone other than Arielle.

Julia exchanged a glance with her friend. She pulled a flat gold cigarette case out of her purse and, taking a cork filtered cigarette out, she put it up to her perfect lips with a sexy movement. Her male companion immediately lit it for her. She took a couple of deep drags on the cigarette and inhaled deeply.

Then, glaring into Arielle's eyes, she blew a thick cloud of smoke in her face. With an obnoxious chuckle, she continued, "Sebastian and I were in love for a very long time," she said. "He was the best bed partner and the best boyfriend I have ever had. It took me a long time to find out that his style is a little, well, *peculiar,* you might say. He doesn't like to hang onto women for too long. I know of many girls he dated and then left when he'd had enough of them. I was the only one that he stayed with for a very long time. I'm here to claim him back," she said. "And I'm not leaving until I accomplish what I came for."

Arielle felt the floor shift beneath her. Her heart was hammering in her chest. Bile rose in her throat. But she knew that she had to keep her composure and try to end this conversation as politely and as quietly as possible. Waving her hand to clear the smoke in front of her face she said, her voice strong and clear, but inquiring, "I'm not sure what you want from me."

"I want you to stay away from him." The look she gave Arielle was full of venom.

Arielle fought not to be intimidated. She knew she couldn't afford to give Julia that power over her.

"I think that will be Sebastian's decision, not yours," she said. She felt Troy's hand on hers, and that made her feel more secure.

"Well, I suggest that you do things my way unless you want to find yourself in a very unpleasant situation," Julia said. Her voice was cold and hard. Fear seeped through Arielle's body, and she started to tremble. To her astonishment, Paul jumped up and got in Julia's face. His voice was firm and strong.

"I think you need to get the hell out of here," he growled fiercely through his teeth. Troy and Arielle reached over simultaneously and pulled him back, knowing he had no idea who he was dealing with. But he didn't pay any attention to them and held his ground.

"Get out of my way, you fool!" Julia shrieked, glaring at Paul. He didn't take kindly to those words. As he moved forward, things went from bad to worse. Everything happened so quickly it was like watching a movie in fast forward. Julia grabbed Paul and threw him clear across the room. He took several people and tables down with him as he hit the floor. Arielle could hear a horrible sound coming from among the broken tables and chairs. Paul was moaning in agony, his arm splayed out in an odd position that suggested it was broken.

"Quick, Paul is hurt!" Arielle cried.

She winced at the thought of the destruction Julia could inflict on this establishment and all the innocent people that had crowded the place just to party for the evening. Troy moved fast. He pulled Paul off the floor and asked Gabrielle to get some help. He was sure several people were hurt. Before Arielle could blink, he was back standing in front of her. Julia and Paola's dates jumped to protect them, not knowing these women were a thousand times more powerful than anyone in the room, with the exception of Troy. It was an unfortunate decision since they now faced an angry Troy. Within milliseconds, the guys were on the floor, unconscious, with several broken bones. Julia and Paola watched Troy move in utter shock. They had no idea how a human could move so fast.

"Amazing," Arielle murmured.

Troy stared straight into their eyes as both women stood still.

They were surprised but still totally unruffled. You could hear a pin fall on the floor as stony silence fell across the room.

"Leave Sebastian alone!" Julia shrieked again, looking past Troy and pinning Arielle with eyes of venom. Arielle glared back at her and pressed her lips tightly together. She could feel a strange emotion taking over her and felt herself getting stronger by the moment. She knew now that no matter what, she wasn't going to back down.

"Get the hell out of my life," she screamed at Julia, taking a stand and not moving an inch as Julia took another step towards her. Suddenly, Arielle could feel a huge emotion boiling inside her—a combination of furious anger and frustration, all rolled into a powerful, forceful energy.

Before anyone had a chance to blink, Julia whirled around and snarled as she grabbed Arielle by the shoulders. Arielle lost her step, tripped over her chair and started to fall, but not before she saw several things happen simultaneously, as if in slow motion. Julia was flying across the room, pushed by some invisible, inconceivable power. She hit the wall so hard the whole place shook. The windows on either side of her broke from the force of the impact. She was screaming in pain and her arms looked like they were literally on fire.

In the stony silence that followed, you could hear the sound of bones breaking. Troy grabbed Paola by the throat and threw her forcefully across the room. She landed next to Julia on the floor and growled from pain. Arielle was startled when she finally hit the floor and felt a sharp pain in the back of her head. Totally disoriented, she tried to get back up on her own but was unsuccessful. She winced with pain and tried to get up again when she felt Troy's strong arms reaching for her and pulling her up.

"Are you all right?" he asked, pulling her close. Arielle could hear his voice, but she was in a fog. She felt something warm and wet on the back of her head, and she was sure that something was terribly wrong. She reached with her hand to feel the warm spot, and when she brought it back in front of her face, her hand was dripping with blood. Troy took his t-shirt off and used it to put pressure on the back of her head.

"Just hold it tight until I can get the medics," he said.

Arielle heard Troy giving orders to the people around, asking them to call for the paramedics and to help the folks that were hurt off the floor. She saw him walk over to Julia and Paola. The two were still on the floor. She was astonished to see him lift both of them by the throat and take them outside. She was in terrible pain as she took a look around; the room looked like it had been hit by a tornado. Arielle sighed and sank back for a moment, overwhelmed. *Oh, where is Sebastian when I need him?*

# Chapter 9

**THERE WERE BROKEN TABLES AND CHAIRS** everywhere. People were beginning to get up from the floor, examining their cuts and bruises. Ian and Eva were among the injured. They had hit the floor when Paul went flying across the room. Arielle's mind was moving backward, trying to sort out what had happened, but she couldn't remember seeing Troy touch Julia at all. Who or what had pushed her that hard? She tried to think clearly but couldn't. Her head was hurting so bad it was making her eyes water.

"Where's Paul?" she cried out suddenly, realizing she hadn't seen him. Gabrielle came over and put her arms around Arielle.

"Where the devil is Paul?" Arielle asked again.

"They took him to the hospital to put a cast on his arm. He has a broken arm and some cuts. What a mess." She sighed and looked around the room.

"Oh, my God, I feel so bad. It's all my fault," Arielle said.

"What in bloody hell are you talking about? How can it be your fault?"

"They came looking for me and look what's happened," she said, crying.

"That's not your fault, Arielle. You need to stop blaming yourself."

Soon the campus police arrived, and within about ten minutes, they had restored order. Since the two women who had started the fight had disappeared, there were no arrests.

Shortly after the paramedics arrived, they took Arielle, Ian, and Eva, along with seven others, to the hospital.

"What a night," Arielle whispered to Troy and Gabby. "I don't think we are ever going to forget Eva and Ian's engagement night, what do you think?" She smiled softly as the pain hit her again and made her grimace. She felt so bad about Ian and Eva she wanted to cry. Their beautiful night had been ruined, and no matter what Gabrielle said, Arielle couldn't help but feel responsible.

By the time she got to the emergency room, Arielle was very dizzy. When they pulled Troy's t-shirt off of her head, she saw that it was saturated with blood. The doctor gave her twelve stitches. It was a painful process. Finally, Troy and Gabrielle drove everyone home. Arielle hugged Paul and gave him a kiss.

"I'm so sorry," she said. He smiled and kissed her back.

"If I had to do the same thing again I wouldn't hesitate for a minute," he said.

"I love you, Paul. Thank you for everything you've done for me."

She felt his gaze on her face and sensed his concern.

"What is it?" she asked.

How could he answer her without letting her know all the images of longing for her that still filled his head? "I love you too, Arielle," he said simply. "Remember, you are my best girl."

Ian and Eva were laughing about the whole thing, which made Arielle begin to feel a bit better.

"Well, this will be a night to remember and share with our kids," Eva said. Ian laughed.

But Arielle's thoughts had returned to the two women and what Julia had said to her. She had said that Sebastian had been her lover for a long time. Another woman who wanted him back. Did he get rid of women when he'd had enough of them? If that were true, what would happen to her? Would she fall into the same category? She began to feel sad. Tears filled her eyes. As she was thinking these sad thoughts, Troy asked her if they could have another word in private.

He pulled her into her bedroom and closed the door. "Arielle, I wanted to talk to you in private because Gabrielle still does not know about me. And I want you to think straight, and not make any assumptions based on what Julia said. Sebastian has lived for five hundred years, and if he dated her for a few years, that is like a drop of water in a huge ocean. The fact that he had a lot of girls in the length of time he has roamed this earth isn't of any importance. Five hundred years is a very long time to be alone. I have had many girls, and many affairs that were longer than a year or two, but they didn't mean anything to me. I have found true love in Gabrielle, and I know Sebastian has found true love in you."

As he spoke, Arielle began to sob. Troy held her in his strong arms, letting her cry out all her fear and frustration. She had complete confidence in him; she knew he would tell her the unvarnished truth.

"I love him so much," she sobbed. "I can't stand the idea of sharing him with anyone."

"You are not sharing him with anyone," Troy said gently but firmly. "These are women who wished they had Sebastian. But he doesn't want them anymore, and probably never really did. Please trust me," Troy said. "Julia is bitter and angry, and she will say anything to hurt you and your relationship with Sebastian. So don't let her do it. I called Sebastian and told him what happened, and he is beside himself. He was ready to pack and get on a plane right away, but I told him we're fine and that I'm here for you. He wants you to call him as soon as you can, though. He is very worried about you."

"Thank you so much, Troy," she said. "You don't know how much it means to me to be able to count on you when Sebastian is not around."

"Then stop sobbing and give me a smile," he said gently. "I want to make sure that you are all right."

"I'm fine," she whispered. "Do you know this is the third time you have come through for me? I owe you my life again!" Troy smiled his amazing smile, so much like Sebastian's that it put her heart at ease. She stopped sobbing and gazed deeply into his eyes. For a startling moment, Troy wondered if she could read his mind.

"What did you do with Julia and Paola?" she asked, wiping her eyes and looking at him curiously.

"They were sent by Annabel, and now they are gone," Troy said. "She will have to face Sebastian herself next time, and that will not be healthy for her at all. And now you'd better call Sebastian." Leaning over, he gave her a peck on the cheek and walked out of her room chuckling.

Arielle sat on her bed and pressed Sebastian's number on her speed dial. He answered on the first ring. His voice was very anxious.

"Hey, baby," he said, and at the sound of his voice, Arielle broke down again, sobbing. She was unable to say a word.

She heard him take a sharp breath. "Please don't cry, Arielle," he murmured, his voice full of concern. "How are you feeling, baby? Are you in pain?"

"I guess I'm doing all right," she sniveled. "I had to have twelve stitches. And my head is hurting pretty bad. I wish you were here," she whimpered.

"Troy told me all about it," Sebastian said, his voice sounding unusually grim. "And I feel so bad. However, I do know that the necklace is working. Troy was shocked and impressed when he saw Julia fly across the room when she tried to touch you. I'm sure that if you hadn't lost your footing, you would have been all right."

"Yes, you're right, and Julia flying across the room was a show stopper," Arielle giggled. "But I'm so angry at her, and so tired of Annabel and her schemes. I could kill her."

"I didn't think that Troy even noticed what happened to Julia."

"Arielle, he is immortal. Nothing escapes him. He knew exactly what happened. I had told him about the necklace. He is my eyes and ears when I'm not near you."

"Oh, so you have spies to watch me?"

"That's the only way I can have some peace of mind when it comes to your safety. He's a godsend, protecting my sanity," he chuckled.

Finally, Arielle was able to smile. "I feel so bad for Eva and Ian. It was their engagement party, and it was ruined." She started to cry again softly, thinking about them.

"I'm sorry about that as well," Sebastian said. "I like them so much. I'll have to apologize to them for Annabel."

"And poor Paul. She broke his arm because he was trying to protect me."

"Yes, I know, Troy told me. I'll have to thank him next time I see him. It sounds like he loves you a lot."

"Yes, he does," Arielle said, "and I love him too, as a friend."

"You must feel extremely rich having all those wonderful people around you. There's nothing like having great friends who truly care for each other. However, I love you more than life. You remember that."

"Julia called me your latest victim," Arielle said. "She said she was here to reclaim you, and that she wasn't leaving until she had completed her mission." She let out a deep sigh and added, "She said you left every girl you dated after you'd had enough." She paused for a short moment, and then added, "What about me? Will you leave me too when you have had enough?" she asked, sobbing again.

Sebastian hissed an inaudible curse through his teeth. He had to put a stop to the endless stream of women Annabel was sending to frighten Arielle.

Worst of all was that she was raising questions in Arielle's mind about the sincerity of his feelings for her. He tried to restrain his anger and the rage he felt as he answered, "Julia is out of her mind. She was always a little eccentric, but I thought it was just a phase she was going through. I want nothing to do with her, believe me. I love you and you alone," he said, emphasizing the last two words.

"Why do you think she decided to show up now?" Arielle asked.

"I saw her in New Zealand a few weeks ago," Sebastian said. "I tried to avoid her, but she was very persistent. She wanted to 'pick up where we had left off,' and I turned her down. That was the first time I had seen her since the 1800s. She was extremely angry when we parted. She vowed to find me and persuade me to stay with her. I remember laughing about it and thinking she needed to get in line right behind Annabel with her crazy threats. But I never thought she would show up and create problems for you."

"She told me that you were the best bed partner she ever had and that you had a lot of girls."

"Damn it, Arielle; we had an affair, nothing more. And that was three centuries ago," he said, frustrated. Arielle fell silent and began crying again.

"Arielle, you have to stop crying," Sebastian said. "There have been a lot of women in my life, but we are talking about centuries ago, not years or months. Eternity is a very long time to be alone."

"Troy said the same thing," she said, "and I'm trying to accept it. The problem is I'm so jealous of you that I can't stand the thought of any other women in your life."

His voice became calm and sweet. "Listen to me, baby. I have no sentimental attachment to Annabel, Julia, or any other woman from my past. You are my whole world, the center of my universe, and you will be my love for eternity."

"But how can that even be?" Arielle said. "Forever means one thing for mortals and quite another for you. How is this going to work? I'll grow old as you stay young? And when I do, will you love me still? It is all quite upsetting to contemplate."

"Arielle, first of all, let me say that I don't think you understand the profundity of my love," Sebastian said. "All I want you to do is trust in me. I don't want you to worry about any of these things right now. I can't breathe without you; I can't imagine my life without you." He paused, then added, "I'm sure Annabel had a lot to do with this visit. You will have to accept the fact that these things will happen every now and then. But we will face them together. I'm sorry you were hurt. I can't stand the thought of you being in pain, and I take all the blame. Please forgive me, Arielle. I love you, and I can't describe the bliss and extraordinary sensation your very existence brings to my life."

As he spoke, his words soothed her soul, and she knew that she should never doubt him.

"I can't hang up unless you stop crying, you know that," he said.

"I'm all right now," she breathed through her tears.

"I want you to call me when you need me. I like to be needed by you. Tell me you are all right."

"I feel much better now."

"I will see you very soon," he said, and with those words her mind raced ahead, thinking of the ultimate pleasure of him and his touch.

"Oh, before you hang up, Sebastian, Troy told me that he will be talking to Gabrielle tonight about, you know… about who he is."

"Let me know how it goes," Sebastian said, a smile in his voice.

"I wish you were here. I miss you so much!"

"You keep that thought, and I'll be there before you know it," he said.

"We'll have Christmas together. I'm very excited about that."

"I can't wait either. *Miss me,*" he said, and then he was gone.

After they had hung up, Arielle lay in bed and closed her eyes, her thoughts turning to Gabrielle and Troy. She knew Troy was in great pain trying to make Gabrielle understand who he was. She had seen how difficult that was for Sebastian. She also knew how frightened and alone she had felt when she had first learned about Sebastian's true nature. *If she loves him half as much as I love Sebastian, she will make the right decision,* she thought. *Still, I should be there for her.*

She walked out of the bedroom and saw that everyone was getting ready to leave. It had been a long, hard day, and everyone was tired. Ian stayed with Eva while Troy took Gabrielle to his house, volunteering to drop Paul off at his flat on the way home.

Arielle went back to bed, and as she drifted off to sleep, her last thought was about Sebastian's amazing face. *I miss him so much. Being with him is all I want. His face is what I want to see before I go to bed every night and the first thing I want to see when I wake up every morning.*

When she next opened her eyes, she realized that she had slept for a long time. She got out of bed and pulled the curtains back, letting the sunlight burst into her room. The sky was clear, but it looked like it had rained all night. She walked into the kitchen and put the teapot on, then jumped into the shower. Her head was still tender, and she had to be careful not to get water on the stitches. When she heard her phone ring, she turned the water off, reaching outside the shower door to answer.

"Hello," she said.

"Hey, baby!"

A huge smile covered her face, and she felt her body go limp with excitement.

"I miss you so much, I can feel it in my bones," she said, giggling.

"What are you doing?" Sebastian asked.

"I'm standing in the shower, dripping wet," she said. "I thought it might be Troy calling, and I didn't want to miss the call."

"Mmmm, I wish I was there," he said, desire in his voice.

"Me too," she said, sighing softly.

"I guess you haven't heard from Gabrielle or Troy?"

"No, but I've been thinking about them. I didn't want to intrude because I know what is going on right now. I'm sure Troy will call me when he's ready."

"Arielle, I don't like this long distance relationship. I'm hurting every moment I'm away from you. I couldn't sleep last night after we hung up. The vision of you is like a burst of stars that keeps me mesmerized. I'm worthless without you."

"I'm happy to hear that you miss me because I don't like being away from you either."

"Finish your shower and call me later."

"I'll call you after I talk with Troy," she promised.

"Miss me!" And once again, he was gone.


She was dressed and finishing up her first cup of tea when her mobile rang again. This time, it was Troy.

"Hey, Troy."

"Can you come over?" Troy asked, voice subdued and filled with concern.

"Yes, I can. Is everything okay?"

"I'm not sure, but I think Gabrielle is very scared," he said. "And she doesn't want me to be anywhere near her," he added.

"Don't worry, Troy, that's exactly how I felt. She will change. And I'm on the way."

"Thanks, Arielle," he said softly, and then he was gone. Arielle took a cup of tea with her as she got into the car and drove to Troy's house. He was waiting for her at the door. "She's in the bedroom," he said. "And she's pretty upset."

Arielle walked into the room. Gabrielle was sitting on the bed looking gloomy, no expression on her face. Her eyes were red and puffy from crying, and she was shaking slightly. Arielle ran to her and put her arms around her friend, who held her tightly.

"I'm so happy you're here," Gabrielle said, beginning to sob uncontrollably.

"Gabrielle, it's all right. I know you love Troy more than anything in this world. He is nice, warm, and loves you. He isn't some wicked person that would ever hurt you. He's just a guy that has lived for a long time, and he's going to live forever. He's not evil. He isn't a ghost. He's immortal, and there's nothing to be afraid of."

Gabby shook her head as if she was unable to understand what Arielle was saying. Arielle took her friend's hands, looked her straight in the eyes, and then asked, "Do you love him, Gabby?"

"Yes, more than anything in this world."

"Would you have fallen in love with him if you knew what he was?"

"I am sure I would have," Gabrielle said. "I don't think I can live without him."

"So, then you need to let him know how you feel. He's so worried about you. He loves you, and he's afraid of losing you."

"How do you know about Troy? Why did he tell you before he told me?"

"He didn't tell me, Gabby. I knew what he was the first time I met him because…because I'm familiar with Immortals."

Gabrielle stared at her motionless, transfixed, as if waiting for her to continue, afraid of what she might say next.

"Sebastian is immortal too," Arielle said.

Gabrielle's eyes were still full of tears, but now her expression was one of shock.

"Sebastian?" she asked. "Your Sebastian? He is also immortal?"

"Yes," Arielle said. "Do you remember when you and Eva asked me where I had found him? And do you remember how he could dazzle you just by looking into your eyes?"

"Yes, I remember that," Gabrielle said slowly, a faraway look in her eyes.

"Well, Troy has the same ability to dazzle anyone at any time. He just hasn't chosen to release it on you as of yet," Arielle said, smiling.

Gabrielle was quiet, her lips pursed in anxiety. But she had stopped crying. Finally, she looked at Arielle. "How did you feel when you found out about Sebastian?" she asked.

"Pretty much like you do right now," Arielle said. "I completely freaked out at first. But as time passed, I realized my heart was telling me that no matter what we belong together."

"I need time to abscrb this," Gabrielle said. "I spent the whole night with him, listening to words that didn't make any sense to me at all. I wouldn't let him touch me," she added. "I was afraid to be near him."

"Gabby, you have to let him know that you love him. He is crushed, thinking that you don't want to touch him because he is some kind of a freak. Rejection is a terrible thing, and that is exactly what he feels right now."

She kissed her friend on the cheek and whispered softly, "He needs to feel your arms around him, he needs to know that you love him. I saw his eyes when I walked in. He is dying. He thinks you aren't going to accept him for who he is."

She paused, searching for the right words. "This isn't something he chose, you know," she said. "This is a life that was given to him by someone else, and he just has to make the best of it."

She looked at Gabrielle, trying to find the right words, the words that would make her understand. "How would you feel if you were unable to make friends just as you and I can? How would you like to see the people you love get old, get sick and die, while you remained young and beautiful forever? Do you think that would be a blessing or a curse? I think it's a terrible curse," she said. "But he has to live with it."

"I'm starting to understand a little bit about the way he feels," Gabrielle said. "I love him so much, and it hurts me to think that things might not work between us."

"Then you will have to do everything you can to *make* it work," Arielle said firmly. "Troy is wonderful, and I love him as a friend. He has saved my life three times since the day I met him, so I also pretty much consider him a guardian angel. Please don't hurt him. He loves you so much."

"You're right," Gabrielle said. "I *do* love him, and he is wonderful."

"You told me yourself he is a great lover—so, as you can see, he is very normal in every way apart from that one small little thing, that he will live forever. Is that so bad?" She couldn't hold back her laughter, and now Gabby even joined in. Arielle was so glad to see her friends smiling face again, and to know that Troy could hear her laughter. Gabrielle's eyes dried up, and Arielle could see a faint smile peeking out.

"Do you want me to call him?" she asked. "I think he is aching for you."

"Yes, I think I'm ready."

Arielle found Troy sitting in the living room with his face resting in his hands, looking miserable.

"She wants to see you now," Arielle said with a smile.

Troy's eyes sparkled as he jumped up, and he gave Arielle a huge hug. "Thanks, Arielle," he said softly, looking back as he practically flew to the bedroom.

As Arielle left Troy's place she was filled with happiness, knowing that her friends were together and that they loved each other. They had a lot of making up to do. Arielle knew the feeling. She too was aching for her beautiful dream, but he was so far away.

*What a great day for them*, she thought as she got into her car and headed home. She hit the button on her phone and her own magical dream answered.

"Hey, you sexy man," she whispered in her most seductive voice. Joyful laughter coming from the other end was his response.

"Are you trying to seduce me, Miss Lizzy?" he asked with a soft chuckle.

"Yep. How am I doing?"

"You've got me all flustered," he said, "and you are lucky I'm not there."

"Whatever do you mean?" Arielle teased as if she had no idea what he was insinuating.

"I think you know exactly what I'm saying," he laughed again.

"Well, you got me so excited I almost forgot what I called you for. I just left Troy's place. They had a pretty wild night, just like we did a couple of months ago."

"How is Gabrielle doing?"

"She freaked out, just as I did, but she's fine now. She loves him, so it doesn't make any difference what he is."

"Well, I'm happy to hear that."

"Mmmm..." Arielle murmured.

"What?"

"I am trying to feel your arms around my waist and taste the amazing scent in your mouth."

"You will be the death of me for sure," he murmured. "I have my eyes closed, and I am holding you now, do you feel me?"

"No, that's not working for me," Arielle snorted. "I need you right here, right now," she replied with a rueful laugh.

"You sound very demanding," he said. "Are you?"

"Yes, I am. Do you have a problem with that?"

"No, not at all. I'll be there soon." Arielle could hear him take a deep breath and exhale as if he were flustered. She chuckled with great satisfaction as she heard him say, laughing as he spoke, "Well, you've succeeded in getting me all rattled. I'm going to have a hard time getting back to work now."

"I am glad to hear that," she said, smiling. "You know they say that misery loves company."

He chuckled again as he whispered softly, "You don't know how lucky you are that I'm not there."

"How lucky am I? Please do tell," she pressed on, and giggled.

"The way I feel right now it could be dangerous to your health," he snorted.

"Bring it on, Gaulle," she said.

"Oh, is that a challenge?" he whispered breathlessly.

"Yes, come and face it, Gaulle. I'm waiting!"

"Oh, my God, woman, you will be the death of me," he said, sucking in a shuddering breath.

"I love you, Sebastian."

"I love you, too. *Miss me*, baby," he said. And the phone went dead.

 *Chapter 10*

**IT WAS GETTING CLOSE TO THE TIME** of her parents' Christmas party, and Arielle was getting very excited. This was going to be a most special time for her. Sebastian, her miracle boyfriend, would be her date for the party. One day, shortly before he was due to arrive, her mother called and asked her to come by the house to check the last minute details for the party. *I guess I can do that. After all, I haven't had anyone trying to kill me in the past two weeks, and I will not be alone,* Arielle thought. She smiled inwardly.

Gabrielle, Eva, and Arielle had made plans to do some Christmas shopping together, so they agreed to drive by Arielle's parents' home on the way to the shopping center. Eva jumped into the shower, leaving Arielle and Gabrielle to chitchat about details of their shopping needs.

"When do you think we can talk to Eva about Troy and Sebastian?" Gabrielle said in a low voice after making sure that Eva was out of earshot.

"I think we should clear that with the guys, and make sure that it's okay with them for us to make their identity known. I don't think that we should make that decision for them," Arielle said, and Gabrielle agreed.

Twenty minutes later they were on their way. When they arrived at the house they embarked onto a delightful Christmassy atmosphere. The house, was freshly painted a soft bone color that enhanced the look of the large white marble staircase leading to the front doors. The front garden was gorgeous. The large green trees and bushes were neatly trimmed, and there were thousands of holly berries glistening like rubies when the sunshine burst over them. There were flowers blooming everywhere, broadleaf evergreen shrubs loaded with little strands of gem-like buds, and finally Helleborus, with its magnificent blooms, amazing against the dark green foliage. All these flowers created a beautiful sweep of colors, making the house indescribably beautiful.

The beveled glass on the two front doors had been cleaned, and it sparkled like diamonds. Two huge evergreen wreaths were hung on the doors, decorated with pinecones and beautiful ornaments. The bottom of each wreath had a large, elegant bow, with ribbons extending close to the ground. Smaller wreaths were hanging in all the windows. There were huge pots full of stunning poinsettias decorating the front balcony and on the stairs leading up to the front door.

*My gosh,* Arielle thought. *If this is the outside, I wonder what it will look like inside.* Gabrielle and Eva noticed every little flower, wreath, and bow pointing out the details with excitement. They all loved this time of the year. They walked around to the back door and went inside.

As they entered the house, they enjoyed the wonderful aroma. Arielle loved the fragrance of freesia potpourri. To her, the familiar scent was part of being home. Inside, the house looked just as fabulous. The chandeliers had been shined and were sparkling. There was pine garland on the staircases, and the four fireplace mantels were all decorated with elegant red bows and sparkly gold ribbons. Everywhere there were gorgeous candleholders with red and green candles.

In the ballroom, a twenty-foot Christmas tree stood loaded with beautiful ornaments. Each ornament was unique, representing some special moment in Arielle's parents' lives—some purchased during various family trips to faraway places, others representing sentimental events. A red velvet tree skirt was embroidered with beautiful holiday designs. A magnificent toy train set up in a large circle the tree made Arielle smile with happiness. Glancing up, she met her father's gaze. Instant recall flooded their thoughts, and they both smiled wide at the vivid memories of Christmas mornings she had spent lying on the floor, making the train run fast and slow, blowing the horn every five minutes, and hearing her father laugh with pure delight. She could almost smell the hot chocolate once again from those memorable Christmas mornings so long ago.

Another large tree in the foyer was also loaded with ornaments, some sentimental, some just pretty. Driving by the house at night, the lights on the tree made the foyer look magical through the beveled glass. There were poinsettias in every corner of the house and in front of all the fireplaces. Gorgeous silk tablecloths covered the tables and mistletoe was hanging on each chandelier and hallway light, giving people ample opportunity to kiss and be merry. Arielle's mother walked into the ballroom smiling; she could tell the girls were mesmerized, and she was very pleased.

"Oh, Mummy, everything is perfect," Arielle cried, giving her mother a big hug.

"I can't wait until Saturday night," Eva cried out joyfully. Arielle's mother smiled, pleased with their reaction.

"We're going Christmas shopping, is there anything you need, Mum?"

"No, dear, have a nice time," she said, giving her a peck on the cheek. "I will see you girls on Saturday night," she called out, standing at the door as they all climbed into Arielle's car and left to do their Christmas shopping.


Arielle already knew what to get for her parents and her friends, but she had to think hard about what to give Sebastian. There was no way she could spend the kind of money he could, but she wanted to find something special, something that would be meaningful to him.

Bristol is a beautiful and enchanting seaside town with seven miles of seafront and tons of places to shop. The girls drove to the oldest part of town, where the Lanes, the girls' favorite place to shop, was located, and parked the car.

There were no cars allowed in the small streets of the open-air mall, allowing people to walk safely from one store to another. The sun was shining, and the girls could smell the fresh sea air. It was very busy, due to the approaching holidays. They walked through the narrow, winding streets full of happy people shopping at the boutiques and specialty shops. It was a nice day, and they walked slowly as if they had all the time in the world. The ocean breeze felt cool on their faces and made them smile with pleasure. Everything was so festive; all the windows were decorated with wreaths, red bows, and candles. It was such a cheerful atmosphere that it was hard not to get caught up in the excitement.

Arielle usually preferred to shop alone, especially when she was planning to spend hours in a bookstore. It was Christmas, however, and it was time to shop with her friends, gossiping and having a great time. Gabby and Eva needed to shop for their parents as well, so it was easy to choose where they were going first.

Arielle's mother was first on her gift list. Arielle wanted to find something that would make her holiday extra special. She wasn't very hard to shop for; she always appreciated everything, no matter how small or large the gift. They walked into one of the boutiques and spread out to look for gifts. Arielle's mother loved clothes, so she purchased a beautiful light blue cashmere sweater to complement her eyes, and a gorgeous multicolored scarf that would look great with the sweater.

"Scarves are one of my mother's weaknesses," Arielle said to the cashier who admired it.

"She's going to love this one," Eva said approvingly, and Gabby nodded. They had their gifts boxed and wrapped, and walked out, pleased with their choices.

Arielle's father was next on her list. She had the perfect gift in mind for him. They walked into one of the oldest bookstores in the mall, and she looked for something she knew her dad would love. It was the first edition of Bury's 1835 edition of Gibbon's eighteenth century masterpiece about the decline and fall of the Roman Empire. It included a huge nineteenth century engraved folio and a map of the Roman Empire under Constantine, with the original outline hand-colored. Arielle knew her father would love this book as he had an enormous interest in the Roman Empire as well as in Constantinople.

Gabrielle found and purchased a rare 1720 Boston edition of Culpeper's *Pharmacopoeia Londinensis*, the first full-length medical book published in the American colonies about household treatments for illness. It was quite rare, with only a few copies in the world. She was so excited, knowing that her father read medical journals day in and day out, and loved anything that had to do with medicine. Arielle caught a glimpse of sadness in Eva's face and knew she was missing her father. She put her arm around Eva and whispered, "Your father is always with you now." Eva squeezed Arielle back and smiled a grateful smile.

The girls' next stop was at a small boutique, where they looked at custom-made jewelry. Arielle knew how much both of her friends loved jewelry, and that is exactly what she found for them. She knew they would be doing the same thing for her, and that made her smile. She also purchased a beautiful blue shirt for Paul, and shirts for Ian and Troy, consulting with Gabrielle and Eva concerning color and styles. Gabrielle and Eva also bought beautiful shirts for Sebastian. Again, they had their gifts boxed and wrapped.

"Well, that's it," Arielle announced as they left the store. "At least as far as family and friends are concerned."

There was only one person each of them still had left on their list, and they knew it would take time and a lot of thought to get the right thing for the men who had given purpose to their lives. The girls walked back to the car and locked their packages in the trunk. They agreed to spend the rest of the afternoon shopping for their new outfits for the party and searching for special gifts for their guys.

They had already been on their feet for a while, so first they decided to sit down at one of the bistros and order some delicious freshly baked pastries and cold drinks. Eva was so happy with her engagement ring that she kept looking at it every five seconds, making Gabrielle and Arielle laugh with delight. They talked about everything and anything. Arielle told her friends that she still didn't have the flight information from Sebastian, and she was hoping there would be an e-mail message waiting for her when she got back to the flat. He was supposed to arrive the next afternoon, and she just couldn't wait.

After a pleasant hour spent at the bistro, the girls moved on to find a boutique that specialized in holiday dresses. Arielle fell in love with a little silver strapless dress that looked amazing on her and found a pair of high heels to complement the dress. She walked into one of the fitting rooms while Gabrielle and Eva were still searching for their dresses.

When she had the dress on, Arielle thought it was the most beautiful dress she had ever owned, and with the high heels, she looked amazing. Suddenly she heard gasping and laughter outside the fitting room.

"What's going on out there?" she called.

"Oh, nothing important," said Gabrielle, still laughing. "How does the dress look?"

"I love it! I'm going to buy it."

"Come out and let us see!" Gabrielle urged, still chuckling.

"What has gotten into you two? What's so funny?"

"Oh, it's Eva, you know how she is," Gabrielle said. She was trying to suppress her giggling but not succeeding very well. Arielle smiled, thinking of Eva and her frequent outbursts of nonsense.

"I'll come out in a sec," Arielle said. She wanted to make sure the dress was right for the party. She was thinking about what Sebastian would say and hoping he would think she looked amazing in it. She fixed her hair and put a little blush on her cheeks, wanting her friends to have a realistic sense of what she would look like at the party.

"Well, can we see it?" Eva asked impatiently.

"Yes, let me know what you think," Arielle said as she pushed the door open and stepped out. Then she gasped in shock, eyes wide, unable to speak. She felt lightheaded and nearly lost her balance. She had to grab onto the door to keep from dropping to the floor. There in front of her stood the most beautiful man on this earth, the love of her life. He looked like Adonis with that amazing smile on his gorgeous face. He wore a pair of jeans with a white shirt that accented the beauty of his body. Arielle was taken aback, not understanding how this was possible.

"Sebastian!" she cried out and flew into his arms. She wrapped her arms around his neck and kissed him without holding back. He looked elated at her reaction. Gabrielle and Eva were laughing with sheer delight.

"But how? When? What?" Arielle stumbled. She had all these questions, but she couldn't seem to get out a complete sentence.

Sebastian pushed her softly back away from him and looked at her from head to toe. His eyes were fixed on her. He let out a long whistle of approval and then pulled her back into his arms.

"You will be the death of me," he said in that hushed voice, adding almost in a whisper, "You look spectacular."

Arielle wrapped her arms around his neck again and pulled herself flush against his gorgeous body. She heard him take a sharp intake of breath and leaning down he brushed his lips against her ear. He pressed gently at the lower part of her back and pulled her even closer.

"Careful," he cautioned in a throaty voice, "you are getting me excited."

She immediately pulled back, giggling, and he released her. "How did you find me? When did you come? I thought you were flying in tomorrow," she said.

"I wanted to surprise you," he said. "And I think I have succeeded in doing exactly that." His lips were curved up into that smile that Arielle knew she would love for the rest of her days. "I flew in this morning, and when I didn't find you at the flat, I thought your parents might know where I could find you. I spent a little time with them and, by the way, the house looks amazing," he said, making Arielle blush with pride. "Your mother told me where I might find you. So I gave it a try. I think I have looked at every store in this area. I was just about ready to give up when I saw Gabrielle and Eva standing here, and I knew that I was in the right place."

"I'm so happy to see you," she said, blushing again.

"I love you, baby, and I wanted to surprise you. I was a little worried about you following our conversation last night."

Arielle fell back into his arms and closed her eyes. She felt safe in that warm sanctuary he was providing just for her. He smiled and pulled her tighter against his body. She gasped.

Every person in the shop was staring at him, not believing that anyone could be as perfectly beautiful as he was. He was hers, and she was elated. She knew every woman in the place wished she were in her place. She also knew that Sebastian had eyes only for her. Finally, he let go of her reluctantly, and she went back into the fitting room to take the dress off. She went to pay for it while her friends were trying on their dresses.

"Let me get this for you," Sebastian said as she took her wallet out of her purse.

"Absolutely not." Her voice was firm, and he didn't say anything more.

"Did you like the dress?" she asked.

"I love it. It makes you look very sexy, but you can't wear it unless I'm with you," he whispered, and leaning close to her ear, he added, "But I like you better with no clothes on at all."

Arielle felt heat spread across the tip of each nerve. His words were seeping into her sanity and stripping her of it. She pulled back and shook her head, trying to regain her focus. "We'd better go and see how Gabrielle and Eva are doing," she said, but he pulled her around to face him. His arms encircled her body, and his voice came out soft and sexy.

"Arielle, I know your reaction when I look into your eyes, so get a hold of yourself, I am about to do that again. I need the energy I get from your beautiful blue eyes."

She looked up at him and started to protest, but their eyes met, and once again it happened. Her heart was hammering in her chest so hard that she was sure everyone could see it pumping. She struggled to take a breath, and she could feel the familiar heat take over her body. She looked away and could hear him laughing quietly, knowing what he was doing to her.

"I wish you would stop doing this," she said.

"Are you all right?" he teased.

"Yes, I'm fine," she said, even though once again she was completely disoriented.

"When we're together next year I think I'll do away with my salve and replace it with just looking into your eyes for the energy I need," he murmured. "What am I going to do with you?" he added, pressing a kiss on her temple.

"You keep asking me the same thing over and over again," she said. "What is it that you want to do with me?"

"Oh, there are a lot of things I would like to do with you, but I'm not sure you would approve," he said, his voice a slight whisper of breath.

Arielle groaned inwardly, knowing that she needed to change the subject.

"I don't understand why I get so dazzled when I look into your eyes," she said. "Is there something wrong with me?"

"There is nothing wrong with you," Sebastian assured her. "I can dazzle people at different levels, and I love dazzling you at the highest level," he said, chuckling.

"Here I come," said Gabrielle from inside the fitting room.

"Sebastian," Arielle said quietly. "I want you to dazzle her when she comes out. I want to see her reaction." Sebastian grinned and nodded at her.

Gabrielle stepped out of the fitting room looking spectacular. She wore a strapless red cocktail dress, and her eyes were sparkling with pleasure. She looked at Arielle first to see her reaction.

"You look stunning. Troy will love it," Arielle said.

Next, she turned to look at Sebastian for his approval, and then it happened. She looked as if she were going to pass out. She tried to mumble something, but no words came out. As she started to lose her balance, Arielle reached out and put her arm around her as both she and Sebastian burst out laughing. She looked so dazed. Sebastian looked away, and shortly after Gabrielle recovered her composure.

"I know what just happened, and Sebastian, that's not fair," Gabrielle said, giving him a look of mock reproval. "Do you think I should get the dress?"

"I think you should," Sebastian and Arielle said simultaneously. "It's beautiful," Sebastian added. Smiling happily, Gabrielle went back to the fitting room in sheer satisfaction.

Next, it was Eva's turn. Eva had picked an attractive black cocktail dress with spaghetti straps; she too looked fabulous.

"Do it again," Arielle whispered to Sebastian as Eva came through the door and looked at Sebastian. That did it for her too. Arielle just couldn't stop the laughter from bursting out as she saw Eva go limp and almost fall to the floor. Sebastian reached out quickly and steadied her with his strong arm. She looked lost and was gasping for air. Sebastian and Arielle shared a knowing look and then looked away. Eva shook her head and appeared dazed. She had no clue what had just happened to her. Once she was back to normal she looked at the dress and then at Arielle and Sebastian, a bit confused. She remained silent for a long moment and finally, shaking her head, she turned back to Sebastian.

"So, what do you think, Sebastian? Should I buy it?" she asked.

"It's very attractive, Eva. Yes, I think you should."

Eva turned to Arielle with a happy smile. "Do you agree, Arielle?"

"That dress is you," Arielle said. Eva smiled and walked back into the fitting room looking pleased.

When they were alone, Sebastian pulled Arielle closer. Bending down, he brushed his lips against her ear. "I want you so much," he purred in a low, seductive voice. Arielle shivered, and looking up, their gaze locked.

"You'll have to wait," she said, pulling back.

He drew in a deep breath. "How long?"

"Only as long as it's necessary to finish shopping," she said, reaching up and touching his lips with her tongue.

"Mmmm," he said, gasping as his arm tightened around her waist. "That's not helping; I hope you realize that," he murmured. Arielle just chuckled happily.

# Chapter 11

**WITH ALL THREE GIRLS OUTFITTED,** Gabrielle and Eva paid for their dresses, and they all walked out of the store together, talking and laughing. Sebastian took Arielle's hand and held it tightly while they strolled down the small streets and bought a few more things. Eva showed her ring to Sebastian, a huge grin on her face, and he made a point of enthusiastically admiring it. She smiled at him happily and gave him a big hug. It made Arielle happy that her friends liked Sebastian, and he seemed to like them. Some of their stories made him laugh out loud, and he seemed to be having a great time.

While holding his hand, Arielle noticed a large silver ring on his finger that she had never noticed before. She pulled his hand closer and looked at it. It was magnificent. A long engraved bar extended along the ring and met with a beautifully etched medieval-looking cross shape on either side. It looked very impressive and very important.

"I don't think I ever remember seeing this before," she said, looking up at him.

"I've been wearing it ever since we met."

"Oh, I guess I've been busy looking at you that I never noticed the ring before," she giggled. "Is the design a family crest?"

"No, it isn't," he said, adding in a whisper, "I'll explain when we're alone."

He snaked his arm around her waist and pulled her closer. Arielle felt she had walked miles since the morning, and they were coming to the end of their shopping day. She still didn't have a gift for Sebastian, but she couldn't do that now with Sebastian by her side. *I'll just have to do that tomorrow,* she thought. *It will be hard to leave him, but I'll have just to do it,* she thought, smiling and pulling closer to him.

Sebastian cocked his head and looked at her quizzically.

"What are you thinking about?" he asked, trying to hide his amusement.

"Just you," she said and smiled.

They were on their way to the car when they heard someone calling Arielle's name. They looked around and saw Andrew running toward them. Sebastian looked at her questioningly.

"It's Andrew, one of our good friends," she explained. Andrew was now in front of her. He lifted her and twirled her around, kissing her on both cheeks, and greeted Gabrielle and Eva the same way.

"Andrew, this is Sebastian, my boyfriend," Arielle said.

Andrew shook Sebastian's hand in a very friendly manner. "You're a very lucky guy," he said. "You've got one of the most beautiful girls around," he added, winking at Arielle.

Sebastian just smiled. "You're right," he said. "I am very lucky."

"What are you all doing? Did you get my Christmas present yet?" Andrew joked. They all laughed, and Andrew walked along with them going in the same direction. He and Sebastian talked about sports. They seemed to enjoy their conversation. Finally, they arrived at the parking lot. Andrew shook Sebastian's hand once again and hugged each of the girls in turn. "I'll be going home for Christmas," he said. "See you next year." They waved and wished him a happy holiday as he walked to his car.

Her friends already knew that Arielle would be leaving with Sebastian, so they weren't surprised when she gave her car keys to Gabrielle. She embraced her friends, and they said their goodbyes.

Sebastian had parked his gorgeous blue Porsche a short walk down the road. On the way to the car, he reached out and wrapped his arm around her back, pulling her closer to his side. He looked down and trapped her gaze. His hand skimmed down to the low of her back and slipped underneath her shirt. His touch was blistering hot, and Arielle shivered with excitement. His fingers moved slowly up and down her backbone, and he heard her take a shuddering breath. A wide smile filled with raw desire spread across his face at the feel of her silky skin between his fingertips. Reaching the car, he turned her to face him and pressed her back against the car. He cupped her chin, tilting her face up until their eyes met. His mouth came down on hers with burning desire, and her lips parted, giving his tongue access to the softness of her mouth. She moaned quietly and the kiss deepened. They were suddenly lost beyond the vigorous need for each other. They drifted into a world of rapture and pure euphoria that made them shatter with startling intensity. The earth swayed beneath Arielle's feet, and she surrendered to his heated ravaging of her mouth.

When he finally drew back, he peered deep into her eyes, and his mouth curved into that amazing smile that she loved. "God, I missed you," he murmured, and his lips were back on hers, moving softly, brushing against her cheek, across her collarbone and down the column of her throat. He growled as a shuddering desire pulverized his body. "All I do is think of you, and I'm on fire," he breathed in her mouth. "What am I going to do with you?" he asked in a husky voice.

Arielle closed her eyes and reaching up, wrapped her arms around his neck and searched for his mouth once again. Their tongues dueled in a wild dance, filling their souls with ecstasy and desire. The taste of his scent intoxicated her. The taste of her scent drove him insane.

Reluctantly, he lifted his head and pulled away. "I think we'd better go," he murmured, out of breath. "I will not be responsible for the outcome if we stay here another moment." He groaned softly and bending down he pressed a soft kiss on her lips. He held the car door open for her as she slid in, unable to breathe after the intense encounter. She watched him walk around the car, looking at her with clear hunger in his eyes. He was so striking that it made her heart skip a few beats, and she couldn't take her eyes away from his face.

When he got into the car, she reached over and set her hand on his thigh, pressing softly, feeling the flexing of his powerful muscles. An enticing smile spread across her face. The fire spread swiftly below his stomach area, and he hissed a tremulous breath between his teeth. Clasping her hand, he moved it away from his thigh and placed it on the armrest. He then laid his hand over hers and met her passionate gaze.

"I can't drive when you get me excited," he said.

Arielle raised her eyebrows, and her lips turned into a pout as she kept her eyes on his face. Sebastian grinned and ran his fingers softly over her hand. Then lifting it to his lips, he trailed soft kissed across her knuckles. "I love you, be patient, we'll be at the hotel shortly," he said and chuckled.

She didn't answer still pouting; she just turned and stared out the car window, her mind in frisson. *The way I want this man is frightening*, she thought and bit down on her lower lip.

His voice sounded like a million miles away. "I'm very happy to be spending Christmas with you. Are you happy to have me here?"

She immediately turned to face him. "Yes," she muttered, eyes wide with apprehension. "Why would you ask me that?"

"Because right now you're pouting, and you don't look very pleased." Sebastian knew exactly why she was pouting, but he was determined to have a little fun with her.

Her face grew anxious. "I'm pouting because you won't let me touch you," she said. "I'm really happy that you're here for Christmas."

"Then show me," he said, feigning dejection.

Arielle placed her hand in his and smiled submissively. "I'm sorry, I love you so much, and I'm happy you are here."

Sebastian smiled inwardly, and pulling her to him, he planted a soft kiss on her lips. They remained silent for the rest of the drive.

The atmosphere at the hotel was festive when Sebastian and Arielle arrived. Christmas decorations were everywhere. Three huge Christmas trees sparkled in the enormous lobby. Sebastian was greeted with smiles by the staff. By now, Arielle knew that he was a very important customer.

"Merry Christmas, Mr. Gaulle," the bellboy said.

"Same to you, Charlie," Sebastian replied politely.

The hotel manager walked up to them and warmly reached out

to shake Sebastian's hand. "Happy holiday, Mr. Gaulle," he said.

Sebastian took his proffered hand and shook it politely, "This is my fiancée, Miss Arielle Lloyd," Sebastian said, to Arielle's astonishment, putting his arm around her waist. The manager smiled at her with a warm smile, "Merry Christmas, Miss Lloyd," he said.

"Same to you," she replied with a sparkling smile.

As they walked towards the elevator, Sebastian pulled her face up toward him and touched her lips softly. She closed her eyes, tasting the sweetness of his lips and giggled.

"I thought we were going to be good in front of people," she said. "What about all these people who are staring at us right now?"

"Oh, I figured sooner or later that was about to happen didn't you?" he laughed, pulling her into the elevator.

"Your fiancée?" she echoed, looking at him with wonder in her eyes.

"Yes, fiancée," he said. "Is there something wrong with that?"

"No, certainly not," she replied. "But shouldn't there be a ring that goes along with that title?"

"All in good time, you beautiful girl, you," he said.

He was holding her so tight that as he shifted his body, she could feel that he was already very excited. She wanted him, and there was nothing else that could make her any happier right now than just being with him. He had an amazing way of enthralling her in bed. The familiar warm sensation spread throughout her body. She stepped out of the elevator into the penthouse, trying to catch her breath as she heard him chuckle softly. He locked the door behind them with one hand. With the other he swept her up in his arms and carried her to the bed.

"I want to keep you in my arms forever. I hate being away from you," he moaned. For a moment, he looked as if he were in deep thought. Then he chuckled.

"What?" she said, looking up.

"When I'm away from you, I can close my eyes and feel your beautiful soft, skin, the amazing feel of your breasts, the joy of making love to you. I'm absolutely under your spell, Lizzy."

Arielle closed her eyes and felt the heat of his body next to hers. Her nerves tensed to a painful peak. Sebastian used that moment to pull away from her and get out of bed.

*What? Where are you going? Come back,* she thought. She kept her eyes closed, waiting for him to return but after a few moments, there was still only silence. Startled, she opened her eyes and found him kneeling in front of her, smiling. He didn't have a shirt on, just a pair of jeans. He looked magnificent. She let her eyes take in all that beauty, wondering how a man like that could love someone like her.

She smiled at him happily, and before she could open her mouth to tell him how much she loved him, he uttered the most unbelievable and unexpected words.

"Marry me, Arielle," he said in a voice filled with emotion.

Arielle stopped breathing and was unable to either move or speak. She felt that the whole joy of the universe had just fallen into her lap. She felt pure joy, bliss, harmony, and fear all mixed up together. She closed her eyes and thought, *I don't have to imagine what heaven must be like, it's right here.* Tears welled up in her eyes, and she started to sob.

"Arielle, I am asking you to marry me, baby, why are you crying?" he said again in his velvety voice.

She reached for him and held him tight as she whispered, "Oh, my God, Sebastian," she sobbed. "I'm ecstatic; I'm elated! And yes…yes… yes… I'll marry you, and I'll love you forever!" she stammered between sobs.

"You mean you'll love me for eternity," he corrected her.

"I don't know about eternity," she said. "But I'll love you for as long as I'm on this earth."

He took her left hand and placed a gorgeous ring on her finger. It was the most beautiful ring she had ever laid eyes on, and it looked as if it was from another era. A large diamond was set in the center of the ring, which was composed of tiny intertwined diamonds and sapphires. Its beauty was breathtaking.

Their lips locked in a hot kiss. Arielle couldn't believe she was engaged and that this gorgeous man was going to be her husband. She put her hand on the nape of his neck and pulled him onto the bed. He lay next to her and pressed his body against hers in greedy eagerness. She could feel his arousal against her stomach, and she moaned anxiously. She stroked him softly but fervently, and he stilled. She pressed her lips at the hollow of his throat and sucked in a deep breath. He moaned deeply as his arms tightened around her body, trying to keep his lips from trembling. He began to make love to her with unbelievable passion. She could hear him moan with pleasure as she rolled her body over his and he stopped breathing. He groaned as her lips brushed his face. Her tongue traced the side of his jaw, across his collarbone and back up, circling his beautiful lips. His breathing quickened, and he moaned in clear anticipation. She felt complete satisfaction knowing that she was the one sending waves of bliss across every part of his body.

She was startled when he lifted her with one quick movement and rolled them both, pinning her beneath him. He brushed her ear with his tongue and whispered eagerly, "You'll be mine for eternity." There was no holding him back again as a shuddering gasp escaped his lips and she fractured.

Sebastian's thoughts whirled in dismay. Day by day, moment by moment, Arielle was proving to be an incurable addiction that was sweltering the blood in his veins. Their lovemaking was hot and wild.

She clung to him gasping, and when it was over, she fell apart and collapsed. Her body went completely numb. Sebastian was to be her husband. It was real now. She felt drunk with elation. Her mind was in a state of ecstasy both from the physical enjoyment of his lovemaking and the emotional thrill from the ring on her finger. This joy was going to be hers for the rest of her life.

Afterward, they lay in bed, unable to move for a long time. He lifted his body on one elbow and with his hand brushed her hair away from her face. He ran his fingers along the side of her jaw as he bent down and gently kissed her lips.

"What an exhilarating state of mind. This is going to be an eternity for us, Arielle, what do you think about that?"

"Sebastian, I just can't imagine feeling this way for the rest of my life. I'm so happy I could scream at the top of my lungs, I want the whole world to know that I'm in love with you." She laughed, and he held her tight, laughing with her, looking like an excited young boy. They lay in bed for a while just talking about their future together, and Arielle spent a lot of time looking at her gorgeous ring.

"I have never seen a ring like this," she said.

"Do you like it?"

"I think it's the most exquisite ring ever, anywhere."

"It's pretty special, and it was made just for you."

"It doesn't look like a modern ring. Is it?"

"No, this is from the Victorian era. Before 1870, they didn't make rings with one large diamond as a center stone. But during Queen Victoria's reign, they started to create this style of engagement ring. I think they are the prettiest rings ever made."

Arielle chuckled as she thought of how Sebastian was always the source of such a wealth of information.

"What is it now?" he asked, smiling.

"How do you know so much about everything? I am amazed at your knowledge, and how smart you are."

"Oh, I'm not as smart as you think," he said. "If you had roamed this earth as long as I have, with endless days and nights to think and wonder, you would learn a few things too." He laughed out loud, and she joined in.

"I just can't tell you how perfectly and utterly happy I am with you, Mr. Darcy," she said, sighing with pleasure.

"All I ever wanted to do is make you happy, Miss Elizabeth," he replied, and held her close. "You are my life, and I couldn't breathe if you weren't with me."

"I have been trying to understand ever since we met how you can love me so much when you are so perfect and so beautiful," Arielle said. "You're every girl's dream, and here you are with me. I'm nothing special, I'm just a simple girl."

"I don't think you see yourself the way others do, Arielle. You are extraordinary. You're smart, you're sensitive, you're warm and so beautiful. When I look into your eyes, I get all the energy I need. Your love supplies me with the very air I breathe. You arouse me more than any other woman I have ever met, and loving you is all I want to do for eternity."

Ecstasy was Arielle's state of mind as she got up and walked toward the shower. She turned the hot water on. Sebastian was suddenly there with her. She laughed at his display of immortal speed. He held her tight against his hot body and let the water run over both of them. He was caressing and kissing her neck as he moaned once. He tipped her face up toward his, and she parted her lips, letting his tongue invade the inside softness of her mouth. His hands tightened around her waist, pulling her closer against him, giving her more pleasure that any human being deserves in a lifetime.

"You will be the death of me," he murmured, his favorite way of letting her know he was extremely happy.

"I can't believe that we're engaged," she said. "I want to call everyone I know and let them know how much I love you."

"I bought this ring three days after I first set eyes on you," he said. "That's how sure I was that you were going to be mine for eternity." He had a brilliant smile on his face, brighter even than the smiles that had made her fall in love with him.

"This is the best Christmas ever!" she said. "And I thought you might not be able to come at all."

"I would never have missed this time with you, Arielle. I had fun just walking and shopping with you and your friends. That's something I haven't had the chance to do for years, for centuries. You make me feel truly young, full of energy, and completely happy. I forget my dreadful existence, I feel like a normal human being."

"I want to call my parents," she said. She picked up her mobile and speed-dialed her parents. It was a warm and exuberant call. Her parents were thrilled. They thought Sebastian was the perfect man for their daughter. They asked to speak with Sebastian, and after a wonderful and cheerful discussion, they hung up.

It was very late when they drifted off to sleep in each other's arms.

 *Chapter 12*

**THE DAY BEFORE CHRISTMAS EVE,** Arielle woke up quite early. Sebastian was already in the shower. She still needed to get his gift, so she reached for her phone and called Gabrielle.

"Can you go shopping with me this morning?" she asked. "Or do you have plans with Troy?"

"No, as a matter of fact I thought you would be busy with Sebastian, and that's why I didn't call you. I was just asking Eva if she wanted to come shopping with me. We need to get our gifts for Troy and Ian. Shall I come pick you up?"

"Oh, that would be great! I have to get Sebastian's gift as well, I couldn't do that while he was with us. And I've nothing for him."

"When do you want me to pick you up?"

"I need to take a shower and get ready, but I won't be that long. I'll ring you as soon as I'm dressed. Is that okay?"

"I'll wait for your call."

She lay back in bed and closed her eyes while waiting for Sebastian to finish his shower. She knew that if she went into the shower now, she wouldn't be able to leave any time soon. The thought made her lips part faintly, and a soft gasp of pleasure escaped her. She was lying there daydreaming when she felt his weight bow the bed. He was pressing himself on top of her, spreading heat, craving, and longing as his arms enfolded her, cuddling her against his chest.

"What are you thinking about?" he whispered as his lips brushed against her ear.

"Just you," she moaned.

"I didn't want to wake you up, you looked tired," he said.

"Hmm," she replied, stretching leisurely.

"Long night?" he asked and chuckled, his eyes filled with mirth. Arielle laughed and pulled his head down; she pressed a soft kiss on his beautiful mouth.

"Sebastian, I have to go and do some last minute shopping with Gabrielle and Eva." She tried to get up, but he pulled her back and gazed into her eyes. He didn't release her. She could clearly see desire, hunger, and want in his eyes. She remained perfectly still. "And you can't come with us. I hope you can find something to do while I'm gone," she added, suppressing her intensifying passion.

"Oh, don't worry about me. But you are not going anywhere right now."

"They're waiting for me to call so they can pick me up," she said, and tried to get up one more time to run to the shower, but she was unsuccessful. Sebastian's grip on her tightened and their gazes locked. He suddenly rolled with her in his arms and pulled her eagerly on top of him, his eyes searching her face for a reaction. She drew a tense breath. Her expression was one of shimmering passion, but she remained silent. His hands moved eagerly, caressing her bare skin, filling him with a desperate want. Her breasts were pressed against his chest, and he growled, totally intoxicated. He moved his fingers to her lower back and pressed her fervently against him until she nearly stopped breathing. He chuckled with pleasure as his eagerness reached a peak. His mouth found hers and he sighed with a deep hunger. It took a short moment and the passion escalated to the ultimate degree of desire. Arielle held her breath practically the entire time. She caressed the planes of his back and felt his hands tightening around her, holding her captive as he pulled her hips tightly against him. She let him devour her lips in his mouth as sensation crashed through her. She was filled with wild anticipation and joy when he suddenly pulled back and looked piercingly into her eyes.

"Do you want to get up now?" he asked, a chuckle escaping his beautiful lips. He knew he had her exactly where he wanted her. Again he rolled, taking her by surprise, and pinned her beneath him.

"Mmmm," he moaned as she shifted underneath him, inviting his next move with vigor and eagerness. He made wild love to her, and she gave into the intoxicating heat of their bodies melding once again. She reached the point of sensual exhilaration, ready to explode into a million pieces. His scent was mind blowing, his body felt hot and soft. Arielle couldn't believe they could do this over and over again, and every time it would feel like the first time. He was the most exciting man she had ever been with—and the only man she had ever met in a sexual way.

With a sudden and calculated move, they reached the peak of rapture together, and they both shuddered. She felt numb with exhilaration, not believing that he would actually be her husband and her lover forever. He rolled off of her, completely spent, and she jumped out of bed. He tried to pull her back again, but she escaped his grip, laughing out loud, and ran into the shower.

"You'll pay for this later, I promise," he said, gasping for breath.

She took a warm shower, then stepped out and wrapped a towel around herself as she went to retrieve her clothes. He was lying in bed, his arms behind his head looking in her direction. His sensuous lips were curved up into that sexy smile of his, and his eyes were full of love and affection, for her and her alone.

"Are you sure you don't want to come back to bed and stay here with me?" he asked, grinning invitingly.

"I'd love to do that, but Christmas is just two days away, and I have run out of time to do what I need to do. I love you to death, and I'll make it up to you, I promise," she said, chuckling as she began to get dressed.

As she was dressing, she picked up her phone and dialed Gabrielle's number.

"I'm ready," she said. "You can pick me up at the hotel entrance." Just as she hung up, her phone rang again. This time, it was Paul wanting to verify the time for the party. The next call was from her mother wanting to know when she would be there. And the one after that was from Andrew, asking if they could meet and talk after he came back from Nottingham, where he was spending Christmas. "That will be great Andrew," she said. "I'm sure we can get together. Call me when you get back."

"Thanks, Arielle, have a happy Christmas," he said. She dropped the phone into her purse and gave Sebastian a sexy smile.

"Well, are you done with all your admirers?" Sebastian asked, a bemused smile on his face.

"Oh, stop, they are friends."

"Paul is in love with you," he said. "And many of the guys I met would like to go out with you. I can read their minds, you know."

"Well, I can't tell people how to feel about me," Arielle said. "All I can do is tell them I'm not available. And I'm ready to show you off tomorrow night to everyone I know."

She bent down to give him a kiss, and he wrapped his arms around her tightly, pulling her down to him. The kiss was hot and very exciting, but she had to go.

"I have to go, Sebastian, please don't make it so hard for me."

"I can't help myself. Every time I set eyes on you I want you," he said.

"Well, you have to wait. So please let me go."

He kept his arms wrapped around her back, still holding her tight. "Kiss me and tell me that you love only me."

She touched his lips softly, whispering in a tender voice, "I love you more than life itself."

He smiled and released her. She straightened her shirt and, smiling, walked out the door.

"Wait!" he shouted. She caught the door before it closed and saw him jump out of bed and go through his jeans pockets. Then he handed her a key to the door. "In case I'm not here when you get back, I want you to wait here for me."

"All right," she said. He kissed her again, and this time, she left. She didn't want to leave at all, but she had to buy him a Christmas gift. He was the most important person in her life now, and she wanted to make him feel special. He made her so happy.

By the time she got downstairs, Gabrielle and Eva were there waiting for her. She jumped into the back seat of the car and stretched her hand between the two of them, showing off her ring.

They both gasped and screamed at the same time.

"When did that happen?" they cried.

"Last night and it was magical," Arielle said dreamily. "That's why I couldn't call you. I can hardly breathe every time I think about getting married to him. I just can't believe my luck."

"Well, I sure hope I get a ring soon," Gabrielle said wistfully. "I'll be very unhappy if I'm left behind." She sounded a little sad, but Arielle didn't want to tell her that Troy had already bought a ring for her and was waiting for her birthday to propose.

"I'm sure Troy will ask when it's the right time for both of you. I hope you do not doubt him," Arielle said.

"No, not at all," Gabrielle replied, and Arielle knew she was telling the truth.

They were heading toward Churchill Square Mall in the center of town. Arielle needed to find something special for Sebastian. She and her friends spent the better part of the morning walking from one shop to the other, finally settling on the right one. It was a small bookstore that had a variety of classic first editions.

Eva and Arielle both were crazy about books, so they spent a little time thumbing through several of them. Gabrielle, on the other hand, seemed to be bored to death, so she walked over to the dress shop next door.

"So, how did it go with Ian?" Arielle asked Eva with a smile.

"I love him so much, Arielle. He's wonderful, and he loves me so much. I find him irresistible. Being with him is the most important thing in my life. He's perfect, and I know that nothing will ever change the way I feel about him."

"I am so glad to hear that! I love you both, and it means a lot to me that you're happy." Eva hugged her and smiled with contentment.

It wasn't long before Arielle found what she was looking for. It was the first edition of *Pride and Prejudice*. Sebastian had told her it was his favorite book, so this was going to be one of his Christmas presents. She was almost sure he already had the book, but maybe he didn't have a first edition. She also purchased the first edition of *The Book of Romance* by Andrew Lang, who was known for his translations of classical literature. The book was more than a hundred years old. She chuckled with pleasure as she placed the books on the counter and asked to have them gift-wrapped.

Next, they stopped at the music store. She purchased a few CDs by composers she knew Sebastian loved: Vivaldi, Bach, Mozart, and Felix Mendelssohn.

Her next stop was a men's shop. "This is going to be a gamble," she murmured as she bought a beautiful brown leather jacket she thought would look stunning with Sebastian's gorgeous emerald eyes. Pleased with the purchase, she had it boxed, and gift wrapped, as she had done with all the other gifts. "Well, I feel pretty good about the choices I made," she said to Gabrielle, who had rejoined them. Eva and Gabrielle had picked some special gifts for their guys as well, and they were almost finished with their shopping.

"How about some lunch?" Arielle asked.

"I still have a few things to buy," Gabby said, "but I'm hungry."

"Me too," Eva said, and they decided to finish their shopping after lunch.

They walked to a nice outdoor restaurant, Summer Wind, on Boyce's Street, a block away from the mall. They were waiting to cross the light at West Street and Boyce when they noticed Sebastian's car coming down the road, passing right in front of them.

Arielle was sure that he couldn't miss seeing the three of them standing there, but he didn't acknowledge them as he passed by. He just kept driving down the street and made a right turn at the corner, moving out of their view.

Arielle was utterly stunned. Her heart hammered in her chest; her pulse pounded her veins, and her mind was filled with wild speculations because Sebastian had not been alone. A beautiful, dark-haired girl had been sitting next to him, and they had been so busy talking and laughing that apparently he hadn't seen her and her friends.

Nausea churned in the pit of her stomach, and she grabbed onto Eva, feeling suddenly lightheaded. Eva and Gabrielle exchanged looks and gazed at Arielle with great concern.

"Are you all right, Arielle?" Gabrielle asked. But Arielle couldn't hear what Gabby was saying. Bad thoughts were pounding through her head, crowding out everything else. She couldn't make any sense at all out of what she had just seen. Who was that girl?

Sebastian hadn't said anything about going anywhere when she had left the room. Tears were welling up, and bewilderment flushed across her face. Tension rippled through her body. She took a couple of deep breaths and asked her friends in a voice that was slightly shaking, "Did you all see what I saw?"

"Yes," they answered quietly.

"Arielle, I wouldn't jump to any conclusions," Eva said. "I don't see anything bad around those two. I'm sure there is a good explanation. Please wait to find out who she is, and don't make any assumptions." Eva sounded very sure about what she was saying, and Arielle should have trusted her. But she couldn't erase the picture of the two of them in the car, laughing and talking, so close to each other. The image played itself over and over in her mind, driving her mad.

Gabrielle took Arielle's hand and pulled her across the street to a table outside a restaurant with a garden view. They sat down.

"Could we have some wine, please?' Eva asked the waiter.

"I just want water," Arielle murmured, but when it came, she didn't touch it. It had only been a few minutes, but it seemed like centuries to her. *I just want to die,* she thought. She could hardly breathe; it was hard to hold back the tears. She knew that to feel jealousy like this would kill her, but she couldn't help herself.

Gabrielle and Eva were shocked. They weren't sure what they could say that would make Arielle feel better, so they were mostly quiet. Arielle looked in her bag to find some tissues to wipe her eyes when she heard Gabrielle clear her throat twice in an attempt to get her attention. Then, Arielle realized someone was standing right in front of her.

"Hello, Sebastian," both Gabrielle and Eva exclaimed. Her head snapped up, and she saw him standing inches away from her, his arm around the same gorgeous girl that she had seen with him in his car.

He reached down with his free hand and pulled Arielle up, pressing his lips to hers. Then he noticed her tears, and immediately he let go of the girl, taking Arielle into his arms tenderly.

"Baby, are you hurt?" he asked nothing but tenderness and love in his eyes.

"I'm fine," she whispered, trying to make her voice steady.

Sebastian looked quizzically at Gabrielle and Eva.

"What's going on?" he said. They both just shrugged their shoulders.

The girl was standing silently next to Sebastian, trying to understand what the confusion was about. Sebastian put his arm around her waist again and pulled the girl close, facing Arielle.

"Arielle, Gabrielle, Eva, this is Loren Dillon," he said, and he smiled. Arielle was astounded as she tried to process his words.

"Your sister?" she asked as her face flushed red against her fair complexion. Relief, embarrassment, and a lingering sense of disbelief joined, leaving her feeling quite confused.

Loren stepped forward and hugged Arielle. "It's wonderful to meet you, Arielle," she said. "Sebastian has told me so much about you. And you've made him so happy." She smiled warmly at Arielle, stepped back, and reaching out to hold both of Arielle's hands squeezed them affectionately.

Gabrielle and Eva moved closer and shook Loren's hand happily.

"Sebastian can't stop talking about you," Loren continued. "He doesn't pay attention to anything I say anymore, and his thoughts are always on you." She was laughing now, and everyone joined in the laughter.

Arielle put her arms around Sebastian's neck and kissed him softly. He leaned over and whispered in her ear, "When are you going to start trusting me?" She looked down, embarrassed that he knew why she had been so upset. She felt humiliated, and she knew he was right. She was going to have to stop mistrusting him.

Releasing Sebastian, she hugged Loren and said, "I'm so happy to meet you."

It wasn't so much that she didn't trust Sebastian and his love for her; it was more that on some level she just couldn't believe how lucky she was. "Yes, I'm so happy to meet you," she said a second time, giggling and averting her gaze from Sebastian.

"Would you like something to drink? Something to eat?" she asked Loren.

"Oh, no, thank you," Loren replied. Like her brother, she was breathtakingly beautiful with the looks of a statue of a goddess, not a real person.

Arielle laughed quietly to herself. *Does Sebastian even know any ugly people?* She wondered. It seemed that all the people she saw or met through him had the same incredible beauty and amazingly musical voices. And of course, they didn't like to eat or drink anything. Sebastian had told her that immortals didn't have a great appetite for human food. It didn't provide them with the energy that salve did. They could eat and drink anything they wanted to if the occasion called for it, but they just preferred not to do so.

"What's so funny?" he whispered as he leaned closer.

"Nothing…nothing at all…" she said in a low voice.

"We'll talk about this later," he said. He cupped her chin, lifted her face toward his, and instinctively their lips were drawn together, irresistibly. Heat surged through her body, and she shuddered, trying to suppress the crazy allure his touch was arousing.

"I thought that you might want to take Loren with you Christmas shopping while I run some errands myself," Sebastian said. "Would that be okay with you?"

"Of course," Arielle said, fully aware of the seduction hiding behind those sexy eyes. "We can start getting to know each other."

Sebastian kissed Loren on the cheek, then kissed Gabrielle and Eva, who loved every minute of it. "Call me when you're done, Arielle, and I'll come back and get Loren."

As he walked away, every eye in the place was on him. He was so elegant and dazzling. Arielle followed him with her eyes, drinking in the sight of him, wishing that she were in his arms. He looked back as he neared the end of the street, waved, smiled, and disappeared around the corner.

The girls spent the afternoon shopping, laughing, and talking about guys, fashion, jewelry, and everything else. Loren was wonderful. Arielle couldn't believe she was immortal. She was so natural and soft-spoken, and she joined in every conversation they had. She was fun and easy to talk to and very kind to Arielle. *It's like I have a sister now,* Arielle thought, and suddenly tears sprang into her eyes again, this time, tears of joy.

Gabrielle and Eva liked Loren too. As they all chatted about the Christmas party, Loren seemed fascinated. "Loren, would you like to come too?" Arielle asked.

A huge smile spread across Loren's lovely face, and she hugged Arielle with enthusiasm. "I'd love to!" she exclaimed.

"Well, then it's settled," Arielle said with a smile.

"I want to see your ring," Loren said eagerly. So Arielle extended her hand and Loren let out a low cry. "Wow! That is gorgeous." She hugged Arielle warmly, adding, "I'm so happy for both of you."

It was getting late, and the girls had tons of bags to take to the car. Arielle called Sebastian and asked him to meet them at the parking lot, giving him directions for where to find them. He was there within ten minutes.

"I hate to say goodbye, Loren," Arielle said, "but we'll see you Saturday night, won't we?"

"Saturday night?" Sebastian asked.

"Yes, Loren is coming to the Christmas party."

A brilliant smile spread across his beautiful face. His lips found Arielle's as he wrapped her in his arms. "I'll see you at the hotel later," he whispered in her ear. Arielle flushed with pleasure.

She got into the car with Gabrielle and Eva. Sebastian and Loren watched them as they drove away. They waved at Loren, and she waved back, a big smile on her face.

*What a strange turn of events,* Arielle thought, and then chided herself. *When will I stop making up bad things in my head? Sebastian is right. I have to stop doing that. I have to believe this is real.*

They drove past the hotel, where Arielle picked up the packages for her family and friends, leaving Sebastian's gifts in his room. Then, they drove to the flat. Arielle took a shower and changed her clothes, choosing snug-fitting jeans with a green silk shirt that she knew would match the color of Sebastian's eyes. She wanted to be sure she would look exhilarating to her new finacé, and she also wanted them to shine as a couple. The necklace he had given her looked amazing against her bare neckline, and the ring on her right hand, with its huge emerald stone, matched her blouse perfectly. The ring made everything real, not only his amazing existence but even more, the fact that he loved *her* and wanted to marry *her*.

She put her hair in a ponytail, grabbed her purse and a light sweater, and drove to the hotel. It was now around four-thirty in the afternoon. Sebastian wasn't there yet, so she poured herself a glass of wine and lay in bed watching the telly. Tired after all that shopping, she emptied the glass and dozed off. When she woke up, his lips were pressing on hers, and he was smiling at her with his sweet, crooked smile. She reached up and pulled him close.

"I love you so much," she sighed, "Do you know that?"

His arms tightened around her waist, and he pulled her face to his, crushing her lips beneath his. Then he laid her on her back and propped himself up on his elbow, looking at her with a sense of wonder in his eyes.

"What?" she asked, a bit uncomfortable with his unrelenting gaze.

"You mesmerize me. I can't get enough of you. What am I going to do?"

"You may get tired of me once we're married."

"That's a ridiculous thought you have had." He kissed her softly and ran his finger down her stomach and back up to her chin. "You are so beautiful."

She closed her eyes and moaned with satisfaction as he rolled on top of her. His lips moved slowly from her face to her neck, back up slowly and down again, methodically.

"I want to marry you," he murmured. "*Now*," he added, accentuating the last word with a kiss.

She pulled back, gazing into his eyes, "What do you mean, 'now'?" she asked inquisitively, pulse intensifying. She noticed his brows were raised in clear amusement, and his lips had curved.

"What do you think I mean when I say now?"

"I don't know. That's why I'm asking."

"Let me clear that up for you. I want you to be my wife today. Now. This very moment."

"Oh," Arielle mumbled, struggling to understand what he was saying. She thought for a minute and then said, "Sebastian, we can't do that. My family would be extremely disappointed if we eloped. I have been dreaming of the day I will walk down the aisle and show every person I love, and every person that has been part of my life, the perfect man I have chosen to be my husband, my lover, and my friend. You."

"I don't think I can wait that long," he frowned.

She reached for his lips and pulled him into a breathless kiss. "It will be soon enough," she murmured while continuing to kiss him passionately.

"We fit perfectly together," he whispered.

"You are perfect, and I'm…well, I'm me," she said.

"Arielle, I have the look of an immortal, and that's why you see me as perfect. You, on the other hand, possess the absolute beauty of a human, without help from anyone or anything, except for the fact that nature was pretty bountiful when it came to you," he said, laughing softly.

Just then her phone rang, and she jumped. Sebastian reached over and handed the phone to her. It was Gabrielle.

"Do you want to go to see a film with my friends, and then maybe go dancing?" Arielle asked Sebastian, holding the phone away from her mouth. He nodded, with clear pleasure in his face.

"Yes, sure, we'll meet you at eight-thirty," Arielle said, clicking off the phone.

She tried to get out of bed, but Sebastian pulled her close again as he softly circled her mouth with his tongue, making her shiver.

"Where do you think you're going? We have plenty of time," he said. He didn't wait for an answer as he proceeded to help her out of her clothes. His lips moved eagerly against hers, and he savored the taste of her. His body shifted and in one move he pulled her beneath him, sending fire through every nerve in her body. That special smile was showing again as his hands moved down to her hips and caressed her silky flesh. Arielle stopped breathing as tension built, and exquisite sensation disjointed her mind from her body. Sebastian groaned as he stroked her, elevating her desire and joining them together again as he moved her into a new position. She felt a tremor of elation that made her shudder as every thought left her mind and the flames of desire doused her. His lips found hers again. She sank into his blazing kiss as the ripples of heat spread, grew hotter, and as he moved one last time, he took both of them to the peak of pleasure.

Sebastian's eyes traced Arielle's face as intensity gave way to gratification. "How do you feel now?" he murmured, still completely out of breath. She closed her eyes, turning into his embrace and seeking the right words to answer him.

"Hmm... deliciously happy," was all she could say, giggling. Their lips met again, spreading pleasure across each and every muscle.

"Thank you for wanting to marry me," he murmured.

She chuckled softly. With an extreme effort she got out of bed and walked to the shower, closing the door behind her. She turned the lever on and stood there waiting for the water to get to the right temperature. A quiet chuckle escaped her when she heard the shower door open. She knew he was standing right behind her, but she didn't turn around. She reached for the soap, but his hand was already there leaving hers lingering in mid air.

"The soap or your life," he purred, brushing his lips teasingly against her ear.

A smile spread across her face, but she still didn't turn around. Pulling her hand away from the soap, she remained perfectly still. He picked up the soap and lathered his hands thoroughly. She felt his hands soft and lathery, sliding up and down her back, caressing her skin. Shivers rippled through her when his hands moved to her lower back and curved around to rest on her flat stomach. She had stopped breathing and was waiting for his next move. He drew in a deep breath and pulled her softly against him. She felt her warm skin flush against his hard-muscled body and trembled with anticipation. His lips brushed the back of her neck. She moved into him, and his control shattered into a million shards. Her heart started to pulsate as his hands started to move slowly upward and stopped when he reached her breasts. He gasped with longing and cupped them eagerly, pressing softly, methodically. She moaned as his breathing picked up. Her breath stopped as his hands started to slide back down, slowly passing over her abdomen and resting much lower. She gasped out loud and heard a soft chuckle as his hands moved around to the outside of her hips and down her thighs, covering every curve of her body with thick lather. He pulled her even closer, and he groaned, filled with an amazing sensation. Her knees buckled when he moved to the inside of her thighs, and she would have been on the shower floor if his hands hadn't held her steadily against his body.

He chuckled softly, his lips brushing her ear. "How am I doing?" he whispered, breathing heavily. She just couldn't take it any longer. She gathered her strength and spun around to face him without leaving his embrace. She met his gaze and got lost in his eyes. She threw her arms around his neck and reached up, searching for his lips. His mouth landed on hers, and they locked themselves in a passionate kiss. She was startled when she heard his husky groan and her feet left the floor. He lifted her up and onto him, groaning deeply as she nearly sobbed. An incredible force of passion pressed their bodies together like a tidal wave, and they melted together as into a swirl of scorching lava.

He was willing to please her for as long as she wanted until all their desire for that night was spent, all the passion had washed over their bodies, and they had both imploded in utter rapture. Afterward, their lips remained locked in an obsessive kiss.

Arielle couldn't help looking at him in amazement; he was more than any woman could ever ask for. She closed her eyes and smiled, contemplating an eternity of this bliss.

Finally, they got dressed and prepared themselves to meet her friends. Giggling, she whistled at him when she saw how handsome he was, dressed for an evening out. He laughed out loud in delight. She took his hand happily as they walked out of the room and down to the lobby.


When the film was over, they went dancing. Sebastian was sociable with the guys, and they all seemed to enjoy being together. Arielle knew he had more in common with Troy, but he enjoyed being with Ian just as much. That night, she was surprised to see Sebastian and Troy enjoying a drink together. She looked at Sebastian quizzically, but he just winked at her and didn't say anything.

The lights were low, and the band was incredible. Arielle and Sebastian danced, holding each other tight. He smiled when she reached up and tasted the sweetness of his lips.

"I love when you do that," he murmured. She moved her lips down the edge of his mouth, the side of his jaw and pressed at the hollow of his throat, making him groan. She knew that spot was very sensitive for him, and she tried to take advantage of it every time she could. He kept his eyes closed and his lips brushed the side of her face.

"I'm completely intoxicated by your touch," he murmured. She couldn't help smiling. She wanted to please him the same way he pleased her. He held her hand on the way back to the hotel and all Arielle could think of was how lucky she was that he loved her. It was late when they got into bed, and she closed her eyes, completely exhausted.

"Hey," he whispered as she began to fall asleep.

"What?" she asked in a sleepy voice.

"I just wanted to hear your voice before you fell asleep."

"What is it?"

"When I touch you, I like to shout from ecstasy." His voice was soft, sweet, and breathless.

"Is that so bad? You make me feel pretty much the same way," she said, moving closer to him. He encircled her with his arms, pulling her even closer.

He sighed. She could feel a longing in him for something, maybe a footprint of his fate as an immortal. She stayed in his arms. Her mind was still struggling to accept the fact that he had died, and now he was here again, full of life, love, and excitement. His body was warm and tender, more alive than any human she had ever known. She turned to face him. He was lost in his thoughts.

"Sebastian, what is it?"

"Oh, I just wish I could be a normal human being and grow old with you," he said. "I need to be with you. I want to be able to breathe, to live a normal life. I wish I could go to sleep and dream!" He paused with a faraway look in his eyes. "I remember growing up so long ago," he continued. "I was a happy child, and I had a great life, with a wonderful family and great friends." He paused again for a long moment, and then continued, "I can't remember exactly how my life was ripped away from me. But afterward, everything I had and everyone I knew was completely gone, as if they were pages that had been torn away from the book of my life and destroyed."

He stopped. He looked so sad. Arielle had never seen him look like this, or heard him talk like that. She tried to think of something to make him happy again. She put her hands on his face and held it close to hers. She kissed his lips softly. "I love you, Sebastian, you are the most important person in my life," she whispered.

He shook his head, and his lips curved up as he whispered, "Don't ever leave me, Arielle."

"What would ever make you say that?"

"It's not a mere request, Arielle, it's a warning. You are mine for eternity and don't you ever forget that. I've warned you." The look on his face was seductive as he added, "You are mine."

"Do you mean to tell me that none of those gorgeous girls you have been with throughout the centuries has ever satisfied you?"

"Jealous, are you?"

"Not at all. I'm just interested."

"Why don't you tell me how many guys I'll have to deal with during the next year?" he countered. "Paul, Andrew, Tristan, and all the others who I haven't met yet?"

"They are my friends, and they are harmless," she said. "No one I hang out with can hurt you. But your girlfriends are powerful and scary. They would like to tear me apart to get to you. How do I fight that?"

"I can't help the women coming after me," he said. "I've made it clear to everyone that I'm not available anymore. You're all I want, and all I need for eternity."

"There you go again, with that word, eternity," she said. "But, Sebastian, I can't be with you for eternity. I'm only human, and I'll die someday. For us to be together for eternity is only a dream. It's not something that can ever happen."

"Oh, but it will," he said mysteriously.

"I don't understand. Don't you want to let me know how you are going to achieve this dream?"

"Let me worry about that. I don't want you to worry about anything." His hands slipped behind her back, palms burning, and he pulled her close. Their lips met in a loving kiss, full of longing and delight. He encircled her in his arms, and they drifted off to sleep.

 *Chapter 13*

**THE MORNING OF CHRISTMAS EVE WAS QUIET** and wonderful. When Arielle awoke, Sebastian's gorgeous face was only a couple of inches away from hers. She smiled and sighed in complete and utter happiness, gently touched his soft lips, and watched as he opened his eyes.

"Good morning, my love," she whispered.

"I love you," was his reply, his lips already curved into the smile she loved so well. She got up and went to the shower, letting the warm water roll over her body. It felt so great.

Life was good, and the most incredible man on earth was waiting for her in the next room. He loved her, and he was going to be her husband. She just couldn't believe it. Could it really be true?

She wrapped herself in a large towel as she stepped out of the shower. She stood in front of the mirror and looked at herself. She was in high spirits, overjoyed even, and Sebastian had everything to do with that. She wanted to make him happy. She wanted to be with him for the rest of her life. He walked into the bathroom, put his arms around her, and held her for a little while.

"Why didn't you wait for me?" he asked. "I love taking showers with you."

"I wanted to make sure we get to enjoy the day outside," she said, smiling. "And I know what happens when we get into bed or in the shower together."

"Are you all ready tired of me?" he asked, his voice plaintive.

Arielle dropped the towel and turned to face him, shocked by his remark. He watched her carefully, a playful smile on his face. "What?" he asked in mock innocence.

"I'm stunned that you would even bother to ask such a question of me. I'm not tired of you, and I'll never be tired of you."

He wrapped his arms around her, and his mouth moved eagerly against hers.

"I was only joking, baby. What do you want to do today?"

"I want to take a walk and enjoy the Christmas spirit and the sunshine with you and you alone."

"All right then that is what we are going to do." He walked to the shower and started to whistle an old tune. Arielle recognized the melody but couldn't recall the name of the song. *I didn't know he liked rock and roll*, she thought. *I thought he was more the classical music type.* She wasn't sure why they had never discussed music with each other. She knew some of his favorite artists, but they hadn't ever really made music a topic of discussion. *That will be something for us to talk about when we take our walk*, she thought. She chose a warm blue dress that made her feel happy. Then, she put her hair up in a ponytail and sat on the bed, waiting for him.

When he walked out of the bathroom, he took her breath away. His hair was dripping water onto his beautiful face, and a little towel was wrapped around his waist. He looked like the perfect representation of a beautiful Greek god, created by a famous sculptor. Only *this* God was smiling at her, showing a set of perfect white teeth and desire in his emerald eyes. She smiled back, unable to take her eyes away from him. Any other day she knew she would end up in bed with him but not today. It was almost Christmas. He put on a pair of jeans and a beautiful blue shirt, and they were on their way.

Outside, the sidewalk was sparkling in the sunshine. Cars were everywhere, and people were walking, holding shopping bags in their hands, laughing, and talking excitedly. She could hear church bells somewhere far away. It made life seem unpretentious and sensible.

She was happy to be walking next to her perfect dream of a man, holding his hand as they crossed the street and walked towards the park. They passed several stores with festively decorated windows, and tons of people rushing in and out.

It was an exceptionally beautiful day. Brighton was bathed in sunny conditions for this time of the year. It was a bit cool, but for the most part, the day was made to order for Sebastian and Arielle. Not a single cloud in the sky.

"What a perfect day," Arielle exclaimed and smiled at Sebastian. "Come, let's go to the park." She took his hand and pulled him toward the park entrance. Underneath the trees, everything seemed so peaceful and green There was a large lake that extended for a few miles into the middle of the park. When they reached a small open area close to the water, Arielle took her shoes off. She closed her eyes and smiled, letting her feet feel the cool grass. When she opened them again, she saw that Sebastian was watching her with curiosity.

"Sebastian, go ahead and take your shoes off. Feel the grass, it's a bit cool, but it's wonderful. Trust me." He hesitated at first, but eventually he took his shoes off and stood on the grass barefoot, taking small steps in place.

"Close your eyes and just enjoy the feeling," she urged.

He did as she suggested. She saw a smile steal across his face.

"So, what do you think?" she asked.

"I'm amazed that I never thought of doing this in all the time I have been on this earth. I never thought that something so simple could make me feel so wonderful. Arielle, you're such a gift to me."

She wrapped her arms around his neck and kissed him tenderly. He was happy to respond.

They sat on the grass together, enjoying their surroundings. A light breeze softly caressed their faces, and the birds chirped happily as they flew from tree to tree, an incredible fragrance from the beautiful flowers filling their nostrils. The lake was picturesque. It looked like a soft blue piece of fabric elusively rippling in the breeze. Ducks and their babies splashed and dove, looking for fish. Children played with their little toy boats on the water. Arielle sighed with pleasure at the sight of the awesome colors and the variety of the foliage. She squeezed Sebastian's hand.

"What is it?" he whispered.

"The beauty of nature, you, and, oh, just everything around us, look. It's so beautiful."

Sebastian smiled and held her tight. "I can't see anything more beautiful than you."

She kissed him warmly and ran her finger down his back. A deep moan of pleasure escaped him. She took his hand and brought it up to her lips, which is when she noticed the ring again. It was so beautiful and mysterious looking. It looked like a ring that might belong to a knight.

"What is the meaning of this ring?"

Sebastian was quiet for a minute. Then he answered slowly, "It's not a family crest," he said. "But it's a lifeline for me. It protects me from being burned by the sun. Do you remember when you asked me what can kill an immortal?"

She stopped and swallowed hard as she looked at him in horror. "Yes," she gulped.

"The sun can kill an immortal," he said. "It's poison to me. This ring shields me with its power so that I can walk outside and enjoy a sunny day. I can never be without it."

His face was sad again, and Arielle had no idea what he was thinking. She was sure that if he wanted her to know he would say something, so she didn't press for any more details.

She touched the ring and couldn't help feeling fascinated that something so small could save a person's life. *It must be magical, like the necklace,* she thought. She smiled and ran her finger over it, back and forth, thankful that it was keeping her love safe from harm. She looked at him with warmth and understanding.

"On a lighter note..." she said with a giggle. "I made a bet with myself that I could go for more than five minutes without looking at your gorgeous face. And I lost the bet miserably. I could only make it for ten seconds." She laughed out loud, and he laughed with her. Then, he reached over and pulled her close for a kiss.

She stood up and walked down to the water's edge to watch the little children guiding their small sailboats, imagining they were captains of real ships. She could read their minds and chuckle at their sweet, innocent thoughts. They were thinking of the perils their boats would be facing—the stormy skies and high waves that would try to sink them—and how they would prevail.

Sebastian was now standing next to her, and he noticed the thoughtful look in her eyes.

"What's on your mind?" he asked, watching her intently.

"Oh, I was just watching the children, thinking about the changes that we go through as we move from young children to adolescence, and then to adulthood."

"What do you mean?" he asked. She turned toward him, and their eyes met. She leaned in and pressed her lips softly to his, and he moaned again softly.

"I was watching the children and thinking about my own life and the changes I have gone through in the twenty-one years I have been on this earth."

"I'd love to hear your thoughts."

"Well, children are fascinating. I used to read a lot, and I would get completely lost in the stories I was reading. I used to create my own mystical worlds and invisible friends. I was enthralled by the stories, but at the same time pretty scared of the unknown. Then as I grew into adolescence, I felt more mature. I thought about the future and what was to come. I thought about boys, and challenges, and new responsibilities. I became more creative and flexible about overcoming the fear that every time I turned around, I was facing another trial." She chuckled. "I think that stage of my life was one of the most intriguing and one of the most complicated. I wanted to start making plans for the future, but I always found myself searching for something," she said, biting her lip and pausing.

"What were you looking for?"

"Sebastian, I don't want you to laugh, but I have realized that what I was looking for, and what was missing from my life was, well *you*. Just you." Sebastian pulled her to him, and their lips met softly. When she pulled back from the kiss, she looked at him and smiled.

"What about you?" she asked. "You had a normal mortal life up to age twenty-two. How did you feel about the changes you went through?"

Sebastian looked thoughtful and a bit sad as he recalled his mortal years. "I have to agree with you," he said. "I went through the same changes you did. I think that my transition from childhood to adolescence was pretty much the same as for any other person. I was happy and ready to take on responsibility and experience my independence. However, the transition from adolescence to adulthood was very dramatic for me. That was the time that I needed my parents' advice about how to handle the opportunities that were coming my way. But that never happened, and those needs were drowned by the emotions surrounding their loss." He stopped talking and looked at his feet despondently.

Arielle watched him for a short moment and then reached out and wrapped her arms around him. "I'm sorry, Sebastian, I didn't mean for you to recall sad thoughts," she said quietly.

He looked up and smiled, pressing his lips on her forehead. They stood there for a few moments, watching the colorful little sailboats float on the calm blue waters, creating a beautiful picture before them. Then, holding hands, they walked across the grass barefoot, carrying their shoes for a couple of miles, talking about everything and nothing, and laughing out loud. Sebastian seemed happy, and Arielle didn't want the day to end. They purchased an ice cream cone and to her surprise, this time they shared it.

"Arielle, I can enjoy human food any time, I wish," he said. "I just prefer the salve because it keeps me energetic and strong."

"Really?"

"Yes, it's no problem at all."

He would never know how happy Arielle was to hear this news. She knew that sooner or later her parents would invite him to dinner, and it would have been awfully strange if he never wanted to eat anything. She laughed happily, but he had no clue why she was laughing. He couldn't read her thoughts as long as she had her necklace on, and she thought that was just fine.

He pulled her towards him and faced her. "What's so funny?" he frowned. "You'll have to tell me what you are thinking. I have to know what's on your mind."

"All I ever do is think about you, so you don't have to worry about my thoughts," she smiled as she reached up, searching for his lips. He bent down and locked them in a passionate kiss.

After they had been walking for a couple of hours, they decided to start back toward the hotel. Arielle felt warm and sheltered just being with him, walking with their arms around each other.

"Thank you for one of the most beautiful and relaxing mornings I have ever had," Sebastian said. Arielle squeezed his hand lovingly, and they walked the rest of the way in a state of profound contentment and delight.

It was noon when they entered the lobby, eager to get ready for the party. The lobby was full of happy people making plans for Christmas Eve. But as they approached the gigantic Christmas tree that was taking up a huge part of the center floor, they stopped in their tracks. Arielle looked up at Sebastian's face, and she could see rage instantly erasing the serene look he had worn all morning. His lips were pulled back in fury, and instantaneously his arm pulled her closer, and he used his body to shield her. Fear seized her as she looked in horror at the three women standing in the middle of the lobby. A cold chill ran down her spine, and she shivered as she felt her legs go limp. This was becoming a continuous nightmare. How many times would she have to deal with these women?

Annabel, Julia, and Paola were standing there like three gorgeous goddesses, smiling coldly, their eyes set on her. Julia spoke out first with a sickening smile on her face.

"Sebastian, my love, I've finally found you, and look who I've brought with me," she said, pointing at Annabel. The coldness and disdain in her voice was nauseating.

"What do you want, Annabel?" Sebastian said in a cold, hard voice. He ignored Julia completely.

"Oh, you know me. I've heard so much about your new love. I had to come and see the miserable, breakable human being for myself. I see now that she's the same girl that came to the house looking for you. What a little liar you are, telling me you were just a friend," she said, turning her eyes toward Arielle with a look of disgust. "I know about the ring you're wearing too. And you should know that what you dream of will never happen, not as long as I'm around."

People around them began to slow down as they passed through the lobby, wanting to witness the outcome of the standoff while trying to be inconspicuous about being intently interested in what was going on. Arielle felt anxious, she knew this encounter was not going well at all.

"Annabel, this is not going to end well for you. Don't push me in front of all these people. I need you to leave right now and take these two horrible creatures with you."

Julia's face turned hard at these words, and her eyes were full of revulsion. "Don't you speak to me in the third person, Sebastian. I am right here. If there is something you want to say, say it to me."

"You miserable, distasteful creature," he said, spitting out the words in disgust. "Get out of my sight before you wish you had never met me."

Julia seemed to ignore his remark as she turned toward Arielle.

"How is your head, breakable human? I should have done a better job with you last time," she said, glaring at Arielle.

Suddenly, Arielle heard a loud growl as Sebastian let go of her, grabbed Julia by the throat, and squeezed her so tight Arielle was sure she had stopped breathing. Nobody in the lobby, including Arielle, was able to follow much of the activity that followed. It all happened so fast, almost like a movie in fast forward. Julia tried desperately to get herself loose but to no avail. Paola jumped in to help her, but she found herself flying across the lobby as Sebastian shoved her hard. She hit the far wall with so much force that Arielle heard a horrible sound and was sure several of her bones had shattered. Annabel used this moment of confusion to her advantage to move toward Arielle, whose mind went completely blank as a cold chill took over her body. She was terrified, and she seemed to be frozen in place. She took a step back just as Annabel's hand was reaching out toward her.

"There's no way that you'll ever have him. I'll destroy you," Annabel hissed in a low voice, her eyes dripping poison, oblivious to everyone but Sebastian and Arielle.

What happened next shocked Arielle to her very core. As Annabel's arm brushed Arielle's body, Arielle saw her go flying across the room and land on her back against the far wall of the lobby, right next to Paola. She was holding onto her arm, which was literally on fire, and screaming with pain, her face was distorted with anguish and shock.

Arielle knew what had happened. It was a repeat of what had happened at the pub. She saw Sebastian turning as he dropped Julia, who was unconscious on the floor. Arielle looked around. There was not a single soul in the room who wasn't standing in shock. They may not have been able to follow all that had taken place, but they could certainly see the aftermath.

Sebastian and Arielle watched as Annabel and Paola tried unsuccessfully to stand up. Julia was holding her throat, trying to breathe. Sebastian moved close to Arielle and put his arm around her, holding her steady against him as she shook uncontrollably.

By now Julia was standing up, her eyes were full of loathing, and she made sure Arielle could feel it. She walked away from them toward Annabel and Paola, who were helping each other stand up. Annabel was still growling with pain, holding her arm and shaking her head. She gave Arielle a look full of venom and walked towards the exit, Julia, and Paola at her heels. Just before they went through the door, she stopped, and completely ignoring every living soul in the lobby, looked hard at Sebastian and then at Arielle.

"Look out, you miserable human. I'll find you alone, and I will destroy you. You'll never have him!" she shrieked.

"Annabel, I'm warning you," Sebastian said, his voice full of disgust and abhorrence that drove a chill down Arielle's spine. "Stay away from us, as far away as you possibly can. Next time it will end up bad for you."

Without a word. Annabel turned and swept out of the room, never looking back.

The manager came over, wanting to know if Sebastian and Arielle were all right. People started to move around again, wondering what in the world all that had been about. Sebastian assured everyone that they were just fine and pulled Arielle towards the elevator.

Annabel and her friends were gone, for now, but Arielle knew her life was moving into an unknown chapter. She felt terribly afraid.


Once in the room, Arielle fell apart. When the door closed, she started to cry. Her body was shaking, and tears ran down her face. All she could see was Annabel's eyes, full of fire and revulsion for her. She sat on the bed sobbing, unable to shake the fear out of her bones. Sebastian held her close without saying a word as she buried her face in his chest. "How am I going to deal with someone like her in my life?" she sobbed while he just held her close.

"Please, Arielle, you don't need to be afraid of her. You have the necklace, and it will keep you safe. You saw what happened down there. I didn't even touch her, and you certainly didn't pull off a throw like that." He smiled gently, watching for her reaction.

Arielle looked at him through her tears and nodded. "I know you're right." But she also knew that Annabel would be coming back, and it terrified her.

Arielle didn't fully understand the powers of immortals, and the unknown was terrifying to her. Seeing the intense hatred in Annabel's eyes and her determination to keep Sebastian to herself had frightened her. The depth of that passion she did understand.

"Do you love me?" she heard him asking in a low voice.

His question startled her and she stared into his eyes.

"What do you think?" Her voice was strong and steady.

"I want to believe that you will be strong and will not fall apart every time you cross paths with Annabel. It may happen more often than you want it to." He pulled her against his body and held her tighter. "Please, Arielle, I don't want you to worry. You saw what happened when she tried to touch you. All I want you to do is make sure you never take that necklace off."

Arielle put her arms around his neck and pulled herself even closer, wanting to feel the warmth and security of his body. She had never thought it would be possible to love someone without limitations. But even in the wake of the ugly incident they had just lived through, now that she was in his arms again, she felt a sense of deep contentment.

They didn't need to get ready for the party for a couple of hours still, so Arielle drifted off to sleep in complete tranquility. Sebastian held her close, happy that the danger had passed. He smiled as he listened to her breathing softly, warmth and harmony surrounding him.

She was just on the cusp of sleep when she felt his lips pressing on hers. She opened her eyes to see his face only inches away, with his lips slightly open and inviting. She parted her lips and welcomed him in, pleased when his tongue stroked hers gently. His incredible scent filled her with unmanageable desire, and he was happy to accommodate her, even as he whispered that it was getting late, and she still needed to go to the flat to get her dress for the party. His kiss deepened, making her moan. She didn't want to move away from his trembling body that could make her senses soar to such amazing heights. She gasped with excitement and sighed. She knew he was right.

"This will be my first real Christmas party," he said with anticipation in his voice.

"That can't be true. You must have been at many Christmas parties through the centuries," she said, trying to shake off the passionate desire she felt.

"Well, I have never enjoyed the holidays with my wife to be," he said. "I want to share everything with you, Arielle. This will be the very first Christmas for us, and I intend to take it all in and make it wonderful for both of us."

"What time is it?"

"Four-thirty," he whispered. She knew it was time for her to get up, but she couldn't move. Not yet. She was elated and so comfortable, and she didn't want to move away from him, not for a second. And he seemed content just to hold her against him.

Eventually, they got up and drove to the flat. The music was blasting, and all Arielle's friends were there, playing cards and drinking. As they walked into the flat door, she could hear the Eagles' "Long Road out of Eden" playing, and it made her happy. Sebastian was singing along softly.

"I didn't know you like the Eagles," she said, surprised.

"There are a lot of things you don't know about me," he grinned.

They stayed for a while, happy to be together. Eva looked beautiful and so happy in Ian's arms. Gabrielle was busy beating all of them at cards. She was jubilant, laughing out loud, making fun of the guys. Her outbursts made Sebastian laugh too, and it made Arielle so happy to see him carefree. He surprised her again by drinking a couple of beers, but she didn't say anything about it.

Finally, Arielle gathered her things and they left. They all agreed to meet at the party around nine. On the way back to the hotel, Sebastian's phone rang. It was Loren. "Hold on for a minute, love," he said and turned to Arielle. "Can Loren bring another couple with her?" he asked.

"Yes, of course, she can bring anyone she wants."

"Thank you, Arielle!" Loren yelled into the phone.

"I can't wait to see you again," Arielle said.

"Her date is Daniel Boellere, and they're bringing Daniel's brother Marcus and his girlfriend, Jeannette Grullon, as well," Sebastian explained after he had hung up. "Marcus and Jeannette will pick up Loren and Daniel. They'll arrive a little after nine."

"That'll be fine," Arielle said, smiling softly. She was wondering what Sebastian was going to wear to the party, but whatever it was, she was sure he would look better than anyone else there. She smiled to herself and giggled softly.

"I don't like not knowing what you are thinking," he frowned, though she could tell he wasn't angry.

"Some of my thoughts are only for me," she said and smiled happily.

"Don't make me take that necklace off," he replied teasingly.

Back at the hotel they jumped into the shower together and enjoyed the warm water running over them. Sebastian seemed to enjoy watching Arielle closely as she prepared for the party. When she finally slipped into her beautiful dress and high heels, he pulled back and whistled with delight.

"You. Are. Stunning," he said, and Arielle smiled, pleased with his reaction.

"Sebastian, get dressed, or you'll make us late," she urged.

He walked into the bathroom, and she could hear him whistling some old song as he was shaving. Once again, she was amazed at how much she didn't know about him. She walked out of the bedroom into the sitting area and poured a glass of wine for herself while she sat down, turning on the telly.

It was seven-thirty; they had ample time to get there. Arielle pulled her little mirror out of her purse and applied some lipstick. She thought about how plain she looked in comparison to the extraordinarily beautiful girls in Sebastian's world.

*What's so special about me that he should love me?* She asked herself for the hundredth time. He was so amazingly good looking, even when he was asleep. He could have any woman on the planet he wanted, but he had chosen her. How strange.

She sipped her wine slowly and couldn't help thinking again how lucky she was. She was ready to take another sip when he walked into the room. Instantly, she forgot what she was going to do and just stared at him. He was quite simply the most exquisite sight she had ever laid eyes on. He was wearing a beautiful black designer suit, with a silver shirt and a black tie. He was magnificent. Arielle just stood there staring at him, unable to utter a word.

"Do I look good enough?" he asked. She approached him and reached out to touch him.

"I just want to make sure you are real," she said, voice trembling. He laughed, pulled her close, and pressed his lips to hers.

"Is that good enough proof?" he laughed.

"How can you do this?" she said incredulously. "How can you look so fabulous all the time?"

"I guess that is the same question I have for you, Arielle," he said, smiling.

As they walked through the hotel lobby holding hands and smiling at each other, eyes followed them to the exit. Arielle was sure it was because of him. She certainly wasn't used to being the center of attention the way she was when she was with Sebastian. It made her feel like someone very special.

# Chapter 14

**THE PARTY WAS IN FULL SWING** when they arrived. Arielle hadn't realized that her mother had invited so many people. As they walked in, the band was playing some of the old sixties music that her parents loved. Many turned and looked at Sebastian with amazement. Arielle wasn't surprised. By now, she was getting used to that kind of reaction.

As they entered the room, her mother approached them and gave both of them a hug. As usual, she looked beautiful.

"Congratulations!" she exclaimed. "Arielle, I couldn't be any happier and more proud, of you than I am right now," she added, her face shining with delight. "Let me see that ring." She reached out and took Arielle's left hand. "Oh, my. It's beautiful!" she exclaimed, and hugged them both again.

"You look so beautiful, Mrs. Lloyd," Sebastian said, kissing her cheek and chuckling. He bowed.

"Why, thank you, Sebastian," she replied, clearly pleased.

"Please, wait here for just a second?" They both nodded amusedly. She excused herself politely and quickly walked off to find Arielle's father. Sebastian and Arielle stood patiently looking at each other, waiting for her mother to come back. It wasn't long until she reappeared holding Mr. Lloyd's hand, pulling him softly toward their direction.

"Hi, Daddy," Arielle called out warmly. They embraced lovingly. Her father tightened his hold on her and planted a huge kiss on her cheek.

"Your mother told me the good news," he murmured against her ear. "Are you happy?" His eyes were quizzical.

"Oh yes, Daddy, I'm *very* happy." Her father gave her a reassuring smile. He kept one arm around her waist and turned to face Sebastian.

"My boy, congratulations. I couldn't ask for a better man for my daughter." He extended his hand with a wide smile on his face. Sebastian took his proffered hand and shook it warmly.

"Thank you, sir."

Then, her parents stood on either side of Sebastian and Arielle, and her father called everyone's attention. "Friends," Mr. Lloyd said, excitement in his voice. "My wife and I are very pleased to make a special announcement this evening. Our daughter, Arielle, has accepted Mr. Sebastian Gaulle's proposal in marriage. Please join us in wishing both of them a long and happy life together."

A loud round of applause and happy cheers followed his sincere words, making Arielle blush and Sebastian smile blissfully. "Lets all drink to their happiness," her father called again. Everyone raised their glasses.

Sebastian pulled Arielle in his arms and placed a soft kiss on her lips. Grinning ecstatically, they walked around to speak with all their friends and her parents' guests. Sebastian had met most of them at Arielle's birthday party. They fell easily into conversation.

Sebastian received smiles of acceptance from the men, who shook his hand warmly, and he mesmerized the women, who couldn't stop staring at him.

"Why am I not surprised?" Arielle murmured to herself, amused. Then, as soon as she could do it gracefully, she pulled him across the room to where Eva was standing with Ian. They congratulated Sebastian and Arielle on their engagement, and they exchanged warm greetings.

Before long, Gabrielle and Troy walked in. Troy too was breathtaking, and many of the women turned around to stare at his immortal beauty as he entered the room. Troy and Sebastian exchanged warm smiles, and it looked like they said something to each other, but Arielle couldn't hear what they were saying. Troy hugged Arielle and congratulated her. He gave her a happy smile. Gabrielle looked stunning and more in love tonight than she ever had before. Arielle was so happy that the six of them were getting along so well. The house looked magnificent, and she couldn't stop smiling. Sebastian had his arm around her waist at all times. He hummed every song the band played.

"Do you like sixties music?" she asked.

"Some of my favorites," he said, smiling.

"What other music do you like?"

"Oh, my taste is pretty diverse," he said gazing at her warmly. "I mostly like classical music, but then the fifties and the sixties were pretty great too," he drawled.

"Yes, they were pretty great." Arielle found herself nodding back. "My parents love the fifties and sixties," she said joyfully.

"Don't promise a dance to anyone because you'll be dancing all of them with me." He pulled her closer.

"Well, I hope we don't have an unexpected guest tonight," she said, and the thought made her stomach clench.

"Unexpected guest?" he said, gazing at her quizzically. Arielle looked up and their gazes locked, emerald and sapphire, a stunning blend.

"You know… I mean someone like Savanna," she said and winced fretfully.

Sebastian looked deep into her eyes. "Oh, I wouldn't worry about that if I were you. Tonight, I'm not leaving your side," he said and hugged her to him tighter.

"That's fine with me, but don't make any promises you might not be able to keep," she said.

Sebastian's brows furrowed. Arielle quickly explained, "You do know that you can't say no to my father."

Sebastian smiled and nodded in agreement. "You're right. But if that happens, I'll get Troy to keep an eye on you."

Ever since she met Sebastian, Arielle's life had drastically changed. She didn't know what the next blow would be, who was going to deliver it, and when? So, she just resigned herself to that fact and sighed deeply.

"Stop worrying," Sebastian said, and bending down he kissed her on the tip of her nose.

Soon after, Paul came in with a date, which made Arielle very happy. He looked handsome in his gray suit with a blue shirt and a gray tie. As usual, he looked stylish, but because he was with a date, he looked even more stunning than usual. He introduced the girl as Marian Walker, the daughter of a family friend. She was very pretty, with blond hair and green eyes, and friendly.

"Paul, Marian, Sebastian and I have special news to announce," Arielle said. "We're engaged."

"Arielle, that's wonderful," Paul said, and shaking Sebastian's hand he added, "You are perfect for each other, and I'm happy for you."

Arielle could see that Paul wasn't quite himself, but she knew that tonight wasn't the time to say anything. She was sure that it had everything to do with his parents. Once again, the newspapers had splashed dirty details about his father's affairs with other women. This had to be awfully hard for Paul. "I have a Christmas gift for you," she said and gave him a hug.

"Oh, thank you," he said, "I've one for you too. It's in the car. I'll bring it to the flat tomorrow."

Arielle turned to face Sebastian and froze in place. "What in bloody hell is he doing here?" she hissed, a little louder than she intended to. Richard Chevaller was among the guests, and that infuriated her.

*He's the last bloody person I wanted to see tonight,* she thought. *He's sure to ruin my good mood.* Gabrielle and Eva walked over to her and teased her, giggling. They knew how Arielle felt about Richard. He didn't seem to understand that when their parents had talked about the two of them getting together, they were only five years old. He was handsome, yes, but he was also one of the most annoying, arrogant, and snobbish people around. Arielle disliked him immensely. Gabrielle and Eva each took Sebastian by the hand, laughing, and gave him the short version of Arielle and Richard's prickly relationship.

"Come stand back here and enjoy," Gabrielle said. "This is an annual tradition between those two."

Sebastian did as he was told and stood between Eva and Gabrielle as they watched Richard and Arielle with curiosity. He didn't have long to wait. Soon, Richard approached Arielle with a wide, stupid smile on his arrogant face.

"Hey, pretty face How's my girl?" he exclaimed and reached

out as if to take Arielle in his arms.

She put her hands up defiantly, keeping him away from her and stepped back, hissing in a low voice. "Richard, please keep your voice down."

"Hello, Richard." Arielle heard a musical sound coming from behind and turning, saw Gabrielle and Eva giggling. She glared at them. Sebastian was standing there watching her, and she could hear his low laughter, along with that of Ian and Troy. They were enjoying her frustration while Arielle was getting angrier.

"'Richard, keep your voice down,'" Richard said, mimicking Arielle's voice. "Is that all you have to say?"

"Richard, why do you keep doing this to yourself? Don't you get it? I want you to stay away from me. How hard is that for you to understand?"

His eyes bored into hers, and his expression turned cross. "Listen, Arielle, I told you, I'm not giving up. We are meant to be together."

"You must be either stupid or hearing impaired," Arielle said with exasperation. She turned her back to him and began to walk away. He grabbed her hand and said, "Please, Arielle, don't do this. Give me a chance. I've been a jerk, and I know it but..."

Arielle spun around, furious, and raised her finger in warning to stop him from finishing his sentence. "Richard, please, keep your voice down before I get mad. Don't ever say that again. I told you before I can't stand it. Leave me alone," she said, emphasizing the last three words.

"I think I love you," he said in clear desperation.

Arielle threw her hands up in the air and sighed. She looked at Sebastian with a pleading look, and he came right over to her side and put his arm around her waist. Looking at Richard, she introduced the two to each other.

"Richard, this is my fiancé, Sebastian. Sebastian, this is Richard Chevaller."

Richard frowned and glanced at Sebastian with a shocked look on his face. He mumbled something, and turning swiftly around he walked away, not even bothering to shake Sebastian's hand.

"He is out of his mind," Eva was saying to Ian. "He has been after Arielle since they were five years old." She laughed out loud.

"Five years old?" said Sebastian "Oh, that poor soul really is in love."

"He's a jerk," Arielle insisted in an aggravated voice, and they all laughed. Just then Arielle's father came back, a big smile on his face.

"Sebastian, can you spare a moment my boy? I want you to meet some of my associates that just arrived, some people you didn't get a chance to meet the last time."

Sebastian nodded in agreement and pressing Arielle's hand softly he leaned closer, "Stay close to Troy. And miss me," he whispered. Then, with a smile, he walked away.

Arielle and her friends went to get something to eat, and as they were coming back from the table, they noticed that everyone in the room was staring at the entrance incredulously.

Arielle followed their gaze and saw that Loren and her three guests were entering the room. They really did look incredibly beautiful—four very attractive people with perfect bodies and flawless features. It was a stunning sight.

Gabrielle, Eva, and Arielle walked up to them and warmly welcomed them to the party.

"Happy Christmas!" Loren said, handing Arielle a huge bouquet of flowers. "Let me see the ring one more time," she added. "Sebastian called Mother before he gave it to you, and Mother said to tell you that she is very happy for both of you. She can't wait to meet you."

Arielle just smiled, pleased.

She was a bit surprised when Loren introduced Daniel Boelliere as a friend, not her boyfriend, but she tried not to show it. Loren then introduced Marcus, Daniel's brother, and Jeanette Grullon, Marcus's girlfriend.

Arielle noticed that her friends looked a little dazed as she made the introductions. She smiled, knowing they were reacting to the breathtaking good looks of the immortals. The men in the room could not take their eyes away from Loren and Jeanette, and the women could not stop staring at Daniel, Marcus, and Troy. They were all charming, and all very friendly. They entered easily into conversation with Ian, Troy, and Paul as if they had known them all their lives.

Arielle and her friends moved towards the ballroom to watch

the band, which was playing a mixture of incredible music from the early sixties up to the latest tunes. People were dancing and having a wonderful time. Arielle introduced Loren and her friends to her mother and her friends, and everyone welcomed them with warm smiles. She whispered something to Loren about Troy, and Loren gave him an understanding glance, which Troy understood. He smiled back at her warmly.

They all danced with each other's dates and had a lot of fun. When the band began to play *Chantilly Lace*, Ian came over and pulled Arielle to the dance floor.

"What?"

"Eva says you and Gabrielle are the bobbers in the group. I love to rock, so come and dance with me."

Arielle laughed, looking in Eva's direction. Eva smiled her approval. "Come on, Arielle. I love to dance, and Eva will not even try to rock 'n roll with me." Arielle knew what he said was true, so she allowed him to pull her onto the dance floor. She smiled as great memories flooded her head, from her younger school years and her then dance partner, Andrew. They danced so perfectly together it seemed as if they had practiced for months. Ian was a great dancer and Arielle had no trouble following his lead. She loved bobbing, and it made her happy.

The school she'd attended had always organized fifties dances each year, a trend that had started in the United States and that British kids also loved. All the students who attended had to dress in fifties outfits and attempt to win prizes by entering the dance contests, which were held all night long. The memories made her smile wide. Arielle hadn't been able to dance rock 'n roll with anyone since she had graduated. But back then, Andrew, Arielle, Gabrielle, and Eva's boyfriend, Jack Wallace, had been the best at those dances, winning some prize each year.

Several other couples were on the dance floor now, having a great time dancing. Eva had never really wanted to learn how to rock. Arielle remembered Jack trying to teach her during their last year of high school, but she had always demurred. Now Ian wanted to dance with her too, and that made a big difference. Arielle was sure Eva was ready to do anything she could do to make Ian happy.

"Lets get her, Ian," she said.

Loren and her friends were standing next to Eva, smiling with pleasure as they approached. They were all talking about school and the dances they had attended when Arielle felt Sebastian's arms around her waist and his body close to hers. He kissed the back of her neck, and she heard him whisper close to her ear, "I wonder how many other new things I'm going to find out about you…"

"What do you mean?"

"You and Ian dancing out there. Have you danced with him before?"

"No, this was the very first time," she said. "I can't believe how good he is. Where were you? I didn't see you come back."

Sebastian pulled her back to the dance floor, and they moved slowly together to a great old song, *Play With Fire* by The Rolling Stones.

His mouth found hers and he kissed her with longing.

"What is it?"

"Arielle, I love you, and I want you to keep loving me for eternity."

"That is exactly what I intend to do, forever," she sighed.

"For eternity," he corrected her.

"All right, for eternity."

His body was so warm and exciting. God, would she ever stop wanting him every time he touched her?

When the song was over, she was still holding him, not wanting to let go. He looked at her questioningly, but she didn't say a thing. Then, still holding each other close, they walked over to shake hands with Daniel and Marcus and to greet Jeanette and Loren. Loren let go of Daniel's hand and fell into Sebastian's arms with a big smile.

"Thank you for giving me such a great sister," she said, looking at Arielle lovingly, as Arielle smiled back at her with appreciation.

As Arielle looked around at the five of them and Troy, it occurred to her that they all looked very similar. All six of them were breathtakingly beautiful, and people were still staring at them. They were all immortals, but Gabrielle and Arielle were the only ones in the room who knew that. They were now part of their lives and they would just have to learn to get used to their extraordinarily handsome looks and their physical perfection.

"May I have this dance?" Daniel asked Arielle with a slight bow and a smile on his face. She accepted, and while she danced with Daniel, Sebastian danced with Loren. Daniel was also a great dancer, and as Arielle leaned on his shoulder, she could smell the same intoxicating scent that Sebastian and Troy possessed. Apparently, that was part of being immortal.

As the night went on, Arielle noticed that Loren and Paul had danced many times together and were holding each other quite closely.

"Do you see what I see?" she murmured to Sebastian, nodding at them as they danced another dance together.

"Well, I think that will be the biggest thing to happen yet," he chuckled as he whispered to her in a low voice.

"I don't take anything Loren does seriously," he admitted. "But who knows? I fell in love with a human, and so did Troy. Why not Loren too? Maybe we will start an immortal colony in Brighton," he joked. Arielle had to laugh at his statement.

Meanwhile, Daniel was busy dancing with another girl, giving no sign of worry or jealousy. Arielle thought that was a bit strange, but she didn't say anything.

The party was amazing. There wasn't a single person, including Eva, who didn't dance all night, eat, and drink until they couldn't dance anymore. When Marcus asked Arielle to dance, Jeanette asked Sebastian to dance. Arielle noticed that Jeannette was dancing just a little too close to Sebastian and that she was flirting with him. That made her uncomfortable. She was glad when the song was finished, and Sebastian came over and took her to the other room.

"Was she flirting with you, or do I imagine things?" she asked, trying to control her jealousy, but not doing very well.

"Jealous, are you?"

"Yes, I suppose I am. Do you mind?" she pouted.

"No, not at all. Because I'm jealous of you too." They laughed and danced one more dance.

It was three o'clock in the morning when they decided to call it quits. Loren told Arielle's parents how much she had enjoyed the party and how thankful she was for them allowing her to bring her friends. She took a little longer saying goodbye to Paul than was strictly necessary, a fact that Arielle noticed but didn't remark upon. They all thanked their hosts and wished them a Happy Christmas. They agreed to meet the following day at the flat to exchange gifts.

"You'll come for Christmas dinner, won't you, Sebastian?" Arielle's mum called as they were leaving.

"With pleasure," he replied. "And on one condition. That you allow me to bring the wine."

The hotel was quiet when they arrived, and there was not a single soul in the lobby, except for the two receptionists behind the front desk. Arielle shivered, remembering the previous day's experience with Annabel. But when she looked up at Sebastian, his smile made her feel safe. She was happy to be with him, but she knew her life had taken a giant leap towards unknown changes. *I love him so much*, she thought. *I'm willing to weather whatever storms may be looming just around the corner.*

They went to their room and straight to bed. Sebastian pulled her tight, and the touch of his skin made her feel as if she were drifting beyond the stars. Lying next to his warm and beautiful body, Arielle felt she had found heaven on earth. When he encircled her in his arms, she knew that she would stay there forever. She closed her eyes, and they fell asleep in each other's arms.

# Chapter 15

WHEN ARIELLE WOKE UP, SHE WAS ALONE. The door to the bedroom was closed, and there was complete silence. The clock on the nightstand showed that it was nine o'clock. She walked toward the balcony and pulled the heavy curtains aside, letting the sun burst into the room. Another glorious morning. She opened the doors and stepped outside to feel the warmth of the sun, and it gave her a delicious sensation throughout her body. She gazed down at her left hand, and a blissful smile spread across her face as the sunlight bounced off the diamond, giving it an amazing, bright rainbow sparkle.

The splendor of this morning crept into her very soul and filled her with gratitude that she was alive and completely in love with the most wonderful man.

From the top floor of the hotel, the sky framed a glorious view of the city below, the churches, the stores, the charming homes with all the Christmas decorations, the picturesque park full of gorgeous green foliage, and behind it, all the ocean off in the distance.

A light breeze touched her face, and she looked up at the clear blue sky with a wide smile on her face. She extended her hand again to take another look at the ring that symbolized her commitment to a gorgeous creature on this earth. Exuberance, elation, bliss flooded her head and took over her whole body. She wanted to scream from happiness as tears welled up and she felt his arms enfolding her body, his lips touching her neck softly.

"Good morning. I love that cute little camisole on you," he murmured, nuzzling her hair. "You'll get a cold, baby. It's sunny, but it's cool out here."

She spun around and threw her arms around this beautiful man who loved her. He was completely startled as he gazed into her eyes and saw the fullness of emotion pouring out of her.

"What?" He was standing in front of her wearing only a pair of jeans, looking like Adonis. She reached out and pulled him close without answering. She crushed his lips with all the passion she possessed. His body shuddered, and his skin was hot from anticipation.

"Mmmm…" she murmured.

"What is it?" he asked, his breath shallow.

"I am overwhelmed with excitement, and it is all because of you, Darcy," she whispered, her voice husky. Her teeth dug into her bottom lip with a low moan.

"Whatever made you do this, please keep it up," he said, tightening his hold on her, deepening the kiss, utterly aroused. She could hear a low chuckle as his fingers slipped under her camisole and pulled her flush against his body. His hot breath floated across her cheek, sending a prickling sensation to the end of every nerve. Arielle gasped at the feel of the strong muscles that gathered her into that familiar sanctuary. Her hands came up, threading through his hair, and suddenly she was panting senselessly. She rose up to her toes and pulled his head down until their lips locked one more time.

Breaking the kiss, she looked into his emerald eyes and said, "Happy Christmas, Mr. Darcy." She giggled.

"Happy Christmas, Lizzy!" He groaned as his mouth glided from her lips down the column of her throat and pressed at the pulse of her heartbeat. This was the essence of Sebastian's excitement. How he wished he had a heartbeat, but that was never going to happen for him. He shut his eyes, overwhelmed by sensual sensation, and his nerves tightened.

"What are you doing to me?" he rasped, panting hard.

"Nothing." She giggled as she caught her breath and pulled back from him. His arms pulled her right back and crushed her against his beautiful body. Her head fell back, and she gasped again with excitement, feeling every bit of him.

"You'll be the death of me. You don't stop when you start something. That was about to set me on fire," he said, his voice full of barely suppressed emotion.

"I'm utterly in love with you," she said. "I don't think I can explain how I feel right now. I want to tell the world how much I love you!" She broke free of his arms and twirled around, her arms extended in the air in exhilaration. He watched her spin, a brilliant smile lighting his face. Then, he crossed the few feet that separated them and pulled her back into his arms.

"Thank you for loving me," he murmured. The expression on his face was pure bliss.

"When did you get up anyway?" she asked, still giddy with excitement.

"Oh, about an hour ago. You looked so peaceful. I didn't want to wake you up."

"I wish you hadn't left me. Your face is what I want to see first thing in the morning. I think that was a request you made of me, and now I'm making it of you."

"All right," he agreed. "I'll make sure that I wake you from now on before I get up. I ordered some breakfast for you, and some tea."

"That's great! I'm pretty hungry, and I would love a cup of tea."

She followed him into the living room. She could smell the eggs and bacon on the table and could see two different kinds of toast, a variety of fruit juices, and lots of fresh fruits.

"You didn't order all that for me?" she smiled.

"No, I *manifested* all that, for both of us," he replied with a chuckle.

"Manifested? What do you mean by manifested?"

"I told you about my gift of being able to manifest anything I wish."

"No, I don't think you ever told me about that gift," she answered with a curious look.

"Oh, my mistake," he said and chuckled again.

"I wonder how many more new things I will find out about you," she said. He didn't reply. "So, why did you manifest all this food if you don't eat?"

"Arielle, I told you. I can eat just about anything I want to, and right now I want to have breakfast with you."

She was a bit surprised, but she moved to pour a cup of tea for herself.

"Would you like a cup?" she asked.

He nodded.

They sat down together, and Arielle ate with a hearty appetite. Everything tasted great, and to her surprise, Sebastian ate pretty well too. It was a bit funny to think she was eating food that someone had just "manifested" rather than ordering from a restaurant. It was a little bizarre. *But then my whole life has turned out to be a little bizarre,* she thought as she took another delicious bite.

Sebastian took the newspaper and started to flip through the pages while Arielle drank her coffee and stood by the window enjoying the view. The quiet was wonderful, and a fantastic feeling swept over her at the thought of spending the rest of her life with Sebastian. If there was paradise, she was sure she had found it here with him.

"What are you thinking?" she heard his voice saying behind her.

"I was just thinking of how happy I am here with you," she replied.

"That's a good thing since you have no choice any more. I'll never let you go." His lips were curving up again, making her crazy with desire.

She walked over to him, sat on his lap, wrapped her arms around his neck, and pressed her lips to his softly.

"Mmmm," he moaned again with pleasure. "What was that for?" he gasped.

Arielle just smiled at him and kissed him again. Then she walked back to the bedroom, knowing that he would follow her. She removed her camisole and stepped into the shower. As she expected, he was right there next to her.

"You always startle me when you do that," she giggled as if she had no idea that he had followed her. He laughed, understanding her surprise, and she chuckled. He held her tight against his body and let the warm water run over them. *There is no word that can describe his beauty,* Arielle thought as she looked at him. His face looked so striking with the water dripping from his amazing hair onto his beautiful face, and his lips were wet and inviting. She reached up and kissed him softly.

It was eleven o'clock when they decided to take a drive to the beach. They didn't have to meet their friends to exchange gifts until later in the afternoon. Afterward, they would return to the hotel and get dressed for dinner at Arielle's parents' house.

While Arielle was dressing, she thought about giving Sebastian his presents before they went out. *Oh, I guess it would be better to wait until we come back from the beach,* she thought and looked into the mirror smiling happily.

It was a magnificent winter morning. They drove to the beach and after parking the car, she watched Sebastian take his shoes off and walk on the soft green grass, which was soaked in morning dew. The dew on the grass sparkled as if someone had tossed diamonds everywhere. He smiled his beautiful smile.

*A smile that belongs to an angel, not a person,* Arielle thought contentedly.

She took off her shoes and felt the cool sensation of the dew on her bare feet. She tried to enjoy the moment, knowing that the sun's magnificent golden rays would make it all disappear in a short time. She took Sebastian's hand, and they walked along the beach. He put his arm around her and pulled her close to his side. Bending down, he nuzzled her hair and pressed a kiss on her temple.

"You have no idea the emotions you have aroused in me," he said. "You are the heavenly gift given to a miserable existence that has been roaming this earth for almost five centuries. Thank you for loving me," he added, his voice becoming husky as he spoke the last few words.

She looked up and reached for his lips one more time. A flare of sunlight covered the ocean, giving it a luminous look and making the soft colors that were created reflect a rainbow of light on the surface of the water. The water rippled in the light breeze, like a picture in motion. They walked slowly, talking about their plans for the year to come. She was shocked to hear that he was planning on buying a house for them in Brighton.

"Why?" she said.

"Because that is what married couples do. And because it's the smart thing to do."

He was thinking like a businessman and she was thinking like a schoolgirl. She blushed at the realization. *Everything that had to do with him seems like a dream,* she thought. *I have a hard time believing that all this is really happening for me. That this is not just a dream.* She smiled at him, knowing he was right about purchasing a house.

"Arielle, I want to give you everything," he said. "I want to make you happy."

"You already have." She smiled and extended her hand, showing him her ring. He looked pleased. He pulled her back into his arms and held her tight as he fell quiet. He sighed, and his arms tightened around her.

"What is it, Sebastian?"

She drew back so that she could look into his eyes. He looked miserable. She couldn't understand what could change his mood so drastically in such a short time. She put her hands on either side of his face and looked deep into his eyes. She knew what was about to happen, but she didn't care, she had to find out the reason he looked so unhappy. Disoriented and breathless, she tried to control her emotions, but she was unsuccessful. She was sure she would never be able to manage the effect of his eyes on her. She looked away and tried to gather her thoughts as she whispered in a voice that only he could hear, "What's on your mind?" she repeated gently.

He pulled her back into his arms and sighed softly.

"There is something that has been bothering me for a while now," he said, "and I've been trying to push it off for another day, and another day. But I think this is the day to talk about it."

"Well, what is it?" She couldn't imagine anything that could compromise the total happiness she felt.

"I can give you the world, Arielle. But I'll never be able to give you a baby. Immortals can't have children. Will you still want to marry me?"

Arielle was shocked, unable to say anything. She had thought about being with him for the rest of her life, but somehow she'd never thought of details like babies. For a moment, she felt a sharp pain as if she were being ripped in two. But the feeling left her just as quickly as it came. She reached up and kissed him softly.

"There is nothing in this world that will keep me from wanting to be with you for the rest of my life, Sebastian. Being with you is the only thing that I want. I want nothing else."

His face became peaceful again, and she saw his lips curve up into that amazing smile as he squeezed her so tight that she almost couldn't breathe.

"I love you more than life. I want you to be happy with me and not to want for anything," he murmured.

Arielle rested her head on his chest, feeling his strength and his warmth. *How can he love a simple human like me when he could have any of the most beautiful women in his immortal world?* She thought. *I'll never understand his thinking, but I'll accept him as a major gift in my life.*

"Sebastian, if we ever wanted to have children we could always adopt," she said. "But please don't worry. This will never become an issue in our relationship."

They walked on the warm sand for a while longer as they talked about their friends and family. That is when he told her about the wonderful friends he had made at the beginning of his immortal life, and how it had all ended badly. He'd had to move away when his friends started to age, and he remained noticeably young, or they had passed on and left him alone with an unbelievable pain over their loss. He never made close friends again.

They drove to the hotel holding hands. He turned the radio on and whistled to an old song that Arielle had never heard before, making her smile. *He is Darcy,* she thought. *He is so passionate, so in love with me.* She felt contentment and a pleasant sense of ease in her life, but she was sure that the pattern would change at some point in time. She knew she would have to deal with Annabel, so full of hatred and revulsion for her. *I'm not going to think about her anymore today,* she thought, pushing the thought from her head. *I'm going to enjoy the day.*

Once in the room, she decided to give Sebastian his presents. She wanted them to be alone and to enjoy his reaction.

"For me?" he asked, looking surprised. She handed him her small pile of packages.

"Yes, and I hope you like them," she said, smiling shyly.

He looked like a little boy, full of excitement as he held the packages in his arms. She smiled, pleased, and watched him open the small package first. A brilliant smile spread across his face.

"Oh, Arielle! This is quite a gift. First edition books. I wish you hadn't spent your money on me. You are the only gift that I'll ever need. But I do love the books." His delight was clear.

"This one is one of my favorites," he said, holding up *Pride and Prejudice*.

"And this one," he added, holding up the other book. "I'm sure it's going to be a great book. I've read several of Andrew Lang's books, and I think he is a wonderful author. I don't know what to say. I'm at a loss for words." He reached out and pulled her close for a kiss.

"Thank you, you are my Lizzy!" he said, smiling. "You didn't have to give me anything at all, but I love it that you did." Next, he opened the CDs, and he was pleased with those as well. "You know the music I like," he said approvingly. The jacket took him aback. He stood up and put it on and stared in the mirror without saying a word. There was silence for a long time. Arielle was hoping she hadn't made some mistake. She moved closer to him and put her arms around his waist.

"Is something wrong?" she asked.

He turned to face her with sadness across his face. He said, "This is the first time in centuries that I have received clothes as a gift. The last people who ever did that for me were my real parents."

She pulled his face to hers and kissed him. "I love you, Sebastian, you are everything to me," she said. He pulled her into his arms, pressing his gorgeous lips on hers in a fervent kiss.

"Thank you so much for my beautiful presents," he said. "Unfortunately, I don't have a present for you, and I feel bad."

"Sebastian, you have already given me everything I could ever want. Thank you for wanting me to be your wife. And what about my beautiful ring?"

His arms were under her shirt now, his warm palms pressed against her lower back, pulling her close. Arielle held her breath as his mouth came down on hers. Time stopped as she fell into a whirlpool of sensual emotion.

"I want you," he whispered and gasped as she unbuttoned his jeans.

"What do you want, Arielle?" he murmured, mirth in his voice.

Arielle looked up and their gaze locked. His eyes were passionate.

"You," she breathed. The excitement was overwhelming Arielle, and she was having difficulty in keeping herself erect. Without warning, he swooped her up into his arms, and she squealed. His soft laughter washed over her, filling her with want.

"What are you doing?" she asked breathlessly.

"I'm taking you to bed."

# *Chapter 16*

IT WAS NEARLY ONE-THIRTY when they decided to get up and get ready. Arielle took a shower and got dressed. She put on a silk chiffon blouse and a short skirt. She pulled her hair back in a ponytail. She felt completely happy.

He held her at arm's length and examined her, grinning with pleasure. "I think this color is beautiful against your skin."

"You'd better get dressed," she said. "We're supposed to be there by around two-thirty." His reply was to kiss her as he walked into the shower whistling.

While they were driving to the flat Sebastian asked Arielle about her friendship with Gabrielle and Eva. "We've been best friends since primary school," she said. "At first, I thought friends were just people to spend time with, to laugh, and to share secrets with," she said. "But when I grew older I realized that friends are far more than just that. Gabrielle and Eva touched my heart, and I truly love them," she said. "Sometimes we spend hours together doing nothing, and we still have a great time just because we are together. We've laughed and cried so much over the years. I've never thought of passing judgment on them, and I know for sure they have never judged me or tried to change anything about me." She stopped and paused, thinking. "I know that friendship is a true gift from God," she said.

"I treasure every moment I spend with Gabrielle and Eva."

She stopped talking and sighed as she looked out the window. She was thinking about the dreadful secret she had kept to herself all these years, afraid to share with anyone except her father. She pressed her lips together as she always did when she was feeling stressed over something. Sebastian pressed her hand gently, and she looked at him.

"Is it something you can share with me?" he asked.

Arielle kept quiet as if she had not heard the question, but tears welled up in her eyes. Sebastian pulled over to the side of the road and looked at her intensely.

"Arielle, what is it?"

She looked down. "I don't want to talk about it just now," she said quietly.

"All right, we will not talk about it, then," he said. "Do you want to go to the flat, or do you want to drive for a while before we do that?"

He was so caring and tender as he put his arm around her.

"It's all right; there is no need to stress over whatever is bothering you," he said. "Just let me know what to do."

She sat quietly for a short time. He reached over and wiped her eyes with his thumb, and smiled lovingly. "I love you," he whispered.

"I love you too, and I'm sorry about this," she said, wiping her eyes. "Don't worry; I'll be fine."

She composed herself. "I'm ready to go now," she said, smiling once again. He stepped on the gas and before long they were in front of the girls' flat. The door was wide open, and Arielle's friends greeted them with happy faces as they walked in. They spent several wonderful hours together, exchanging gifts, laughing, and having drinks. Arielle could see that Sebastian was having a great time, laughing and talking with the guys. That filled her with happiness too.

She feigned surprise when she got her gifts from Gabrielle and Eva even though she already knew exactly what she was getting. The girls loved the jewelry she had chosen for them.

Next, Arielle walked over to Troy, put her right arm around his back, and handed him his present.

"This is a very small gift, just a token really, for someone who has saved my life three times. I love you, Troy, and I treasure your friendship." He looked at her, completely taken aback as a smile spread across his face. He pulled her close and gave her a warm, friendly hug.

"Thank you, Arielle. You didn't have to do this," he said. "You have already given me the gift of support with the most important step in my life." He smiled and looked over at Gabrielle, and Arielle knew exactly what he meant. He kissed her on the cheek looking extremely pleased.

Next, she walked over to Ian and handed him his gift, along with a huge hug.

"Happy Christmas, Ian, I love you as well. And I treasure your friendship more than you will ever know. Thank you for making Eva so happy." He wrapped his arms around Arielle and gave her a warm and loving embrace.

"I love you, too, Arielle. Thank you for being so thoughtful." Arielle looked across the room at Gabrielle and Eva and thought of how much she loved them. *They have been better than sisters to me*, she thought with a sudden rush of emotion. She was happy that the three of them had found love at the same time, and the most important people in their lives liked each other. It would be so sad if they didn't. She hated that she and Gabrielle were keeping Sebastian and Troy's nature a secret from Eva. *But it's not easy to explain*, she thought. *I know we will find a way to do that in the future, but not now. Not today.*

As Arielle handed Paul his gift, he held her close and kissed her on the cheek. "You are still my number one girl," he whispered. She knew Sebastian could hear a pin drop miles away, so she was sure he had heard Paul's remark, and she saw an uneasy look cross his face. She smiled at Paul and hugged him back.

"You know that I'll always be there for you," she said. "I love you, Paul, and thank you for always being there to support me."

Ian, Troy, and Paul were all happy with the shirts she had chosen for them, and Paul gave her a beautiful sweater that matched the color of her eyes. Sebastian was thrilled with Eva and Gabrielle's gifts to him. He looked Arielle's way a couple of times, grinning, and he could see the warmth in her eyes.

Time went by quickly, even though they were there for several hours. But finally, it was time to go and get ready for their dinner with Arielle's parents. It had been a beautiful day, but by the time they were driving to dinner it had started to drizzle. Looking at the sky, she could see that there was more rain to come. The roads were wet and glowed from the streetlights. Arielle stared out the window wondering what the future held for her. Sebastian took her hand and pressed it lightly, making her turn toward him. When she did, he leaned in and kissed her tenderly.

"You are drifting away from me again," he said. "I don't like not being able to read your thoughts. I need to know what you are thinking."

She smiled and kept quiet. He was right, but she was not sure of what to say. He didn't press her with any questions, and before long they were standing at her parents' front door. Sebastian carried her packages in one arm and wrapped his other arm around her, pulling her close. Arielle was carrying the bottle of wine that Sebastian had chosen for tonight.

"Are you all right?"

"Yes, I'm fine," she said. She pushed the doorbell and shortly after her mother was standing in the doorway, looking happy to see them.

"Your father is in the living room," she said in a low voice. Arielle handed her the bottle of wine and her mother chuckled with pleasure.

"You do keep your promises," she said, gazing up at Sebastian warmly.

"Always," he replied pleasantly.

Arielle's father was sitting in the living room reading a book. He looked tired. Arielle crossed the room and hugged him affectionately. "Happy Christmas, Daddy, I love you," she said.

He stood up and shook Sebastian's hand with a big smile. They sat and talked for a while about business, about the previous night's party, and about the plans, Arielle's parents had for taking a trip to Africa. Arielle was happy to hear that they were going to go somewhere alone to enjoy some time together, away from everything. It had been a long time since she had seen them go anywhere without friends or family.

Arielle's father talked about Africa and all that he had read about it, and Sebastian joined in. He told them about several trips he had taken to Johannesburg and Cape Town and gave Arielle's father suggestions about places to visit, expeditions to take, and restaurants where the food was excellent.

"Regardless of when you decide to take an African safari it will be a rewarding experience for you," he said. "It's something you'll never find anywhere else in the world." His magical voice had taken all three of them to another place just by listening to him.

"This is fascinating, Sebastian," Arielle's father enthused. "Thank you so much for all these great bits of information. It will make our journey so much more interesting."

"Please excuse me for a few moments," Arielle's mother said, standing up reluctantly. "I'd better see about dinner."

"Arielle, can you play something for us?" her father asked. At first, she demurred, but Sebastian and her father urged her to play the piano for them.

She chose an appropriate piece for the night, an excerpt from Tchaikovsky's Nutcracker Suite, the elegant "Christmas" waltz. She loved that piece. When she finished, Sebastian remained transfixed, overcome with pleasure, and her father had tears in his eyes.

"Dinner is ready," her mother called. When they walked into the dining room, she gave Arielle a huge kiss.

"I love to hear you play the piano," she said. Arielle smiled shyly and sat down next to Sebastian. He reached over and held her hand under the table, pressing it softly.

The table was dazzling, and the food smelled wonderful. There was a beautiful arrangement of pine and holly in the middle of the table. They ate hungrily since they'd had nothing since breakfast. They drank champagne to celebrate everyone being together.

After dinner they exchanged gifts. Arielle's father was very pleased with his book, thumbing through it with extreme interest. He opened the map and put on his glasses to study it closely. He almost looked like he was lost in another era. *How ironic*, Arielle thought to herself. *Sebastian is the one who really has been lost in other eras.* Finally, he looked up from the book, his eyes moist, and said, "Thank you, pumpkin. Your gift is perfect."

"I'm so happy you like it, Daddy. I know you will enjoy reading it."

Arielle's mother took the sweater out of its box and exclaimed with joy. "My favorite color." She went into the other room and came back wearing it. It was perfect, and the color made her eyes look brighter than ever. She threw the scarf around her neck and smiled a brilliant smile full of delight.

"Thank you, dear, I love my gifts, and I love you." She came close to Arielle and gave her a hug. "I love you too, Mum." Arielle said. "I love you with all my heart."

Arielle's gift from her parents was an Apple notebook and a digital movie camera. She was ecstatic. She needed the computer badly since the one she had was ready to die at any moment. She was happy about the camera because she had left hers back in St. Jean de Luz.

"I couldn't be happier," she said, looking at her parents. "Thank you so much!"

"Arielle, come and see what Sebastian gave Daddy and me for Christmas," her mother said. "They arrived yesterday, and they're gorgeous." She took Arielle's hand and walked to the front door. Outside Arielle saw two of the most exquisite planters she had ever seen set on either side at the entrance to the house. Arielle's mouth dropped as she looked at Sebastian in wonder.

"Oh, Mother, they are beautiful."

"Sixteenth century French," her mother said. "Finished in unglazed terracotta. They are from St. Jean de Fos. Aren't they gorgeous?" Then, she turned and hugged Sebastian.

Arielle looked at him and saw a smile of deep satisfaction spread across his beautiful face. *I couldn't love him anymore than I love him right this moment,* Arielle thought. *He's so amazing, and he never stops surprising me with how generous and how thoughtful he is.* She was so happy to see her mother in such a state of delight it filled her heart with pleasure.

When they walked back inside Arielle saw her father looking at Sebastian, letting him know how much they appreciated his gift. Then it was time for coffee and dessert. They chattered happily about the wonderful meal Arielle's mother had prepared and everyone's delight with their Christmas gifts.

It was getting late, and Sebastian and Arielle were preparing to leave when Arielle noticed her father and Sebastian exchanging strange looks. She didn't think too much about it until she saw them getting up and asking her to follow them. She looked at her mum in confusion, but she just looked away. Arielle saw a faint smile touch her lips.

"What is it? What's going on?"

"Just follow me, darling, and you'll see," was her father's reply. She followed her dad towards the door leading to the garage and watched him as he flung the door open and waved her ahead of him. By now her curiosity had reached an incredible height. He flipped the light switch on, and Arielle's mouth fell open. She was shocked speechless. Right there in front of her was a brand new, bright red Porsche Boxster with a huge red bow and a big sign on the windshield with the words "Merry Christmas, Arielle" written across it.

"Daddy, what have you done?"

"What do you think of Sebastian's present?" her father asked while her mother was beaming from ear to ear. She spun around, and Sebastian was standing right behind her with an amazing grin on his gorgeous face. He wrapped his arm around her and pulled her close.

Finally, she was able to speak. "Sebastian, I can't accept something like this, I just can't," she said finally. "It is incredibly beautiful, but it's far too expensive. I just can't accept it."

Her parents smiled and walked into the house leaving Sebastian and Arielle alone. He pulled her even closer and looked into her eyes. He released his immortal dazzle on her again.

"Arielle," he said. "I had this car specially ordered for you. I can't give it back." He was looking intently into her eyes. She was unable to reply since she couldn't breathe. It seemed as if his voice was coming from inside a tube.

"You do know that I have the power to compel you to accept it," he said. "But I'd rather hear you say that you'll accept it of your own free will. If you love me, you'll accept the things that I give you because it makes me happy to do so. Everything I have is now yours, Arielle."

Arielle looked away and finally found her voice again. "But it's so expensive. I could never give you anything like this car. How do you think that makes me feel?"

"It's not a contest of who gives what to whom, Arielle. I love you, and I want to make you happy. You've given me a feeling that I have lived without all my long life. That's something you can't put a price on."

He hadn't loosened his grip on her, and he didn't seem to want to let go. He passionately pressed his lips on hers and gazed into her eyes, trying to dazzle her again.

"Please say yes," he murmured.

She stared into his amazing face and smiled inwardly. She wrapped her arms around his neck and pulled his head down to capture his lips in a scorching kiss. Her lips parted, giving him access to the softness of her mouth. He lifted his head reluctantly, gasping for air.

"Don't do that here," she heard him stammer. She closed her eyes and inhaled deeply, struggling for strength to keep herself upright. She finally opened her eyes to find him watching her carefully.

He moved slowly and dropped a set of keys into her hand. She looked down and stared at the keys, dumbfounded. He pulled her toward the car and opened the driver's door. "Get in, baby," he said. "Let's go for a drive."

She slipped in behind the wheel. It was a perfect fit. Sebastian got in on the passenger side and looked at her with an expectant smile. She was so excited she didn't know what to do. She pushed the start button, and the engine purred. She backed out of the garage slowly, but when she got on the street, she pressed down on the gas pedal. It was still raining, but Arielle didn't seem to notice.

The car was gorgeous, and she had sitting next to her the most beautiful man, who loved her unconditionally. Once again she had the feeling that this couldn't be real, she must be living in a dream.

"So, will you take the car?" he laughed, watching her as they drove away from her parents' home.

Unable to stop grinning, she looked back at him and nodded happily. "Thank you, Sebastian, I love it. But I still think it's way too much."

They drove back to the house in a happy silence. When they walked back into the house, her parents were very discrete and didn't ask any questions.

"I guess I'll keep it," she said with a shy smile, and they seemed pleased. They loved Sebastian already. *Maybe he's put a spell on them too*, she thought.

She had never seen her father or mother react to anyone else the way they had with Sebastian. Not that she had brought a parade of guys trooping through the house, but they had never acted the same way with any of the boys she had known in school. Since he was the man she would be with for the rest of her life, this pleased Arielle immensely.

# *Chapter 17*

**IT WAS QUITE LATE WHEN THEY PULLED AWAY** from the house, leaving Arielle's new car in the garage. Sebastian reached over to take her hand as he always did. Just then, Arielle noticed a car parked down the street. As the headlights swept over their car for a quick second, Arielle thought that she saw two women sitting in the dark. They looked awfully familiar. Her heart skipped a beat, and a cold chill ran down her spine, to think that she was being watched. *It's pretty silly to think that every person I see wants to harm me*, she thought. She knew that Sebastian hadn't noticed anything because he had been looking at her when they passed the car. But he noticed her apprehension.

"What's wrong?"

"A car was parked across the street from my parents' house, and I thought I saw a couple of people in it as if they were watching us," she said uncertainly.

"Do you want me to go back?"

She didn't hear his question because she was trying hard to see the faces in her head.

Sebastian turned around, but when they got there, the car was gone. Arielle's uneasiness grew. She was sure now that they were being watched.

"Are you sure?" Sebastian asked.

"Yes, I'm sure. They were right there, but I'm not sure they were there for us. I'm just always worried, knowing that Annabel is out there plotting something."

Sebastian put his arm around her and pulled her close. "Don't worry, my love, she can't hurt you as long as you wear your necklace. We'll find a more permanent solution shortly. But nobody can keep us apart. Not Annabel. Not anyone." He gave her a reassuring look that made her feel safe again.

"I hate going to a hotel with you," she heard him saying. "It diminishes my true feelings for you. You're going to be my wife, so I'll be getting us a home soon." His voice was full of concern.

Arielle couldn't wait until they could have a place of their own. It was so hard for her to believe that this perfect man had been "dead" for more than five centuries. He was tender, loving, warm, and an unbelievable lover. She loved him with every beat of her heart, with her entire soul, and she had accepted him for who he was.

It wasn't long before they were in their room. He folded his arms around her as soon as the door closed behind them and pulled her close.

"I have been waiting to be alone with you all day. I'm under your spell. I'm the happiest man alive," he said, chuckling at the last remark. She joined in.

"I think you are pretty remarkable yourself," Arielle said. "I don't think I can love you any more than I do right now."

He started to undress her, and she let him. His palms were hot, sending waves of pleasure across her skin, making her quiver. His lips covered hers in a scorching kiss, sending unrestrained exhilaration that spun her senses into oblivion. He moaned with hunger as he lifted her up in his arms and carried her to bed. His scent was mesmerizing.

She poured every emotion into that kiss. His hands pulled her flush against him so she could feel his obvious need. She hung onto him, recognizing his deliberate intent, and she could think of nothing else except that she needed him. His fingers slowly skimmed over her soft skin, and she shuddered. Scorching sensation traveled down her spine. She surrendered as he rolled over, taking her with him and pinning her beneath him. She felt fire surge through her veins and an inexpressible heat that burned her skin as if she were literally on fire. Her hands traced the planes of his back, and her nails dug into his skin, making him moan with excitement. Their lips remained locked in a passionate kiss as he stretched over her; there was no holding back. He groaned, and she gave herself to him with a complete exhilaration that made her sob in sheer bliss. She could hear him suck in a deep breath as she was whirling in a sea of desire. Joy blasted across every fiber of her body like a cosmic explosion, and they both savored the moment, gasping for air. Her pleasure reached an incredible height, and she tried to please him the same way he pleased her. How could someone make love all night long, and how could every time seem like the first time? That was something she kept asking herself when they were together. She just could not explain any of it.

"Arielle," she heard him groaning, "What are you doing to me?" he sighed, breathless. She smiled with exuberance as he fell on his back, exhausted. He gathered her in his arms, and they fell asleep, utterly sated. Her last thought before closing her eyes was that this had been the best Christmas of her life.


This was the night that her dreams should have been nothing short of wonderful, but they were wild and frightening. She saw a bright light far away and the shadows of three women, tall and threatening. As she got closer she tried to see their faces, but they were standing at the very edge of the light, and the glow prevented her from recognizing them. She had a horrible feeling that it was Annabel and her friends, but she couldn't make out their faces, so she was unsure. It looked as if they were holding something, and they were waving it wildly back and forth. She couldn't clearly see what it was. As she walked by, they looked at her, and cold air blew her way, making her shiver. She began to tremble in fright. She looked back and saw them moving towards her. She tried to run, but her feet were glued to the ground. All she could do was watch the women approach. Panic consumed her.

They were but a few feet away when their faces suddenly became clear, making her cry out in desperation. It was Annabel, Julia, and

Paola, their eyes red like fire and filled with pure loathing. Their faces were distorted in anger, and they were laughing wildly as they raised daggers over her body. Arielle was sobbing out loud. Her body convulsed from sheer terror.

Her eyes snapped open, and she stared, confused, into Sebastian's alarmed gaze. She felt his hands gripping her shoulders, and she was being shaken awake.

"Arielle! Arielle, wake up. Oh, baby, you are having a nightmare."

She was completely disoriented. When she came to, she fell into his arms sobbing. She was trembling and couldn't stop crying. "It was horrible, it was horrible," she kept repeating.

"It was only a dream, my love, calm down. I'm here, and you are safe."

He held her tight, continuing to speak soothing words, and she stayed in his arms a long time until she finally fell asleep, the warmth of his body against hers.

It was later in the day when she opened her eyes again. Sebastian was sitting next to her, watching her carefully. He smiled at her and moved closer to put his arms around her.

"You scared me last night. How are you feeling today?"

"I'm okay," she whispered, but the memory of the nightmare came back and left her feeling unsettled.

He stood up and pulled the curtains open. She looked out the huge windows. She could see the sun peeking slowly up in the clear blue sky, filling the room with a burst of golden light, warming her. She felt safe and reached out for him. He lay next to her and touched her lips with his in a soft and tender kiss. She put her arms around his neck and pulled him even closer.

"Sebastian, please hold me, I need you close to me. I feel so exhausted, so unbelievably worn out. I just don't understand it."

"I'm here, and I don't want to be anywhere else. However, I think if you get up and take a shower you might feel a little better."

She knew he was right, and she did exactly that. The water made her feel better, but she was still tired beyond belief. She brushed her teeth, put her hair up in a ponytail, and wrapped a bath towel around herself. When she came out of the bathroom, he was waiting for her with a cup of coffee. She smiled at him, a thankful look in her eyes.

"Thank you for loving me," she whispered and touched his lips. "You are the most important person in my life."

The coffee was delicious. Arielle walked over to the window. Sebastian stood next to her, and they both gazed out at the beautiful view of the park.

"Is there something you would like to do today?" he asked.

"I just want to be with you."

"I'm not going anywhere, Arielle. I'm going to be with you until you get tired of me, and I sure hope that never happens." He paused, and then added, "I wanted to know if there is something in particular that you would like to do today. I've made arrangements with a realtor to look at homes tomorrow. I thought that would be a good thing to do for the next three or four days. I'm sure we will find something we both like."

"Oh, that sounds so great," Arielle said. "I've always loved looking at homes—especially if it's going to be for us. The lease on our flat is up at the end of the month," she added. "Eva is going to move in with Ian, and Gabrielle with Troy."

"Well then, that works out extremely well. I was a little worried about that. I didn't want to interfere with the decisions or arrangements you had made with your friends."

"I don't make any decisions anymore if you are not included," Arielle said simply. Sebastian grinned wide. He took her face in his hands and kissed her tenderly. Then picking up the newspaper, he made his way to the sofa and left her to finish her coffee.

She was filled with excitement over searching for a house. The thought of being with Sebastian every day and every moment of her life was intoxicating. She couldn't imagine anything better. Beaming with happiness, she walked over to the sofa where he was sitting, put her arms around his neck and kissed him gently. He set the paper down and wrapping his arms around her waist held her close.

"Do you want to see a film later?" she asked.

"All right," he agreed. "Do you want to ring your friends and see if they want to go with us?"

*He'll never know how happy I am to hear him say that,* Arielle thought. She was worried that she might have been pushing her friends on him too much, but here he was now asking to spend time with them. *I love him so much*, she thought happily. She rang Eva, only to find out that they had been planning to ask them the same thing.

"What film do you want to see?" Arielle asked, and then, as she listened to Eva's answer she began laughing out loud, unable to stop.

"What is wrong with you?" Eva asked.

"Nothing, nothing at all," Arielle answered, yet she was unable to stop giggling.

They agreed to meet at six-thirty at the pub to get something to eat first. When she put down the phone, Sebastian was looking at her curiously.

"What was all that about?" he asked.

"Do you know what film we are going to see tonight?" Arielle said with a chuckle. He looked at her, clueless.

*"Pride and Prejudice,"* she said, starting to laugh again. This time, Sebastian burst out into a hearty laugh as well.

"That's pretty funny, I have to admit," he said, grinning.

Arielle was still laughing as she walked out onto the balcony to feel the warmth of the sun on her skin. Sebastian came right behind her, wrapped his arms around her and pulled her against him. Leaning close he whispered, "We have been invited to my parents' home for a New Year's Eve ball, do you want me to accept for us?"

Arielle spun around without leaving his embrace and gazed into his beautiful eyes. "Of course. I would love to see Loren again and meet your mother," Arielle said. "I can't think of anything else I would rather do on New Year's Eve."

"Thank you, baby," he murmured, and his lips moved against hers as his hands stroked her hips.

"What are you doing?"

"I am trying to stimulate you, am I doing a good job?" he asked, laughing out loud. She threw herself at him and held his body close as his grip on her tightened. It was as if they were trying to make each other understand the depth of their love. He threw her on the sofa and made love to her with a wild hunger.

"Is this going to happen all the time when we live together?" she asked breathlessly.

"Do you have any objections to it?" he replied, gasping for air.

"No, not at all," she giggled. "I just want to make sure that I understand the rules."

He laughed again, holding her tight, not wanting to let go.

They turned the telly on and stayed there relaxing, just enjoying being with each other.

"What am I going to do with my car?" she asked suddenly, realizing she now had two of them.

"Well, I think you should sell it," he said. "Your new car is all paid for, and the insurance is covered, you don't have to worry about any of that."

"You've done so much for me, Sebastian," she sighed. "I don't know how I can ever repay you."

"First, I want you to marry me," he said kissing her again. "Then I want you to finish school and be happy. You are going to be my own private engineer," he chuckled, and kissed her again, this time on the tip of her nose.

"I have to move my things out of the flat by the end of next week," she said. "Today is the twenty-sixth, so we have only five days left on the lease."

"But there is a whole month before classes start. So you have plenty of time to do anything you want," he said. His musical voice always made her feel secure.

"I also have a lifetime to love you," she said. She felt utterly blissful.

"I think you meant to say that you have *eternity* to love me," he corrected her again.

"Okay. I have eternity to love you."

"Thank you," he whispered in her ear. He sighed contentedly.

They had a wonderful time at dinner, and then settled in at the cinema, anxious to see the film together. Sebastian had his arm around Arielle and every time Darcy or Lizzy was on the screen he gave her a little squeeze. In the part when Darcy tells Lizzy that she had bewitched him and that he was hopelessly in love with her, Sebastian leaned over and searched for her lips. She turned to him, and their lips met in a passionate kiss.

"I love you, Mr. Darcy," she whispered.

"I'm hopelessly in love with you, Lizzy," he answered softly and chuckled.

What both Sebastian and Arielle loved about the story was how Jane Austen suggested that both Darcy and Elizabeth had lives that continued beyond the ending of the book. That was a very intriguing point for both of them. Arielle also related to Elizabeth having to deal with the burden of secrets, secrets she couldn't confide in her family or friends. *That's exactly what I have been doing with my dreadful secret,* Arielle thought. *I guess I could find tons of things in this story that would relate to my life and my beautiful dream, Sebastian,* she thought and sighed happily.

They walked out of the cinema discussing the details of the film and comparing it with the book. Then, they decided to go dancing. Once again, they got back to the hotel late. Arielle giggled blissfully, remembering that tomorrow they would start house hunting. Then, Sebastian gathered her in his arms, and she snuggled close to him. By now it had become a wonderful routine. *I don't think I'll ever be able to sleep without him by my side;* Arielle thought as they drifted off to sleep.

 *Chapter 18*

THE NEXT MORNING, ARIELLE WOKE UP EARLY. Sebastian was still next to her, looking like a sleeping angel. She drew a deep breath and took a minute to take in his amazing looks. He was so perfect, and the warmth of his body sent a surge of desire across her. She bent down and pressed a soft kiss against his lips. Strong arms wrapped around her so fast that she was startled.

He laughed out loud, enjoying her surprise. He had been pretending to be asleep, but in fact, he had been awake for a while, lying in bed waiting for her to wake up.

She traced her fingertips over his bare ribcage and trailed them down to his flat stomach. He moaned with pleasure and gathered her into his arms, cradling her against his chest. She nuzzled his neck, and he groaned his approval. He cupped her chin and lifted her face to meet his gaze. "I love you so much," he murmured, and his lips claimed hers in a swift move.

She pulled back gasping for air. "I love you too," she purred, and her hot breath coursed beyond his skin, right into the core of his soul. He parted his lips and let her taste his sweet scent. He didn't try to move away, just stayed in her arms, moaning with the thrill of her touch. *He brings me to such incredible heights*, she thought. She could never have imagined such pleasure, such joy.

"We're meeting the realtor at ten," he said tenderly.

"I'll be ready," she smiled.

"What are we going to be looking for?"

"I would love to find a house with huge windows looking out at the ocean. And a beautiful garden."

"Mmmhmm… That sounds a lot like what I had in mind."

"I guess we won't have a hard time knowing when we find the perfect place, and it's going to be perfect for us," she said.

"You are perfect for me."

She just giggled and, framing his face with her hands, she pressed her lips hard against his. He moaned and closed his eyes, savoring her touch.

"Remember where we left off," she said giggling as she jumped out of bed and ran into the shower.


Their first day of house hunting was uneventful. They saw many beautiful homes, but nothing that especially appealed to them or fit their plans.

On the second day, they stopped in front of a brand new home that captivated Arielle before she even got out of the car. It was a very large two-story home with huge windows facing the ocean. The garden was full of beautiful trees, green foliage, and hundreds of blooming winter shrubs. Beautiful winter hazel, with colorful bell shaped flowers, winter jasmine with branches cascading like waterfalls, and Edgeworthia chrysantha, with tiny yellow flowers mixed with a creamy white covering. In the center of the garden was a large fountain. Golden streams of water lit by the bright sun flowed from the top tier fountain to the bottom.

Sebastian took Arielle's hand, and they walked up the large marble staircase and through the beautiful front door. She was completely mesmerized.

A striking young woman was standing in the middle of the foyer. As they approached, she smiled widely at Sebastian. Arielle immediately stopped breathing.

"Good morning Mr. Gaulle," the woman said brightly, her voice soft as velvet.

*What?* Arielle thought. *Is she an immortal? She looks like immortal, and she talks like and immortal. What is she doing here?*

"Good morning, Sonia," he replied, smiling at her. He clasped Arielle's hand and pulled her closer. "This is my fiancée, Arielle Lloyd," he said. "Arielle, this is our realtor, Sonia Dankworth."

Sonia smiled politely and approached Arielle, offering her hand. They shook hands amicably. "Good morning," Sonia said politely.

"Good morning," Arielle replied, giving Sebastian a sidelong, quizzical look.

"Please look at the house and if you have any questions I will be happy to answer them," Sonia said. Then she walked into the other room, leaving them alone.

Sebastian gazed down at Arielle, noticing her stunned expression. "What is it?" he asked curiously.

"Is she...?" Arielle began to ask, but she couldn't finish the question.

"Is she what?"

"Is she an immortal?"

"No! Why would you think that?"

"She is stunningly beautiful," she whispered.

"Are you immortal?" he asked without replying to her question, mirth in his voice.

"What do you mean?"

"Well, you are stunningly beautiful too, much more beautiful than this woman. Are you immortal?"

Arielle chuckled, and he folded her in his arms. "Sorry, I just thought..." she said, her voice trailing off. "Oh, I don't know what I thought," she added, waving her arms in frustration.

"Come on, baby, let's check the house out," he said and pulled her through the foyer's archway deeper into the house. When they reached the back of the house, Arielle gasped. The view was simply breathtaking.

The magnificent white beach below extended as far as her eye could see. It was a full view of the ocean, the ocean she adored. Floor to ceiling windows provided a clear, unblocked view of the magical beach world as if they were framed paintings untouched by human hands. Arielle looked at Sebastian, her eyes filled with tears of excitement. He took her hands and drew her against him. He nuzzled her hair and set his lips to her temple.

"It seems that you like this house," he whispered.

"I love it!" she exclaimed. "I love watching the water in Brighton. It changes so often. Sometimes, it is as dark blue as sapphires, at others, it's green, like your eyes. Sometimes, it is as gold as, oh, as when the sun is slowly replacing the dark skies at dawn!"

"I think this is my favorite house too," he chuckled. His lips brushed her ear.

He walked over toward the realtor, and they exchanged a few words as Arielle stood to stare out the window.

A few minutes later he came back, and putting his arms around her; he fastened them tightly at her waist. He held her against him and bending down he whispered, "It's settled. This is going to be your new home, and it's very charming, I have to agree. However, I still prefer you by far."

He grinned and bending down their lips met. Arielle forgot how to breathe. She was full of excitement; her heart overwhelmed with exhilaration.

All the way to the hotel she talked about the house enthusiastically. Sebastian watched with delight as she chattered happily. When they got back to the hotel, she fell into his arms, exhausted. He held her tight and sighed against her lips. "I love the house just as much as you do," he said. "I can't imagine being any happier than I am right now."

Arielle fell onto the bed and closed her eyes. She had the impression that she was living a dream. She was going to live in the most extraordinary home ever, she was to drive a magnificent car, and she had a perfect man to love for the rest of her life. She was overwhelmed with contentment.

"What are you thinking?"

She opened her eyes and saw that his face was an inch away from hers, his lips parted in that sexy smile of his.

She leaned in and kissed him. "You will never know how happy I am right now. This has to be a dream. It just can't possibly be real. It's not just the house or the car, it is the fact that you, the most beautiful person in the world, want me and love me. Why is that? I just can't understand it."

"Arielle, you are my life. We have gone over this before. There is nothing for me in this world if you are not in it. I can't breathe if you don't love me." He paused for a moment, gently tracing his fingers over the contours of her face. "Let's go out and look for some furniture that you might like to have," he said, breaking into a huge grin.

"Oh, I'm not very particular about furniture," she said. "I don't like modern furniture, it's always so very uncomfortable. But I love most traditional styles. I love your taste, Sebastian, and I would be happy with anything you choose."

"Well, okay then. You can move your things to the house and be out of your flat by the end of next week. Do you want me to call a moving company?"

"I don't need movers. We rented the place furnished, so I don't own any of the furniture. All I have to move is the telly in my bedroom, my clothes, and a few small personal things."

Two days later, they took a ride out to look at the house again. Sebastian drove slowly, enjoying the day and holding her hand as he always did. She looked at his perfect features and thought to herself how lucky she was. She couldn't imagine even one moment without him. As they got out of the car, he dropped a set of keys in her hand.

"Here you go, Miss Lloyd, soon to be Mrs. Gaulle, here are your keys to your new house."

"*Our* house," she corrected him.

"Our house," he repeated, amused.

He put his arm around her waist and pulled her towards the front door. Her hand was shaking as she turned the key. "Let's open it together," she whispered. He put his hand on hers, and they pushed the door open together. He swept her into his arms and carried her over the threshold. "I love you," he murmured, stepping into the foyer. He set her lovingly down onto the marble floor, and she let out a cry of surprise.

The house was completely furnished. There was a gorgeous round table in the middle of the foyer with a huge flower arrangement in the center and two stunning antique chairs placed against the wall.

A magnificent grandfather clock stood between the two chairs, giving the entryway the look of a picture in a home decorating magazine. Arielle gasped as an overwhelming sensation of joy pricked through her. She turned and looked back at him with wonder in her eyes.

"Let's go in and take a look at the rest of it," he urged.

The living room and dining room were beautiful, filled with antique furniture. The dining room table was carved with amazing designs. Everywhere she looked she saw beautiful, fabulous things. The family room was warm and inviting with comfortable furniture. By the large window overlooking the ocean was a beautiful baby grand piano. Sebastian closed his hand about her waist tightly and whispered, "That piano is for you, my love. I want to hear you play, only for me. Will you do that?"

Arielle was speechless. She couldn't imagine anything prettier than what she was seeing. All she could do was look at him and nod. He pulled her into the master bedroom. The king sized bed featured a magnificent backboard with intricate sycamore inlay carving. It depicted the beauty of nature with floral forms including roses and vines. The other four bedrooms were furnished with exquisite taste, and the kitchen was equipped with all modern appliances. The final touch was the beautiful heavy blue silk curtains and under curtains that hung from every window, caught with rope tiebacks.

"Sebastian, when did you do all this? You've been with me most of the time..."

"I have the power to manifest anything I want any time I want it," he said mischievously. "I know I told you about that a few days ago."

She looked at him puzzled. "What do you mean? That nothing in here is real?"

"Oh, it's very real. I just don't do things the same way as humans do."

Arielle didn't really comprehend what he was saying, but she was trying.

"So... are you saying that these things will all disappear at some point in time?"

"No, they will never disappear unless I will kill them to disappear." He grinned, aware of how difficult it must be for a mortal to understand how any of this could be true.

"Okay, I don't understand anything you are saying, but I'm not going to try anymore. The more I ask, the more confused I get," she said, laughing.

"Do you like it?"

"I love everything about this house, every little part of it. I love it so much I can hardly breathe."

"Do you love it more than you love me?"

"Sebastian! I love nothing in this world more than I love you. I'm willing to step into an unknown and sometimes chilling world of yours only because I'm completely and utterly in love with you. I can't live without you, either. You are my world, and honestly, I'm scared that one of these days I'll wake up and you'll disappear like a beautiful dream. In fact, please hold me right now. I want to make sure I'm not dreaming all this."

He drew her close. His hands framed her face as he bent down and set his lips on hers. Arielle threw her arms around his neck and moved as close as she could to him. Their kiss deepened, becoming more fervent, more passionate, and they were lost in each other's warmth. Sebastian broke away first and held her gaze. He could see the fire in her eyes and he could feel her eagerness and desperate need for him, while an obsessive desire burned his soul.

*My addiction*, he thought, and chuckled. Arielle closed her eyes, moaning breathlessly, and his breath hitched. He fought for control and coughed to clear his throat.

"I'm going to leave you for a short time to go and check out of the hotel," he said. "Then, we can pick up where we left off, or just talk about moving your things later today or tomorrow. What do you think?"

Arielle's eyes snapped open wide. "Now?" she asked, staggering back and hauling in a trembling breath. Sebastian chuckled softly, and gathering her close one more time, he set his lips on hers passionately.

"I shouldn't be long. Don't forget where we were," he snickered.

Arielle watched him walk away. "I'll be happy to stay here and explore this beautiful house," she said, frowning a bit. She heard a soft snort in reply.

When Sebastian left, she called Eva. She told her all about the car Sebastian had given her for Christmas and the house he had just bought for them.

"You must be so happy," Eva said. Her voice too was filled with happiness.

"Eva, I'm so overwhelmed that I think it's a dream. He's so amazing. But he is doing so much for me, and I can't do anything for him."

"I'm sure you do a lot for him," Eva said. "He looks so happy when he is with you. I've watched his face when you are together, and he looks like he wants nothing else in this world but to be with you. I love you so much, Arielle, and I'm so happy for you both."

"I feel the same way about you and Ian, and Gabrielle and Troy. You all seem to be so very happy together. I'm very fortunate to have you in my life," Arielle said, sighing happily. "I was thinking about moving my things later today. Will you be there?"

"I was going to call you and talk to you about Gabrielle and I," Eva said. "I'm moving my things right now, so I don't know if I'll still be here when you come. Ian is helping me move into his place. He has a beautiful house on the beach, and I know I'll be so happy with him. I can't stand being away from him. I feel complete when we are together."

Arielle laughed. "I know exactly what you mean. I feel the same way about Sebastian. What did you want to tell me about Gabrielle?"

"Troy and Gabrielle moved her things this morning. I guess he's pretty wealthy. Gabrielle said his house is like a palace, and she just can't get used to the size of it."

Arielle chuckled again with delight.

Soon after she hung up the phone, it rang again. This time, it was Troy.

"What's up, Troy?"

"Arielle, I'm going to propose to Gabrielle next Saturday on her birthday. I know I told you this before, but now I need your help with my plans."

"Oh, Troy, she'll be so happy! I know how much she has wished for this moment. Just let me know what you want me to do, and I'll be happy to take care of it."

"Thanks, Arielle. You have been a true friend."

"I love you both, so don't worry, everything will be taken care of, whatever you ask."

"Thanks, Arielle. I'll call you later with the details."

She put the phone down and walked out into the backyard. It was just as breathtaking as the garden in front. Huge gorgeous trees were everywhere. Arielle looked around and smiled wide. She could just imagine how it would be in the springtime. She could see blooming multicolored flowers, blue, white, and pink hydrangeas, and green foliage covering the entire area. She could vividly see jasmine climbing the walls that surrounded the property, and almost smell the lovely scent of freesia everywhere. It would be a small piece of paradise.

Her attention shifted to the goldfish that were swimming back and forth in a small fountain by the back of the garden. There were three different areas equipped with comfortable furniture, with plenty of places to sit and read a book, or just relax. *What a paradise,* Arielle thought again.

As she looked out at the sea, her mind wandered. She was enjoying all the wonderful things that life could offer, but a strange feeling crept up on her. She couldn't quite put her finger on it, but it was making her feel more than a little peculiar.

Suddenly, a vision of Julia took over her mind, and she could hear her words about all the women Sebastian had been with and how he had left them after he'd had enough. It was the same thing Savanna had told her at her birthday party. Could these things be true?

*Will he leave me too, after he has had enough?* she wondered. Had he ever asked any of the others to marry him? Had he ever told them that he loved them? She tried to push the feeling into the back of her head, along with every other bad thought or feeling she had ever had. "I don't want to deal with any of that today," she murmured, but the thoughts wouldn't go away.

Now, she sat down and stared at the water, moisture covering her eyes. *What in the world is going on with me? Why do thoughts like these enter my mind?* She wondered if life would have been simpler if Sebastian was just a normal human guy.

She stood up and walked down the end of the property and looked at the beautiful homes that were built on the tops of the cliffs on either side of their home. The hillsides were covered with grass and big bundles of red and white valerian. The view was spectacular. She was so absorbed in her thoughts that she didn't hear Sebastian approach. Suddenly she turned, and she was caught in his warm, tight embrace, so tight that she struggled for breath. His face was beautiful, and his lips found hers, holding her in a passionate, tender kiss.

"What were you thinking about?" he asked, grinning. The grin faded when he noticed the moisture in her eyes.

"Are you crying?" he asked, voice full of concern.

"This place is out of this world, and it makes me very happy," she said. "I always cry when I'm extremely happy."

A cool ocean breeze made her shiver. Her thoughts drifted to a faraway place again, so much so that she forgot that Sebastian was still standing there, watching her. She felt his arms tightening around her, and his eyes pierced hers. His effect on her was as intense as ever, but now she could hear his voice loud and clear.

"Arielle! You are tormenting me now. Something is wrong, and I can't read your mind. You have to tell me what you are thinking." He shook her lightly, and she snapped out of whatever was making her act like a crazy person.

She looked at him and saw worry in his face. *How can I hurt him like that? He doesn't deserve to pay for my insecurities and petty jealousy. I need to stop these thoughts.* She sank into his warm embrace and sobbed, "I'm sorry Sebastian, please forgive me. I am just being stupid."

"I don't understand. Is there something I did?"

"No, not at all. But when it comes to you I'm full of insecurities."

"What are you insecure about?"

"Losing you, of course."

"Again, I don't understand."

"You don't want to hear what I'm thinking."

"Now, that's where you are wrong. I want to know all your thoughts."

She stopped for a couple of minutes and looked towards the ocean. Finally, she said in a low voice, "I'm scared that am just a fad for you."

His arms gripped her tightly, and he spun her around to face him. He was clearly shocked, and he stared at her with astonishment.

After a few minutes she heard his voice again, this time hard and angry, "Is that what you think of me?" he said through clenched teeth.

"I'm sorry, Sebastian. I know that I'm acting like a jealous teenager and not a mature individual."

"What could you possibly be jealous of?"

"Oh, just life itself."

He put his arm around her waist and pulled her into the house. He shut the door behind them. They stood in the middle of the kitchen. "I love you, Arielle. I can't breathe if you are not near me. I don't want to live if I can't have you. I want to marry you, today, now! All you have to do is say the word. So I simply do not understand how you can be jealous of anything at all."

"You're right. I'm such a fool," she cried. She wrapped her arms around his neck, and standing on her toes; she searched for his mouth. She touched his lips with her tongue and his kiss draped her in sheer passion. His hands pulled her tightly against his body as his lips moved from her mouth down to the hollow of her throat and she moaned with desire. The smoothness of her skin excited Sebastian to a painful level. Intense desire elevated his need and his muscles locked. He was ready to fulfill every single one of her needs. Her hands moved slowly and unbuttoned his shirt. She pulled the shirt away from his jeans, and pushed it wide open, exposing her eyes to the amazing sight of his body. Her mouth went dry trying to absorb the magnificent sight that took over every single fiber of her existence. She moistened her lips and set them on the planes of his chest, trailing his skin with soft kisses. She skated her tongue slowly across the hard muscles. His breath hitched as heat spread across single nerve, every single fiber of his body. She moved her hands slowly, lower and lower, and unbuttoned his jeans. Sebastian swallowed hard and groaned.

"You will be the death of me," he said with a low chuckle. He picked her up and carried her inside to their new bed. His hands were now on her bare hips, and all she could think was how much she wanted him. He was frantically removing his clothes and gasping for air as he pulled her beneath him, gently reeled her into a fascinating world of passion, and claimed everything that he knew was his and only his. She closed her eyes and moaned. He was so perfect. Once again, she was lost in the beautiful world that he had provided for her.

Afterward, he lay next to her completely satisfied, a smile spread across his beautiful face. She closed her eyes thinking how lucky she was that he loved her when his arms suddenly pulled her on top of him and held her tight. His lips were curved up into that inviting smile. He kissed her softly.

"How are you feeling now?" he whispered.

"Pretty extraordinary," she said with a giggle.

"I love you, Arielle, don't ever forget that."

"Your eyes are so beautiful," she whispered. He grinned, drawn in by the beauty of her face, and he kissed the tip of her nose.

"I'm in love with your eyes too. They give me the energy I need to breathe," he murmured.

She laughed. "I could spend the whole day just telling you all the things I love about you."

She rolled back onto the bed and stretched to feel the full effect. She was exultant, and the bed was soft and very comfortable. He kept his arms about her, resting silently, totally satisfied for a very long time.

They must have both dozed off because when her mobile went off, Arielle was startled. She jumped out of bed and caught it on the second ring. It was Eva asking if Arielle wanted to go shopping the next day for a New Year's Eve outfit. She was going to the Taylors' annual New Year's Eve party, and so were Arielle's parents. This year, Arielle would be going to the Dillons' party with Sebastian instead.

Their parents had arranged the annual parties for as long as Arielle could remember. Christmas was at the Lloyd's house, New Year's Eve at the Taylor's, and Mardi Gras at the Winters' house, up until Eva's father had passed away.

"Hang on, just a sec, Eva," she said. "Sebastian, do you mind if I go shopping with Gabrielle and Eva tomorrow?"

"No, darling, you go ahead."

"Do you want me to come and pick you up?" she asked Eva.

"No, I would rather pick you up. Ian's sister is coming with us."

"Oh, that will be great. I can't wait to meet her. See you tomorrow then."

She gave Eva her new address and jumped back into bed where Sebastian was waiting for her. She fell into his embrace, her lips parted, and Sebastian repossessed them ravenously.

"Whom are you going to meet?" he murmured without leaving the kiss.

She pulled back gently. "Oh, Ian's sister is coming with us. I've never met her, and I think it will be wonderful. I also found out that Troy will be proposing to Gabrielle next Saturday on her birthday. I'm so happy for her. Both my best friends are going to be engaged. I can hardly believe how our lives have changed—especially mine."

She grew quiet. She closed her eyes and tried hard not to think about all the other women that had been Sebastian's lovers in his long immortal life, but she failed. Agonizing details began to consume her imagination, and she pressed her lips nervously. She knew Sebastian could sense her fears and anxieties. She was afraid that he might even guess what was twirling around inside her head. At least he couldn't read her thoughts. She was happy about that.

Late in the afternoon they drove to her parents' house to pick up her new car, and from there they drove both cars to the flat to pick up most of Arielle's things. It took a few trips to get everything out of there. They finished moving in the early evening, and the last trip was to pick up Arielle's old car, her little Volvo and bring it back to the house. Then they went out to eat, but Sebastian didn't touch a thing. Afterward, they spent their first night in their new home just enjoying the house. Sebastian made Arielle play the piano and sat next to her with his arm around her waist and a happy smile on his face as she played. Every so often he would lean in and kiss her. Arielle couldn't imagine being any happier.

 *Chapter 19*

**AROUND ELEVEN O'CLOCK THE NEXT MORNING,** Gabby and
Eva arrived. Ian's sister Rachel was very friendly. She was quite
pretty and looked a lot like her brother. Arielle took them on a tour
of the house, and they all loved it. "After we go shopping, I would
love to see your new places," she said, and her friends agreed.

At the mall, they found some amazing dresses for their New
Year's celebrations. Arielle chose a strapless black cocktail dress with
a narrow blue sash around her waist. It was short—about four inches
above the knee—and very attractive. She also bought a pair of black
leather high heels and some stockings.

They decided to buy some sexy lingerie next. "For after the party,"
Gabby said with an arch smile, and they all laughed. They had fun making
their selections, and then they headed out, happy with their choices.

The first stop was at Gabrielle and Troy's new place. The house
was amazing, Eva had not been kidding. It was full of antiques, not
surprising considering Troy's history. There was a huge library full
of amazing books, some very old. Troy was very hospitable. *He is
going to make Gabrielle so happy,* Arielle thought.

They were standing in their bedroom when Gabby leaned close
to Arielle's ear and whispered, "Arielle, he is the most amazing lover."

Arielle chuckled, knowing exactly what her friend meant. She leaned over and whispered in Gabby's ear. "Well, he has had centuries of experience, remember that." Gabby couldn't hold her laughter back, and everyone wanted to know what was so funny, especially Troy.

"Oh, nothing," Arielle said, rolling her eyes. "Girl talk."

Next, they went to Eva and Ian's charming place.

"It's amazing that we all live by the ocean," Arielle exclaimed gleefully. The three friends had been spending time together by the sea ever since they were very young girls. "Ian this is amazing. This has to be some omen," she laughed as they all joined in.

Arielle got home around seven-thirty. "Thanks for driving, Gabby," she said. She had a funny feeling as she walked up the big staircase leading up to the front door, realizing that this was her new home. The door swung wide open just as she put the key in the keyhole. Sebastian stood in the doorway looking perfect beyond belief wearing only a pair of jeans. His sensuous lips were curved up in the most amazing smile. His magnificence stole Arielle's breath away. She just stared at him, speechless. Her heart filled with warmth and excitement. Would she ever get used to his astonishingly good looks? How could this man be real? The feeling of ecstatic disbelief seemed impossible to shake.

"Welcome home," he said softly, reaching out and gathering her into his arms. Her eyes came up and met his scorching gaze, and her breath caught in her throat. His mouth came down on hers, and he kissed her affectionately.

"Did you miss me?"

"Ah! That's my line," he chuckled, eyes hot as fire.

She giggled and slid her arms around his beautiful body. Her lips traced across his bare chest, and her palms stroked the planes of his back. He moaned with pleasure as sudden heat surged though his body like wildfire. She pressed hard against him, and her body felt a warm, palpable sensation that touched every single grain of her existence.

"I don't like being away from you," he murmured, capturing her lips in a hungry kiss.

"I have to do things," she said, gasping for air.

"You can do them with me."

"No, I can't, I like to do girl stuff with my friends."

"Well, I guess I'll have to get used to that."

"Sebastian, what are you going to do about your job if you are in school next year?"

"What made you think of that?"

"Well, we were discussing our classes for next year, and as usual, you were on my mind," she admitted coyly.

"Don't worry. I have done this before many times. I have certain abilities that allow me to do things a little differently than humans. The thing that bothers me is when I have to travel. I can't stand being away from you, so that will be a challenge for me."

"I don't think I'm going to like that part either."

"Did you get something to eat?"

"Yes, after we went shopping we stopped and had something to eat. I haven't had any time to go grocery shopping, so there's no food in the house."

"Oh, but that's where you are wrong. I went shopping for you."

"What?"

She let go of him and walked into the kitchen. She opened the fridge and couldn't believe her eyes. It was full of vegetables, fruits, eggs, milk, juices, everything she would need. He had stocked the cabinets as well. "Did you manifest all this too?"

"No, I went to the store," he said happily.

"You did? I'm amazed."

"Arielle, did you think that just because I don't eat I don't know what a home should have?"

"No, I didn't mean that at all."

"By the way, the bottles in the back of the fridge are for me. It's the salve, which is very important for my survival."

She nodded, and her gaze drifted from his face to the contents of the fridge. She flinched at the thought that some liquid like salve could be his lifeline.

She kissed him softly. "Thank you so much, baby. You are perfect," she said and walked into the bedroom.

"Are you going to bed?"

"No, I'm going to take a shower. Would you like to join me?" she said with an inviting gesture.

"I thought you would never ask," he replied and followed her with a soft whistle.

In bed, she lay utterly ecstatic encircled in his arms. She thought about where she was, and the man who was sleeping next to her. She still felt like she was living in a dream, that she would wake up any moment, and it would all be gone. Her heart started to race, so she reached over and touched him to make sure he was really there. He moaned softly.

"What's the matter?"

"Nothing, I was just making sure you are still here," she said. He pulled her closer. She felt the warmth of his body and closed her eyes. For a moment, Annabel's face flashed in front of her, and she shivered knowing that one of these days she would have to face her nightmare again. But for now, she was safe and happy. She pulled herself closer to Sebastian and drifted off to sleep.

Early in the morning she woke up and stretched back, feeling warm and comfortable. She sighed lazily, and blinking a couple of times; she decided to crawl out of bed and walk to the back window. She drew back the heavy curtains and held her breath as her eyes took in all the beauty the world was offering, for free. The water looked magnificent under the bright sunlight. The tide was out, and in the morning light, small sailboats created a remarkable picture that no painter's hand could have captured.

Arielle was absolutely in love with the house. *I don't remember ever having had this kind of feeling standing in front of any window at any place I have ever visited,* she thought. She looked at her angel, still fast asleep, and went to the kitchen to make coffee. Beams of morning sunlight impaled the windows of the kitchen, brightening the room. Soon the house was filled with a wonderfully rich aroma of the brew. Taking a cup of coffee, she went out the back door. The grass was still wet with the morning dew. Arielle let her toes feel the moisture and beamed with delight.

The day was gorgeous. It was warm. She could feel the sun heat her skin. This had been an extraordinary year as far as the weather was concerned. The usual weather for December in Brighton was drab and wet but not this year. The days had been a bit cool but overall too warm for this time of year. She was not complaining at all; she was just taking in the weather change with extreme pleasure. She was wearing a skimpy camisole that she had purchased the day before. It was a bit cool, but she didn't mind. She held the cup with both hands and closed her eyes, letting her senses become aware of the earth beneath her feet, and her body become infused with the unexpected warmth of the sun. What a wonderful feeling.

*I should call Mum and Daddy*, she thought. *I would love for them to see the house before they leave for Africa.* She thought of all that she had to look forward to, and she was filled with extreme happiness. Sebastian would be with her every day. He would share her bed every night. She laughed aloud with pleasure and threw her head back, letting the sun caress her face.

Opening her eyes, she took a sip of coffee and turned to walk back inside. Sebastian was standing at the family room window watching her. Her Greek god, with a wide smile on his sensuous lips. She smiled back at him and waved. He was in front of her before she could even cross the threshold.

"Good morning! I do wish you would not leave the bed without waking me up. Your face is the first thing I want to see every morning, remember our agreement?"

"I just thought you might want to sleep in. You looked so peaceful and so beautiful, I didn't want to disturb you."

He reached for her, and she fell into his arms, trying not to spill her coffee. He put his finger under her chin, pulled her head up to his level, and softly pressed his lips to hers.

"You look so beautiful. I like this little camisole, did you just get it?"

"Yes, just for you," she smiled, reaching for his lips one more time.

"How am I ever going to get anything done at school if I feel this way all the time?" she asked. "All I want to do is be with you. That's just not normal."

"Why would you ever think that it's not normal? I'm sure that anyone who shares the kind of love that you and I share has the same feeling."

She shook her head and took another sip from her coffee.

"Would you like some coffee?" she asked. He declined and poured himself a glass of salve. They sat in front of the huge picture window, enjoying the ocean view.

For a long time, they sat quietly and didn't say a word. Finally, Arielle announced that she needed to call her parents, and got up to get her phone.

"Hello, Mum, how are you? And how is Daddy?"

Naturally, Arielle's mother wanted to know all about how she liked the house. Arielle happily chatted on for about thirty minutes without stopping, gushing about the house, about Sebastian, and about how happy she was while her mother just listened. Finally, she said, "Do you want to come and see the house?"

"We've been there, darling. Sebastian invited us to come over while you were out shopping with your friends. It's wonderful. Sebastian was a perfect host. He and your father spent a lot of time talking about business and you."

Surprised, Arielle finished her call. Putting down the phone, she looked at Sebastian. "Did you do that for me?" she asked. "Invite my parents over, I mean?"

"There is nothing I wouldn't do for you, Arielle. I love you, and the way you feel affects me directly."

She sat on his lap, sighed, and they held each other in complete contentment. She leaned close and breathed in his intoxicating scent. She closed her eyes and grinned, realizing the intense heat that his proximity was creating. Even with her eyes closed she could feel his penetrating gaze. Opening her eyes, her gaze met that warm green emerald ocean that made her heart thud at such an exhilarating speed.

"What?" she asked, flushed.

"I know you are lost in your thoughts, I can feel it," he whispered. "What were you thinking? What's bothering you?"

"Noth…nothing…" she stammered.

Sebastian looked at her, amused. "Well, it has to be something. So, out with it."

"I was thinking about how much I love you," she replied, and leaning in she pressed her lips on his passionately.

"That's a good thing," he commented, letting out a soft sigh.

After a short pause, she added, "Sebastian? I do have one small question."

"I knew that something was smoldering in that pretty head of yours," he said, chuckling. She laughed too and continued.

"If Immortals can't have children, how come the Dillons had a child?"

At first, the question caught him by surprise, then quickly another thought darted through his mind, making him shiver lightly. He looked directly into her eyes and held her gaze for a long moment.

Arielle could see his anxiety. "What is it?" she asked, eyes wide open.

He pursed his lips, and his voice came out all quivery. "Are you asking because I told you that I can't give you any children?" he asked, his voice low. "Because if you are, I'm sorry, but it is the absolute truth." He pursed his lips anxiously and added, "I do feel terrible about that."

"Sebastian, please, baby, I love you. I don't care about that, I was just curious," she said, gently cupping his face in her hands and kissing him. "Forget it," she added, "we don't have to talk about it."

"No...no..." his voice trailed off. "I think you have a valid question."

Arielle moved her legs and curled into his lap, laying her head on his chest. Sebastian bent down and took her mouth in a loving kiss. His voice came out soft and slow, "Immortals can't produce children," he said.

"Well, then how can Loren be the daughter of an immortal couple?"

Sebastian took a deep breath, hesitated for a moment, and then told the Dillon's story.

"Olivia and Christian Dillon were married in 1425. One early morning, the servants found a small bundle left at their doorstep. To their surprise, it was a baby girl. The Dillons fell in love with her and decided to raise her as their own. Loren grew up to become a true beauty and a wonderful daughter who loved her parents. She had no clue about their immortality, and the Dillons didn't think they needed to tell her anything about it until it was necessary.

"It was on Loren's nineteenth birthday that Christian took his daughter riding on her new horse. A few miles away from the house they ran into a group of drunken riders that wanted to have some fun with Loren. Christian and Loren tried to dismiss them politely, but things seemed to get worse by the minute. Something about the three men didn't seem right, but Christian thought that as an immortal he would not have any trouble protecting his daughter. But he became alarmed when he saw the speed with which they dismounted their horses and how quickly they were able to pull Loren off her horse. This let him know they were dealing with immortals. Christian jumped off his horse and fought them hard, but he lost the fight. He was shot in the chest and collapsed at his daughter's feet. The assailants didn't bother with Christian any further. They turned their attention to Loren. In the time it took for Christian to heal and regain his faculties, they had assaulted Loren and left her bruised and traumatized young body sprawled on the ground half naked, clinging to life by a mere thread."

Arielle let out a soft cry and covered her mouth with her hand. Sebastian tightened his arms around her and pressed a kiss on her temple.

"What happened then?" she asked anxiously.

"Christian attended to his daughter's injuries, and when it became obvious that she wasn't going to make it, he had one choice and one choice alone. He didn't hesitate. Unwilling to let her die, he gave her immortality. She had become his whole world. And that's the whole story, in a short version."

He looked down at her, and her lips trembled. She had been captivated by the story. There was moisture in her eyes, and she gulped down a sigh. Sebastian tilted her head up and set his lips on her forehead, kissing her gently. He then moved his lips over her eyes, and with his tongue, he tasted the salt in her tears. He moaned tenderly. They stayed quiet holding each other.

Finally, Arielle broke the silence. "Are you saying that Loren and her family have been around for over six hundred years?"

"Yes."

"Wow," she said and shifted again on his lap. She laid her head on his shoulder trying to absorb all that information.

"Does it make you sad that I can't give you children?" he asked, cupping her chin with his hand and turning her face toward him.

"No...no...not really..." She shook her head. "I don't care about that." She kissed him tenderly, and he replied with a soft moan. "Sebastian, all I want is you," she murmured.

"Thank God for that," he replied, squeezing her softly.

"It was just a question out of curiosity."

"And a very good one," he said. How he wished that he were human so that he could give her beautiful children—girls—who would look just like her. He smiled at the thought. "I should have explained that when you met Loren. I have been fortunate to be part of their family for more than five hundred years now. I love them dearly." His arms held Arielle tightly against him, and she didn't ever think of moving, not even an inch away, from that warm embrace.

When it was time to get ready for the ball, Arielle let Sebastian get ready first while she made up the bed. When he walked out of his walk-in closet, he took her breath away. He looked stunning. He wore a black suit with a white shirt and a burgundy tie. His hair looked amazing, and his perfect face was magical. She walked up to him, touched his lips softly with hers, and was startled as he grabbed her, pulled her tight against his body and kissed her hungrily.

"I don't want to mess you up, you look perfect," she said, gasping for air as she tried to push him away.

"I don't care about being messed up by you," he grinned. "I want you right here, close to me."

"Sebastian, I need to get ready, let go." She pushed against his chest softly, and he let her go, chuckling.

As she jumped into the shower, he called out, "Do you want me to come in there and help you?"

"No, don't you dare," she yelled back, knowing what he was capable of.

When she was finished with her shower, she fixed her hair and makeup, applying a soft pink lipstick that accentuated her lips. The blue sash of her dress matched the color of her eyes perfectly. She took a last look in the mirror, pleased with the beautiful girl that she saw looking back at her. She so wanted Sebastian to be proud of her. This night was very important to her, and it was the night she would meet his mother.

As she stepped into the living room, he turned to look at her. The look in his eyes made her heart skip a beat. He let out a long, low whistle, and his mouth dropped open.

"Gosh, Arielle, how do you do that?" he exclaimed. "How can you surprise me every time I turn around? You are dazzling. I'm going to have to keep you by my side all night long. I don't trust anyone there. You have to understand that immortals are always out there, searching for their next victim. Most of them only want a night of pleasure, not a lifetime partner. You will get hit on many times tonight. Do you understand? You are such a sight. You will not be ignored by any male in the room, especially being a human—that is like the icing on the cake."

"Don't worry, Sebastian," she said. "I'm a big girl. I can take care of myself."

He walked up to her releasing his dazzling power, and she lost control. Her heart was in her throat and her lips parted in a moan. She didn't seem to be able to draw any air into her lungs. She lost her balance, and he had to reach out and hold her steady while he laughed with pleasure. She forced herself to look away from his eyes and begged him as she tried to catch her breath, "Please, don't do that to me," she said. "Let me look into your beautiful eyes for once without dazzling me. I know you can do that. It's a choice you make when you look into people's eyes, isn't it?"

"Yes, you are right it's a choice. But I love dazzling you. I love the way you look when you are disoriented and trying to catch your breath. You're totally irresistible."

He pulled her closer and put his finger gently on her lips. "I love this color on you," he said. "But it prevents me from kissing you, and I don't like that. I will have to mess it up at one point or another."

"Try not to do that. I'm sure you can hold off for a little while," she said, giggling.

"Oh, I can't promise anything like that. Touching you and kissing you is part of what I need to sustain me," he said and laughed again with pure pleasure.

 *Chapter 20*

**IT WAS DARK WHEN THEY LEFT THE HOUSE,** and the streets were poorly lit, with a few light posts set every two hundred feet or so apart. But it was New Year's Eve and the traffic was thick with partygoers. The feeling of celebration in the air made Arielle happy. Sebastian reached over and took her hand. He pressed it softly, making her turn to look at him. His eyes were shining with love and affection.

"I love you," he said in a firm voice. "And I want you to save all the dances for me. I'm a very jealous man; I'm warning you," he added teasingly, squeezing her hand and letting a soft chuckle escape him. Arielle sent him a sweltering look, and "humphed" playfully.

As they entered the gates of the Dillon estate, Arielle felt they had crossed a time zone. There were a million bright lights illuminating both the grounds and the estate, changing it from night to day. The house was a colossal piece of architecture and stood like a magnificent testament to greatness on the back section of the property. Many of the huge windows gave a clear view of the interior. There were chandeliers everywhere, making the house seem even brighter. Through them, Arielle could see people moving about with happy looks on their faces. It was an atmosphere of exuberance.

They pulled up to a round driveway where two valets were waiting to help them out of their car. Sebastian put his hand around

Arielle's waist and gently led her toward the grand entrance. Again, she had a feeling that she was stepping back in time. She remembered having the same feeling when she had visited Sebastian's home in St. Jean de Luz.

There were beautiful paintings hanging everywhere and amazing statues she was sure had been created by famous sculptors. The rooms were huge and furnished with exquisite taste. Richly detailed tapestries hung from the long walls of the foyer, giving it a Gothic look. Arielle was mesmerized. She loved looking at the house and every detail in it. Sebastian pulled her close and pressed his lips softly to hers.

"You didn't even make it for a short time," she teased. "Did you mess up my lipstick?"

"No, it still looks great, but I want to know where you are drifting off to…"

"This house is amazing!"

"You are amazing, you look beautiful, and very sexy. I want you to stay very close to me tonight," he whispered softly in her ear.

"Where am I going to go?"

"Trust me; I know what I am talking about. You'll be a very challenging game for the men attending this ball."

As soon as they stepped into the ballroom, they noticed a lot of people turning and staring at them. Many of the guys came up to Sebastian, shook his hand and waited to be introduced to Arielle. Girls walked up and hugged him warmly, paying little attention to her.

They had been standing there for a few minutes when she heard the delightful voice of Loren calling her name. "Arielle, I'm so happy you came!" she cried out, running towards her and giving her a huge hug.

"Let me see the ring again," she exclaimed. Arielle stretched her hand out, her eyes sparkling.

"Oh, that's so gorgeous. Let's show Mother."

"Is Father attending this celebration?" Sebastian asked.

"No, you know Dad, he doesn't like any celebration."

"What do you mean?" Arielle asked. "Not even the New Year's Eve celebrations?"

"No, not even those," Sebastian answered this time. "A new year is of no importance to an immortal. It's just another day in the very long journey of eternity," he added sadly. Arielle squeezed his hand gently.

"So where is he?" he asked, glancing at Loren.

"He's in his study with his friends discussing horses, as always," Loren said, giggling. "He did ask for one thing more than once," she furthered. "He wants to meet Arielle."

Marcus and Jeanette, who had attended Arielle's birthday party, walked right behind Loren and the conversation ended. Arielle didn't see Daniel anywhere, and since he was supposed to be Loren's boyfriend, Arielle wondered about that.

She received a warm hug from Marcus and a smile from Jeanette, who seemed, however, to be more interested in Sebastian. Arielle shook her hand politely and Sebastian, after offering a soft hello, turned to greet a friend, at which Jeanette clearly looked disappointed. Arielle resisted the impulse to roll her eyes. She glanced at Sebastian. He appeared to be totally transfixed with someone or something across the room. Following his gaze, she could see a young woman surrounded by a group of men who were fighting for the girl's attention. She looked back at Sebastian, who was still focused on the group.

"Who is that?" she asked.

"Who?" Sebastian said, turning his gaze to Arielle.

"The girl across the room."

"Oh, that's Arianna McCaffy."

"She's stunning," Arielle said. A pang of jealousy suddenly hit a nerve.

"She's all right, I suppose," he replied uninterestedly. Arielle tried to remain quiet, but words seem to slip out of her mouth uncontrollably.

"She must be a lot more than all right. She seems to be holding your attention."

Sebastian's brow rose, and he looked down at her face. "What makes you think I'm looking at her?"

"Well, aren't you?"

"No," he said, his tone smooth. Arielle pressed her lips together and remained quiet. Sebastian moved closer to her, one arm slipping around her waist pulling her hard against him, the other cupping her chin, lifting her face to his. His eyes bored right into hers and a wide smile covered his sensuous lips. "When, oh when, are you going to start trusting me?"

"How can I do that in a room full of such stunning women?" she protested as Sebastian bent down and took her mouth in a scorching kiss.

"You are the only stunning woman I'm interested in," he assured her.

He kept his arm around her while he walked around the room, stopping to pay his respects to a few distinguished couples, introducing Arielle as his fiancée. He had to let go of Arielle as he shook hands with several of his friends and received hugs, some of them from especially eager females and a bit more lengthy than Arielle thought appropriate.

Arielle looked around the room. She felt like she was standing in the middle of a modeling agency. Everywhere she looked she saw unbelievably beautiful people. Each one had distinct differences, but they all were stunningly beautiful with gorgeous facial features and amazing bodies. *Good Lord,* she thought. *How could any normal human being have a chance around so many amazing people?*

Loren hugged her again. "I'm so happy you came, Arielle, have you seen Paul here?"

"No, I haven't seen Paul since Christmas day," Arielle replied, a bit surprised by the question.

Sebastian moved toward her and took her in his arms, holding her with affection.

"Why are you so interested in Paul?" he said to Loren. "Is there something you would like to share with your brother?"

Loren looked down and kept quiet as Arielle gave Sebastian a meaningful look, motioning for him not to press Loren for answers. He understood right away and didn't say anything more, just gave his sister an affectionate kiss.

"Loren, the type of welcome you gave to Arielle is usually reserved for me. Am I playing second fiddle to her now?" he joked. Loren just smiled and fell into his arms, giving him a huge kiss on the cheek.

"I'm sorry, Sebastian, but Mother has been waiting anxiously to meet Arielle. Can we take her there?"

"All right," he said. "I'll be back," he called over his shoulder to some of his friends, and they moved to the main ballroom. Everyone was busy socializing, and some were dancing while a twelve-member band was playing a variety of modern melodies and classical compositions. Several couples were already on the dance floor.

*Well, that sure fits the surroundings,* she thought and chuckled. The room breathed of immortality, creating a highly memorable atmosphere. Arielle felt that she was truly living in another era.

They walked towards the west wall, where Arielle could see several women standing in a circle. They all turned around as she approached, and she heard Loren say in a clear, excited voice, "Mother, this is Arielle."

A tall, attractive woman stepped forward. She reached out and embraced Arielle warmly. Then, she took her hand and looked at the ring, a beautiful smile on her face.

"Congratulations, my dear, and welcome to the family," she said in a kind voice. "Sebastian has told me so much about you, and I'm so pleased to meet you." She gave Sebastian a warm kiss on the cheek. "I'm happy to have you here, darling," she said.

She introduced Arielle to her friends and Sebastian greeted them all with a smile. Then, Olivia took Arielle's hand and pulled her closer. "Please come and sit with me for a while," she said. They walked toward a large sofa against the wall, and Olivia asked Arielle to sit next to her while Loren and Sebastian sat on her other side. She kept Arielle's hand in hers and gazed into her eyes as if she wanted to read into her very soul. Immediately, Arielle thought of the reaction she had to Sebastian's gaze, and she went rigid, not wanting to be dazzled, but to her surprise she had no reaction to Olivia's gaze at all.

"You are a very beautiful young woman. I'm happy to see that you are wearing the necklace," she said approvingly.

"I want to thank you for that," Arielle replied. "It's a magnificent gift, and I love it," she added, running her fingers over the necklace as she spoke.

"Tell me a little about you, and your family, dear."

"Well, my family has lived in Brighton for thirty-five years. They are originally from York. My father owns BMLS industries. They build commercial airplanes. My mother is involved mostly in charity work and sits on several boards of directors. She helps to acquire monies for hospitals and museums, and institutions that need the funds to help with illness or abuse."

"Sebastian says you are in college. What are you studying?"

"I'm an engineering major. I'll be graduating next year and

moving on to graduate school."

"What type of engineering do you want to practice?"

"Um, that is a very good question," Arielle said, smiling. "The only other person that has ever asked me that question was my father, whom I adore."

Olivia seemed pleased with this reply. "Tell me," she urged.

"Well, I would like to be hired by an engineering firm that will make it possible for me to design commercial buildings or bridges across the world. That's my passion."

Olivia was now looking at Arielle with tremendous interest. Sebastian was also studying her face as she spoke, a loving grin on his face.

"I don't think I've ever met a woman your age who has been so sure about where she was going in life. I'm extremely pleased about this. Sebastian told me that you were exceptionally smart and very beautiful, and he is right on both counts. I know that he has made an excellent choice. I'm so proud of both of you." She then leaned closer to Arielle and whispered, "He is my son, and I love him deeply, so please don't hurt him. I know he loves you more than anything in this world. He has never really loved another girl. This is all new to him, I want him to be happy, and I will do anything I can to help you both if you need me."

Arielle smiled softly, and when she spoke, her voice came out as a whisper. "Mrs. Dillon, I love him more than life itself. He is everything to me, but I know we don't belong in the same world. He is unbreakable, undying, strong, magical, and gorgeous. I'm only human. I am not sure how it will all end up, but I know I can't live without him."

After speaking these words, Arielle felt a sudden sadness. Olivia noticed and cupping Arielle's chin in her hand she tilted her face up so that Arielle could meet her gaze. Sebastian reached over his mother's lap and took Arielle's hand.

"What are you all whispering about?" he asked. He heard every single word spoken, but he wanted to be involved in the conversation. Both women ignored his question as Olivia continued talking in her soft, tender voice.

"Don't worry, dear, it'll all workout. Sebastian is an amazing young man, and he'll make it work. Just trust in him and be happy."

Then she kissed her on the cheek, and turning to Sebastian she said, "Sebastian, I think you should introduce your future bride to our guests, don't you?" Sebastian nodded in agreement and rose to his feet.

"Have you seen your father yet?" Olivia asked.

"Not yet, but we are heading that way," he replied and placed a gentle kiss on his mother's cheek.

"We will talk again before you go," Mrs. Dillon said firmly as Loren, Sebastian, and Arielle walked away.

As they walked, Loren began chattering nonstop, telling Arielle everyone's business. Arielle chuckled happily.

"I don't see Daniel anywhere."

Loren gave her a surreptitious look, and leaning closer she whispered back, "He's history." They laughed. Through it all, Sebastian kept a firm arm around Arielle's waist, as if he were afraid to let her go. Several young men walked up and asked her to dance, but he told them politely, and firmly, that she had promised all the dances to him.

As they were mingling, a beautiful young woman walked up to Sebastian and took him into her arms. Arielle thought she saw some familiarity in the look he gave her, and again she felt a pang of jealousy. But she just looked at him and met his gaze steadily. He smiled lovingly and introduced her.

"Arielle, this is Sylvia, she is the wife of a dear friend. We've known each other for many years." Then, turning to Sylvia, he said. "Sylvia, this is my girl. She is the woman I'll be spending the rest of my life with."

He couldn't have said anything that would have made Arielle feel happier or more secure. He bent down and pressed his lips to hers while she noticed a flash of jealousy in Sylvia's eyes.

Arielle looked away quickly and let Sebastian pull her towards the next room. As they entered, several girls walked up to him and hugged him, some lingering for a long time in his arms, some kissing him as if they knew him well. Arielle was so jealous she was ready to scream. She pressed her lips together, and instantly he noticed. Nothing she did escaped him.

"What is it?"

"Nothing," she said, keeping her lips pressed tight.

"Something is bothering you, and I want to know what it is," he insisted.

"How come you know all these women so well?"

"Arielle, come on, they are just people I've met through the years."

She remained quiet while he tried to make her look at him.

"Are you jealous?"

"Yes, extremely," she said in a stiff voice.

"Mmmm, I like that," he said and pulled her tight against his body. "Do you still love me?" he asked, chuckling.

"You should stop asking that..." she said, a bit anxious.

Just then, two guys walked up and introduced themselves to Arielle as Taylor Wells and Roman Brannon. Loren seemed to know Roman, and they moved onto the dance floor. Taylor was striking. He was tall, with bright blue eyes, dark hair, and a brilliant smile. His voice was warm and exciting.

"Sebastian, ol' man. Where have you been keeping this beauty?" he asked.

"Taylor, this is Arielle Lloyd, my fiancée," Sebastian said irritably.

"Your fiancée? When did this happen?"

"Earlier this year," Sebastian replied, enunciating his words crisply.

Taylor's gaze never left Arielle's face. "You are gorgeous, my dear," he said charmingly.

*What's with the "ol' man" and "my dear" bit?* Arielle thought. *He sounds like he's back in the eighteenth century.* Arielle suppressed a giggle.

"Can I have the next dance?" he added with a flirtatious grin. Sebastian's arm became rigid around her waist. His jaw muscles tensed.

Arielle smiled softly at Taylor. "Thank you, but I've promised all the dances tonight to my fiancé."

Taylor returned her smile courteously. "Sebastian, ol' boy, you've always been a very lucky man," he said. He gave a nod to Arielle, and turning around, he walked away. A quiet curse escaped Sebastian's lips as he pulled Arielle away from that side of the room.

"What was all that about?"

"I have never liked that guy," he scowled. "There's something disturbing about him. He is an old adversary of mine. I never thought he would be here tonight. It wasn't Arianna that attracted my attention earlier, it was Taylor."

"Oh…" her voice trailed. "I supposed you don't want to talk about this right now, do you?"

"No, not particularly."

"All right then," she said softly. "We'll talk about it later."

Sebastian chuckled, and pulling her close to him, pressed his lips ravenously against hers.

"I love you, my Lizzy." Their eyes met, emerald to sapphire. Then, their lips met again. Sebastian held the kiss for a very long time.

"Sebastian," a beautiful velvety voice called out behind them. "Can I have one of those kisses?" A cheerful laughter followed. Sebastian and Arielle turned around and came face to face with a striking woman. She looked a lot older than Sebastian, yet utterly gorgeous. Her smile was mesmerizing. Sebastian's muscles clenched. His eyes narrowed to slits. He became absolutely still.

"You haven't forgotten me have you, darling?" she continued, never taking her eyes off of his beautiful face. She reached out to brush his hair away from his forehead, but Sebastian pulled back quickly, avoiding her touch. The woman flinched, but kept a wide smile on her face. She seemed to be purposely ignoring Arielle's presence, just keeping her gaze focused on Sebastian.

"Hello, Elizabeth," he stammered awkwardly. Arielle felt his body stirring uncomfortably.

"Just hello? No hugs, no kisses, darling?" she pouted. Sebastian paused for a short moment, struggling to regain his control as he instinctively pulled Arielle tighter against his side.

"Elizabeth," he said firmly. "This is my fiancée, Arielle Lloyd."

"Fiancée? You're going to… be hitched?" she asked, laughing disagreeably. She shook her head in denial. "I'm having a hard time believing that any woman could claim you for her own," she said, laughing again most unpleasantly.

Arielle felt an immediate dislike for this woman. *Who is she?* She wondered.

Finally, Elizabeth acknowledged Arielle. "My dear," she said, accentuating the words, "Sebastian and I go way back. He was one of my very best customers," she chuckled.

Arielle looked up at Sebastian, utterly puzzled. His face was tense, and his lips were pursed. He had a dreadful look in his eyes. Arielle realized that whoever this woman was, she was making Sebastian extremely uncomfortable. Her thoughts whirled wildly in her mind. She didn't like the sound of the woman's words, but could see that she was determined to finish this conversation.

Arielle slowly turned and gave the woman a stern glare. "Your very best customer? What type of business are you in?" she asked, totally puzzled by Elizabeth's next statement.

"Oh, let's just call it the ultimate gift—for men," she said and broke into another ill-mannered laugh.

Sebastian gazed down at Arielle, and pulling her softly toward him; he murmured, "Let's go, baby." Arielle shifted, letting him know that she was going to get through this conversation. She continued to keep her gaze on Elizabeth.

"What types of gifts did Sebastian purchase from you?" Arielle insisted.

"Oh, he wasn't the one purchasing the gifts," Elizabeth said, chuckling distastefully.

"Then, I don't understand. How he could be your best customer if he didn't purchase any of your gifts?"

Elizabeth continued to hold a tactless smile on her face. "It was the ongoing crowd of women that were buying gifts, trying to get Sebastian into their beds," she said. "So, as you can see, indirectly he became one of my very best customers."

"Elizabeth, be careful," Sebastian spit out, his voice icy cold.

Arielle ignored Sebastian's statement. "Well, it sounds to me that you should be grateful to Sebastian for boosting your business," Arielle said, holding her own. She was sure this discussion was going somewhere, but she wasn't sure where.

"Oh, indeed, I'm most grateful," Elizabeth said, looking up at Sebastian, who remained rigid. He wished very much that Arielle would listen to him and move away from Elizabeth, but she was insisting on standing her ground. He pursed his lips in frustration, but he knew he couldn't force her to move.

Now, Elizabeth turned her gaze back to Arielle, and when she spoke again, her voice came out slow and venomous. "Sebastian was loved by many, but he chose me," she said. The smile widened, and she pierced through Arielle's eyes deliberately. Arielle's jaw dropped in astonishment, a sight Elizabeth seemed to enjoy. But she quickly regained her composure and stared back at Elizabeth with pure revulsion.

"What are you doing here, Elizabeth?" Sebastian interrupted. His voice was now hard as steel.

"Oh, didn't you hear? I married Lord Winston, one of your mother's dear friends," she said.

"Will you please excuse us? I want Arielle to meet the rest of the guests," Sebastian said, giving her a meaningful glare.

"Oh, no, not before Arielle has a chance to hear all about you, my darling," Elizabeth replied venomously. Once again Sebastian tried to pull Arielle away, but she held firm. She wanted to hear what this woman had to say.

"What is it that you would like to tell me?" she asked, pursing her lips.

"Oh, not much, just that I was the one who transformed Sebastian from a boy to a man, and what a man. If you know what I mean…" She winked conspiratorially at Arielle, who instinctively recoiled. "He became my one and only bed partner for many wonderful years," she added with a blissful sigh.

Arielle felt the blood draining from her face and bile churning in the pit of her stomach. But she struggled to remain poised. *What in bloody hell? Another woman to torment me?* She thought and winced.

Sebastian cursed quietly. He tightened his hold around Arielle's waist. Giving Elizabeth a severe look, he warned her through clenched teeth, "Elizabeth, that's enough! I suggest for your own good that you walk away from us this instant." His glare was icy enough to freeze the blood in Elizabeth's veins. She staggered backward. She started to say something but Sebastian's clenched fist, hard expression, and another low curse that escaped his lips pushed back and halted every word she had at the bottom of her throat. "There is no excuse for your behavior," he hissed. And he pulled Arielle away forcefully without saying another word.

Elizabeth stood frozen in place, watching them walk away. She was shocked by his reaction but pleased with herself. She knew she had succeeded in delivering a hard blow to Arielle.

Elizabeth was married to a prominent older man that provided her with the life of luxury she desired, but the invitation to the Dillon ball had brought back exciting memories of her encounters with Sebastian, and she couldn't wait to see him again. They had lost touch a couple of centuries ago. It had taken her a very long time to fill the void. This isn't how she imagined her reunion with Sebastian to be. Meeting Arielle had filled her with a venomous jealousy. She hated the idea that he had chosen a mortal to share his bed. She would have never dreamed that Sebastian's rejection would so devastate her. She pushed through the crowd, looking for her husband. When she found him, she feigned boredom and asked him to take her home.

After they had broken free of Elizabeth, Sebastian moved Arielle through the balcony doors and into the garden, away from curious eyes. Arielle staggered lightly, feeling faint. When they reached the garden, he helped her sit down on a small wooden bench by the fountain. He could hear her heaving, trying to breathe. He was at a loss for words. Everything Elizabeth had said was true, so there were no excuses; only the fact that what had happened had taken place centuries ago.

It was evident that Arielle was terribly disturbed by this encounter. She shuddered and began to sob. His stomach clenched tightly. A quiet curse escaped him, but other than that, he remained silent.

Finally, he leaned close to her and whispered, "Baby, would you like me to take you home?" She looked up and met his despondent gaze.

"No, I'll be all right, just give me a minute."

Sebastian sat next to her and slipped his strong arm around her waist, pulling her close. "Arielle, please," he murmured. "It was a very long time ago."

"Sebastian, I do understand, but I can't help feeling overwhelmed every time another beautiful woman comes after you."

"These women were in my life centuries ago," he said with deep sadness in his voice.

"Would you be concerned if a man after man kept showing up to claim me back? First, it was Annabel, then Savanna, then Julia, now Elizabeth. How many more will there be? How many more?" she muttered and began sobbing again. He remained silent.

"When was the last time you had a girlfriend?" she asked quietly after a few more minutes had passed. She swallowed hard as she waited for his answer.

He stood up, and taking her han; he pulled her up to face him. He gathered her tightly in his arms and gazed deep into her eyes. "That would have to be more than a century ago."

"Oh, come on, that's a ridiculous statement."

"Arielle, I don't lie. I was tired of a life filled with frivolous affairs. I was looking for something that would bring meaning to my existence," he said thoughtfully. "And then I saw you…and you are now my life. I can't be in this world if you are not in it. I love you; you are my girl, my only girl. I want you to marry me, now, today this moment. I want to be your husband, your friend, and your only lover." His arms tightened around her and swooping down he took her mouth in a fevered kiss. "Please tell me that you love me."

"I love you, Sebastian," she whispered, lost in the heat of his embrace.

"Can you forget about this incident and go back in the house, or do you want to go home?" he asked softly. "I wouldn't mind taking you home."

"No, we don't need to go home. This is your mother's party, and I'm not going to allow any impudent female to drive me away," she said stubbornly. "I can forget about her and about every other gorgeous woman that comes looking for you," she said, giving him a meaningful look.

"Loving you has made incidents like this one just a way of life for me," she chuckled bitterly. She wrapped her arms around his neck and pulled him down for another hot kiss. She was hungry for his touch, eager for the feel of him.

"I want you, Arielle Lloyd," he said, their lips still locked in a ravenous kiss. His hands stroked her back. She moaned, and as she did, he nearly lost control. The heat of her body was intoxicating. The wonderful fragrance of freesia in her hair drove him wild.

"We need to go in before we lose control," she chuckled, flashing him a brilliant smile.

"I love you, baby," he murmured. They pulled themselves together and with great effort, she climbed the steps to the veranda and walked right back through the wide-open balcony doors with the man she loved by her side.

As they reentered the room, he put his arms around her and pulled her close to his body. "You are not going to dance with anyone but me tonight," he said. "I've seen the looks in their eyes, and I know what they are thinking. I'm not letting you out of my sight. As you can see, I'm more jealous of you than you are of me."

"You don't have to be jealous of me. I don't want anyone but you."

Arielle closed her eyes and enjoyed the feeling of whirling around the room in Sebastian's arms. *I wondered why Sylvia seemed angry when he kissed me,* she thought. She felt a strange anxiety taking over again as she thought about how many beautiful girls he had been with, wondering how many she would have to worry about.

She heard his voice soft and tender. "I'm going to remove that necklace from you. I can't stand the feeling of not being able to read your mind."

"Most of the time I'm thinking about you, so you don't have to worry about that," she laughed. "I would like to know, though, about all these women that seem to want to kiss you and hug you and get as close to you as possible."

"I don't give a damn about any of them. They are of no importance to me. What they think and what they want is their business, not mine." His voice sounded a little angry.

Arielle was pleased, but she didn't want him to think that she would give in so quickly, especially now that he couldn't read her mind. He gave her a squeeze, and she stopped breathing.

"I can't breathe!" she gasped.

He pressed his lips on hers, hard and passionate. "Tell me that you love me before I lose my mind."

She was quiet while a smile touched her lips. He squeezed her a little harder, and she began to fear that he would break her ribs, so she answered quickly, breathlessly, "Okay, I love you," she said with a giggle.

"I've noticed that many of these people talk, and act as if they are still in another era," she added, chuckling.

"Well, in a way they are," Sebastian said. "Remember, we were all born and raised centuries ago, and it is hard to lose everything that is part of you. Time moves on, but sadly enough we remain unmoved."

Arielle had to agree that he was right once again.

"Let's dance," he said and spun her around. She was becoming lost in thought, safely enfolded in his embrace, moving to the sound of a mesmerizing melody.

"May I cut in?" The velvety voice came from directly behind Arielle and caused her to snap out of her haze. Opening her eyes, she looked up and met Sebastian's eyes. He was smiling wide. Slowly, unwillingly, he let her go. Turning around, she came face to face with one of the most strikingly handsome men she had ever seen. He was immaculately dressed. His eyes pierced right through her very soul. She heard Sebastian's soft chuckle.

"Arielle, I'd like you to meet my father, Christian Dillon," Sebastian said. Her mouth dropped, and her eyes widened. "Dad, this is my fiancée, Miss Arielle Lloyd."

"Arielle, it's a pleasure," Mr. Dillon said, and he gave Arielle a soft hug. His eyes lingered on her as he pulled back and turned to Sebastian. "How are you, my boy?" he said. "I haven't seen you for over a month."

"I'm good, Dad," Sebastian said. "I've been quite busy with IIRL."

"Yes, I heard about the issues you have been having from your mother. How are you doing with that?"

"Everything is under control," Sebastian replied politely.

"I was sure you could handle it," he said, patting Sebastian on the back. "I'm very proud of you. He turned his attention back to Arielle.

"Would you like to dance with me, dear?"

By then, Arielle had been able to collect her thoughts. She smiled shyly, and said, "I would love to." Moving away from Sebastian, she took Mr. Dillon's hand.

He was an amazing dancer. It didn't take long before they were moving effortlessly around the dance floor.

"I'm pleased to see Sebastian so happy," he said quietly. She looked up and met his gaze nervously.

"Oh, I don't know about that."

"I'm sure you're the reason, and I thank you for that," he said, an appreciative look on his face.

"I think you're giving me too much credit," she said. "Sebastian is an amazing man; I can't think of a woman who wouldn't like to be in my shoes." *Some would even like to kill me to get me out of the way,* she thought.

She saw his lips lift. He was silent for the remainder of the song.

*I guess he already knows a lot about me through Sebastian, Loren, and their mother,* she thought. She couldn't believe how comfortable she felt with him. He was a wonderful man.

When the song was over, he brought her back to where Sebastian was waiting. "Thank you, Sebastian," he said. "She's lovely, and I couldn't be happier for you."

"Please come back and visit us," he said to Arielle as he turned and walked away.

"That was interesting," Sebastian said.

"What do you mean?"

"My father rarely leaves his friends and their discussions about horse racing—their one and only passion. Whatever my mother told him about you must have intrigued him and made him eager to meet you."

"Well, I hope that I didn't disappoint him," Arielle said.

"Oh, I doubt that." He pulled her back into his arms and a sensuous kiss.

They danced all night and had a wonderful time. When it was time to go, Mrs. Dillon embraced Arielle warmly. and Loren promised to call her soon. They drove home talking about the night happily. Sebastian held her hand and seemed exuberant.

"You were the best looking girl in the whole place," he said more than once.

"Please don't say that. Those women all looked like paintings. They were perfect."

"Arielle, those women look like that because they are immortals. You, however, are a natural beauty, and each one of them would give their life to be what you are: human."

Arielle didn't say anything. She sat in silence the rest of the way home. Sebastian kept looking at her but didn't press her to talk. It was very late when they got into bed, and he pulled her into his arms eagerly. He found her mouth and kissed her, assuring her that she had nothing to worry about.

It was late the next day when they left to go to her parents' house for dinner. The following day, the Lloyds would be leaving for four weeks. Arielle wanted to make sure that they would let her know how they were getting along from time to time. She was a little worried about them being gone for so long because of her father's incident with his heart the year before.

They had a wonderful time together, talking about the holiday parties and her parents' upcoming trip. As they were leaving, Arielle hugged her parents tightly.

"Please drop us a text now and then and let us know how things are going."

"Don't worry, dear, we'll keep in touch," her mother said with a soft smile.

"Sebastian, dear boy," her father said, putting his arm on Sebastian's shoulder. "Please take care of my little girl."

"It'll be a sheer pleasure to look after Arielle," he said, flashing one of his brilliant smiles. He shook her father's hand firmly and gave a warm hug to her mother.

On the way home Sebastian reached for her hand as he always did.

"I'm worried about my father," she whispered. Sebastian pressed her hand tenderly. He understood her concern.

"What is it that you would like to do?"

"I just don't feel that long trips are good for him," she said thoughtfully.

"I know what you mean," Sebastian said. "But I think it'd be a big mistake if you tried to stop him from living and doing the things he wants to do. That would most certainly drive him to an early grave."

Arielle pursed her lips and turning, gazed at his beautiful face. "I know that you're right again, once again," she said. "I love you so much, Sebastian," she said, and leaning in she gave him a soft peck on the cheek.

 *Chapter 21*

**THE NEXT WEEK ROLLED BY QUICKLY.** Saturday was Gabrielle's engagement party, and Arielle was looking forward to that. Troy had chosen to hold the party at Sotherbees, one of Brighton's finest restaurants.

Finally, the day had arrived, and it was time to prepare. Arielle took her necklace off and jumped into the shower. She let the warm water run over her body; the heat made her skin tingle. She closed her eyes, and suddenly the words spoken by Julia and Savanna came to mind. "He is not your white and shiny knight. He is the dark prince that leaves broken dreams on the way to his kingdom." "His style is a little peculiar, you might say. He doesn't like to hang on to women for too long. I know of many girls he dated and then left when he'd had enough of them." She pursed her lips and tried to push the thought from her head. *I should know better; I shouldn't doubt him,* she thought.

But what if what they had said were true? What if he did just satisfy his desires and then left her, just as he had done with all those other women who were so much more beautiful than she was?

*He's so perfect, so absolutely gorgeous. Why would he ever fall in love with someone like me?* She thought, her eyes welling up with tears. She pressed her lips together in distress. *I don't think I could live without him anymore,* she thought. *Losing him would be the worst thing that could ever happen to me.* The love she felt for him, the affection she held in her heart, was real. The mere thought of him was enough to make her body go taut with exhilaration.

She was still in deep thought as she turned the water off and reached for the towel. She was startled to see him standing there, disappointment spread across his beautiful face.

"So… is that what you think of me?"

Instinctively, she moved her hand up to her neck even though she already knew the necklace wasn't there.

"Do you really believe that I'm here to use you and then leave you?"

Her eyes were moist, and all she could do was press her lips together.

"Is this what you're looking for?" He raised his hand, her necklace dangling from his index finger. She reached out to take it, but he pulled it back out of her reach. "So, all this time you have never believed or trusted a single thing I've said to you?" There was clear displeasure in his voice. She didn't reply as she reached out again, and taking the necklace from him put it back on and clasped it.

"Arielle, I have read your mind, and you can't take this information back. How could you ever doubt that I love you?"

She shrugged her shoulders like a child, helpless to answer.

"I told you a long time ago that you were going to be my wife. There is no man on this earth that wants to marry a girl more that I want to marry you. I have never asked another woman to marry me, and I have never told another woman that I love her. You are everything to me."

Totally embarrassed, Arielle looked down at her feet at a loss for words. Now he knew about her petty jealousies, and all the silly things in her head. She wasn't sure how to answer his question.

"Arielle, look at me, please."

"I can't."

Sebastian put the towel around her and pulled her into his arms, forcing her face to look at his face. Her hair was dripping onto her shoulders and getting his shirt wet, and her eyes were full of tears. He picked her up and carried her to bed as if she was a doll.

"Now, you can stay quiet and not say a word, but eventually, you will have to say something. I'm not going anywhere, and neither are you."

He looked determined, and she knew she would have to say something.

"It's just that you are so perfect," she said finally. "I find it hard to believe that you could want me to be with you forever."

"Well, you are correct about one thing. I don't want you with me forever, I want you with me for eternity," he said, bending down and kissing her.

"Sebastian, you have to admit that it's very hard for a simple human to accept that someone like you, who can have any gorgeous woman in your immortal world, has chosen to be with me. And though I want nothing more than to believe you, and mostly I do, sometimes the things those horrible women have said to me about you come back to haunt me, and I begin to lose faith again."

"Well, you'll have to accept the fact of my love for you because I'm not going anywhere, and neither are you. You have already agreed to marry me, and I'm going to hold you to that promise."

"But how will this ever work? I'll get old, and you will stay young. I'll eventually die while you will stay alive for centuries to come." She was now sobbing.

"I'll never let you die, I made that promise before. Why don't you just trust me? You are not going anywhere. You are staying with me for eternity."

The tears were rolling down her face. Sebastian reached over and pushed the hair out of her face. With his finger, he pulled her chin up so that he could look in her eyes.

"Arielle, you have to stop crying, I can't bear to see you like this. Why don't you come and talk to me when you have worries like this? I can't live without you, I'm sure I've told you that before many times." He paused, and after thinking for a moment, added, "I guess that insecurity has to be a human emotion. But really, you have to start trusting me. Don't let things worry you so. Can you do that for me? Please?"

"Yes," she said reluctantly. "I mean... I hope I can."

"You don't sound very sure about that, Arielle. Do you promise to trust me?"

"Yes, I promise," she said, cautiously lifting her eyes to meet his.

"Tell me that you love me and I'll let you get ready. I hope you realize how hard it is for me to let you get out of this bed with just that little towel wrapped around you," he added, laughing softly.

She took a deep breath and looked directly into his eyes. She reached over and pulled him close as her lips met his in a warm, fervent kiss. "I love you more than life," she whispered, and he moaned with pleasure.

The restaurant was beautiful, and the food was fantastic. Arielle watched Sebastian try the meal. He ate very little, but he did have a couple of drinks. After dinner, Troy stood up and turned Gabrielle's chair around as he got on his knee and asked her to marry him. She cried, and so did Eva and Arielle. The ring was beautiful, and Gabrielle's face was an amazing sight. She sparkled from happiness. When their lips were locked in a passionate kiss, Sebastian reached over and took Arielle's hand. His lips were hardly moving, but she could read on them the words "I love you." She smiled and pressed his hand softly. Everyone was jubilant, and they drank champagne to their happiness. The guys were busy talking about various things, as the girls admired the ring. After wishing Gabrielle and Troy happiness for their engagement, they left the restaurant.

When they got to the car, Sebastian opened the passenger door for Arielle and held it for her as his sensuous lips pressed hers softly in a luscious kiss.

"You are a great friend, and Gabrielle loves you more than you will ever know," he said.

"Oh, but I do know. I know much more that you think I do," she said softly.

"What do you mean by that?" he said, giving her a quizzical look.

"I... I," she started to say, but immediately she stopped.

"What?"

"Nothing."

But he wasn't going to let it go. "What did you want to say?"

"Sebastian, I have a terrible secret that I've been keeping since I was very young from everyone, including my best friends. The only person that knows is my father. I always thought that you knew about it since you could read my mind, but you've never said anything about it."

"Now, you have my undivided attention," he said, looking at her intently.

"Tell me the truth, have you not seen anything different about me at all?"

"Honestly, Arielle, I've no idea what you are talking about."

"I find that hard to believe but, oh well."

"Is it something you can share with me now?"

She slipped into the passenger seat while he walked around the car, never taking his eyes off of her. She could see the curiosity on his face. He was sitting next to her in no time at all. He took her hand as he always did, only, this time, he was watching her carefully.

"What's the secret? Out with it now," he said gently but firmly.

"I can hear people's thoughts," she said in a barely audible voice.

His body went rigid, and his eyes displayed extreme shock. "What!"

"I said, I can hear people's thoughts. Well, not everyone's. There are some people that I can't hear at all, but most of the people I meet I know what they think or feel or desire. I can hear people's pain and anguish. And I hate it."

Sebastian's jaw dropped. "Are you serious?"

"Yes, that's one dreadful gift that I've never shared, like I said even with my best friends, or anyone else. Only my father, Troy, and now you."

He was still looking at her, astonished. "Can you read my thoughts?"

"No, I can't hear anything from you or any immortal, so you don't have to worry about me finding out your secrets. You are safe."

"I don't have any secrets from you, Arielle. I'm just curious."

"I have set a place in my head that I call the special place, and that's where I put all the thoughts that come in uninvited. I have learned through the years to depress the noise because sometimes it drives me crazy."

Sebastian looked puzzled. "I just can't understand how I could have missed something like that. I never saw anything in your mind but your thoughts and your desires. That's unbelievable. Well, maybe I'm not as gifted as I thought," he chuckled. "I don't think I have ever met any human with such an ability, or anything even close to it. That's pretty bizarre. I knew there was something very special about you. I just didn't know what."

"Gabrielle and Ian are two of the people that belong to that special group in my head. Eva's thoughts are mostly clear to me, but sometimes they are clouded, and I can't hear anything. The reason for that is… okay, are you ready for this?"

"What?" He gave her a curious look, wondering what revelation possibly be next.

"Eva has special powers as well. She has visions and premonitions, and she can see things in the future."

He looked thunderstruck. "I just can't believe what I am hearing."

"Eva was the one that warned me every time one of your crazy ladies showed up, ready to do away with me."

"Oh, my gosh, that's just unbelievable." He was looking out the windshield, a stunned look on his face.

"So, you can read people's thoughts, and Eva can see the future."

"Yes, that is just about it. I can read their thoughts, and that is why I know they are my very best friends. They really truly love me, and I trust them with my life. You look shocked."

"I'm trying to understand how I missed this," he said, completely baffled.

"One of these days I'll have to tell them. I'll have to come clean because I hate keeping secrets. I want them to love me even though I can clearly read their minds," Arielle said. She already felt a bit unburdened being able to discuss this with him.

"They have been your friends for all these years, they'll understand."

"I'm not so sure about that. If one of them could read my mind I would like to know," she said, tears welling up and spilling onto her face.

He reached over and wiped the tears from her cheeks tenderly with his thumb.

"Would you not forgive them?"

"I suppose I would, but I'd be pretty disappointed that they didn't come clean sooner. They'll be afraid to be close to me, knowing that their private thoughts are completely exposed. That's the reason I kept it a secret for so long. I don't want them to think I'm a freak."

"I don't think you are making the right assumption. They're your best friends."

"And now Gabrielle and I have another secret, your immortality. It's so hard to explain, and how will Eva or Ian ever understand that?"

"But you could see inside their heads, so you knew how they felt about you. Why did you not trust them?"

Arielle was silent because she knew he was right. There was no good reason for her to have kept this knowledge from her friends. She should have trusted them to love her no matter what.

"I guess it is too late now?" It came out as a question, not a statement.

"Don't ever say that. It's never too late when you have the chance to fix a problem that will make your life easier."

Again he was right.

"I know that Eva is wondering about Troy and me," he said. "I know she's trying to figure out what is so different about us. I also know that she's one of the nicest girls I've ever met and that she is very trustworthy. I feel the same way about Gabrielle. You are three very exceptional girls and very lucky that you have each other. They love you unconditionally, and they are genuinely happy for you and me."

"I know, that's why they are my very best friends," she said, smiling through her tears.

"Why did you only tell your father and not your mother too?"

"My mum thought that I was living in an imaginary world, and she wanted me to grow out of it. It would have been too hard to make her understand."

"Did you ever try?"

"Yes, I did a couple of times, but she thought it might be a good idea for me to see a psychiatrist to talk about the things I was hearing from other people. That wasn't something I wanted to do."

Sebastian turned the ignition on and pushed the gas pedal. They drove for a while, and then he finally said, "Don't worry, Arielle, everyone has secrets. Some secrets are more significant than others. I would not lose sleep over this."

"What do you think about me, now that you know my secret?"

"I think I love you more," he said with a smile. "And your father?

How did he take it?"

"This is the interesting thing about my father. His mother had the same abilities, so he was not shocked. He didn't think I was crazy."

"So, he was open about it?"

"Completely. He told me that this would be a gift that I could use to separate my true friends from my enemies. He said that my grandmother used it to help her get through many difficult times."

"Well, I think he is right about that."

"I think he would be right if I had a normal life, but I don't. My boyfriend is immortal and so are my enemies."

"What do you mean by that?"

"I can't hear what you are thinking, and I can't hear the people that want to hurt me. So what kind of a gift is that?" Pure frustration spilled out of her as she spoke these words.

"Well, that's a very interesting point," he said, but he sounded skeptical.

"I know that not all immortals can read minds," she said.

"How do you know that?"

"I asked Troy if he could read my mind but he said he didn't possess that gift."

"He's right, not all immortals do. But Nathan can see the future, just like Eva, and that's an extraordinary gift."

"Troy also told me that immortals couldn't read each other's minds."

"Well, I want to believe that. However, I have enormous reservation about that statement."

"Why would you say that?"

"Well, I've been wondering for a very long time how Annabel knows who I'm with and how I feel about them. And when I say a long time, I mean centuries. No matter where I moved, somehow she always seemed to find me. She always knew that none of my affairs were serious, so she left me alone. But if she can't read my mind then how does she know all that? I just can't accept the theory of an informant. I can't believe that anyone close to me would be providing her with all the details about my life." He looked deep in thought.

"What about me?" she asked. "What if she can read my mind?"

"I don't know, Arielle. I have no theories and no facts. She may be able to read your mind. Now that I think about it, that's a probability."

"It makes sense that she could, but I really hope she can't," Arielle said, voice trembling.

"I thought it might be someone in my mother's household that was telling her what I was doing and who I was with. But your point makes more sense to me now. She knew about the ring. She knew that you're not just a passing affair for me." He was now staring out the window.

"Sebastian, you are scaring me!"

"I am right here, Arielle."

"But you're not with me all the time."

"You have your necklace for now. And Olivia is working towards a more permanent solution. And you have Eva with her premonitions and Troy, who is going to protect you when I'm not here. I think you're pretty well covered," he said, smiling comfortingly.

"Well, you know, there are many ways to hurt a person without touching them. And I'm certainly no match for Annabel."

He looked at her again and then turned to stare out the windshield. She could see frustration all over his face as he pinched the tip of his nose. She had only seen him do that once before when he was extremely angry and full of anguish.

He gave her a quick look again and turned away, staring in front of him, his eyes piercing the night without saying a word. She wasn't sure if she should say something. And if she should, what would it be? So, she just kept quiet and stared out the window, her head full of bad thoughts. She was sure that her encounters with the crazy immortal women were going to become very complicated. She had great fears about the outcome but no solutions.

Sebastian was still holding her hand and stroking the skin softly with his thumb. He sped up the car as his voice broke the silence, low and soft as velvet. "I don't want you to worry about this," he said finally. "I'll deal with the consequence of my actions."

"I don't understand. What actions are you talking about?"

"I was well aware of the warnings from Annabel and that she is not very stable. I should have dealt with her before I got you involved."

"But you didn't 'get me' involved. I wanted to get involved. I fell in love with you."

He was quiet again, and she didn't know what he was thinking. She wished she could use her gift to find out his thoughts and take away the torment he was going through. But that wasn't going to happen. So, she just waited for him to talk again.

But he didn't say anything. Instead, he pulled the car into the garage and came around to open her door. Their eyes met, but she didn't get the same reaction she usually did when she looked into his eyes. He wasn't unleashing his magical power because he was deeply preoccupied.

As she got out of the car, he gathered her into his arms and held her without saying a word. He sighed a deep sigh, but he didn't let go of her. She didn't move until he bent down and took her mouth in a voracious kiss. Her fingers locked at the nape of his neck and held him tight. His tongue found his way into the softness of her mouth and relished the sensation of her sweetness. He groaned with desire, but this time, there was a hint of sadness in the sound.

She pulled back from the kiss and releasing him, she steadied herself by leaning against the car. "What's going on in there?" she asked, pointing at his head. He smiled vaguely as he put his arm around her waist, and pulled her through the door.

"Let's go in," he said, voice uneasy.

She looked at his flawless features and saw that he suddenly looked very tired. There was a crease across his forehead, and his eyes had turned a dark green color. He walked into the kitchen and took a large glass of salve, and drank it down without taking a breath. She watched him take his shirt off and throw it onto a chair, exposing his beautiful chest. At the sight of it, she involuntarily drew in a deep breath. Amazing defined muscles filled her eyes, and a shiver rippled down her spine as her breath caught in her throat. She watched him walk out into the backyard in silence.

She stood in front of the big window and looked at him standing in the twilight. He looked as stunning as ever, but she knew he was deeply troubled. She didn't fully understand his change of mood, but she knew that she needed to leave him alone.

She walked into the bathroom and washed her face. The water made her feel better. She brushed her teeth and combed her hair, staring at her reflection in the mirror. She was worried about Sebastian. She had never seen him this way before.

He was still standing out in the middle of the yard like a statue lost in thought when she walked into the kitchen to get a glass of water. She didn't turn any lights on because it was quite bright in the house with the moonlight coming through the huge picture windows. She watched him quietly for a few minutes, and then went to bed.

She had no idea how much time had passed—she must have drifted off to sleep—when she suddenly felt him next to her. His arms encircled her body, and his lips found her mouth.

"Are you okay?" she whispered against his lips.

"Yes, I just needed to think."

"Can I help?"

"No, you really can't. It is all my doing, and I will have to deal with it."

She held him close, wanting to make him feel safe.

"You are my life," she whispered.

"I know. I just wish I had been smarter about the whole thing and gotten rid of Annabel long before I ever set eyes on you."

"I knew what I was getting into when you told me about Annabel," she said. "I chose to stay, so you see, it's not your fault."

"It's completely my fault. This is something I should have resolved centuries ago. I just never dreamed that this amazing feeling could exist until I met you. I have lived without it all my life, and that is a very long time. Now I regret not doing anything about Annabel."

"Please, let's talk about it tomorrow."

"Are you tired?"

"No, not really, I just don't want to talk about Annabel," she said.

He kissed her neck and moaned pleasurably.

She was dozing off when she heard him saying. "What do you think about all of us going to St. Jean de Luz?"

"What do you mean, all of us?"

"I mean the six of us. Let's make it a gift to all of us to celebrate our engagements, from you and me."

"You are joking."

"Not at all. What do you think?"

She turned around to face him, her eyes full of surprised delight and exclaimed, "I think it's fantastic! I can't wait for them to see your house. It's the most beautiful place I've ever seen."

"I'm glad you feel that way because it's your house now too."

"What?" she said.

"I said it's your house now."

"My house?" she repeated.

"Yes, Arielle. You are going to be my wife and the lady of the Gaulle manor. What I have is yours, including my very soul."

Her head was spinning; it was all too much to comprehend. She felt an incredibly warm feeling taking over her. Of course, what he was saying made sense, but she just couldn't believe that she would be the lady of that awesome house.

His voice interrupted her thoughts. "I thought it might make you happy to have all your friends at the house before the new semester begins," he said.

"It's a wonderful idea," she said, looking at him affectionately.

He was smiling as he pulled her even closer and pressed his lips to hers gently. She was now deep in thought as she rolled on her back and stretched leisurely. She locked her hands behind her head and stared at the ceiling thoughtfully. She closed her eyes, imagining the effect the house would have on her friends. I know how it affected me as soon as I stepped through that door, she remembered.

Then suddenly she recalled something else, and the face that popped in front of her made her body shiver, her heart thud in her chest, and her lips tremble with anxiety. It was the sight of Annabel glaring at her with all the loathing she held for her. What if she showed up when they were all there? What if she tried to hurt someone? The thought made her tremble, and she felt an instant tightening in her chest. She moved her arm and squeezed Sebastian's hand with unusual pressure, making him look at her with concern.

"What's wrong?"

"What if she shows up at your house while we are there?"

He was quiet for a short time. Finally, he spoke in a low voice, "I don't think she will do that. But if she does I'll handle it, and remember, Troy will be there as well. He is just as powerful as I am."

"I wish all my friends knew the truth. It would make it easier for them to decide if they wanted to take the chance to take this trip with us," she said.

Sebastian paused before answering. "I think that's a pretty big step to take with them such a short time before we leave."

"When were you thinking of leaving?"

"I thought Monday or Tuesday would be good if they all agree. I'm paying for their trip, it'll be our gift to them as I said before."

"You are paying for all of us to go there?"

"Yes, of course," he said, and she smiled at him.

"That's amazing. You are the most giving person I've ever known."

His eyes were closed, and he looked so beautiful. Arielle rolled onto her side and kissed his eyelids before she assumed her normal position cuddled in his arms. *How will I ever sleep when he's not here?* She thought. *Well, I guess I'll just have to stay up until he comes home.*

She giggled at the thought and closed her eyes, blissfully secure.

 *Chapter 22*

**THE NEXT DAY WAS A GLOOMY, RAINY DAY.** Rain pounded against the windows and Arielle could hear the wind gusting through the trees, making them sway in all directions as a steady noise rose from the beach from the waves thrashing against the rocks below. The weather had been wonderful during the holidays, but now it was getting back to the more typical boring and dreary conditions they were used to in January in Brighton.

Arielle got out of bed and gazed across the ocean, which looked murky and shadowy. The cliffs on either side looked uninviting. She shivered slightly and jumped back into bed, making Sebastian laugh out loud.

"What are you doing?" He opened his arms and let her fall into them. He held her close, making her feel warm and safe.

"I don't want to get out of bed. The weather is terrible, and there is not a single place I want to go."

"What do you want to do?" She smiled and searched for his mouth with her eyes closed. He was glad to help her in her search and let his sensuous lips find their way to hers. He kissed her and let his hands caress her gently.

"Why do you bother to wear anything in bed?" he asked.

"I guess I am used to it, why?"

"Why? That's a silly question, do you really have to ask?" he asked, his lips curving into a seductive smile.

She wound her arms around his neck, and his lips parted to welcome her into a scorching kiss. He groaned as his lips moved from her mouth to the hollow of her throat and pressed softly. Arielle moaned and drew a deep breath, losing touch with reality for a short moment. His palms were sizzling as they slid downward over her breasts, bare stomach, and around her magnificent hips, making her shudder with pleasure. Sebastian hauled in a sharp breath and felt thrilling tension through every muscle in his body. He smiled wide as he moved his hands lower and gently stroked every soft spot and sensitive nerve.

Arielle gasped for air as heat spread across her body. Sebastian's touch was hypnotizing, and all she could think about was how much she needed him. She gasped when he rolled on top of her and her gaze fell into the deep, passionate green ocean of his eyes, filled with desire and anticipation. He took her mouth in a fevered kiss, and they merged  passion coursing every fragment of their bodies, spinning their minds away from reality to another level filled with ripples of passion, ecstasy, and intense rapture. His body was glorious, and she was completely under the influence of his magnificent presence. He thrilled her with utter fulfillment, and she knew that she too was taking him to an unbelievable level of pleasure as he imploded, taking her with him on an amazing, utopian journey.

Afterward, he lay still for a long time with his eyes closed, totally spent. He finally opened his eyes and gazed adoringly at Arielle, who was still lost in a delightful stupor. His lips found hers one more time and held her to a long gentle kiss. Then he rolled off of her and lay flat on his back, letting out a deep sigh of contentment.

"You will be the death of me, I know it," he said, laughing. His voice was breathless, and she laughed joyfully as she lay back, closing her eyes. She loved hearing those words every time they made love. Afterward, they lay there together wrapped in the aftermath of their incredible encounter. Arielle was feeling lazy and content, and she wasn't going to move out of that bed anytime soon.

They dozed for a while, and when they woke up again, Sebastian reached over, picked up his phone, and called Troy. Arielle couldn't hear everything he said, but she could tell that the conversation was about making arrangements for the trip to St. Jean de Luz, so she was sure he had accepted Sebastian's invitation. When he got off the phone, he looked pleased.

"Well?"

"He said he would talk to the others, but he thought it was a great idea, and he was sure they would all love to go."

Next, Arielle's phone rang, and she was surprised to see that it was Loren calling.

"Hello, Loren," she said. Sebastian turned around and stared at her, a curious look in his eyes.

"What's up?" Arielle asked. Loren began to talk, her voice full of excitement and passion. She went on for several minutes without stopping at all while Arielle just listened. Her face must have changed expression because Sebastian was now standing very close to her, trying to hear what Loren was saying. When Loren finally stopped talking, Arielle said, "I'm so happy for you, Loren. I hope everything turns out the way you want. I'm here for you anytime you want to talk, or if you need my help." Then, she closed her phone, a stunned look on her face.

"What? What!" Sebastian exclaimed.

"You are not going to believe this one."

"Oh, my God, Arielle, will you please tell me what's going on?"

"Loren is in love with Paul, and Paul is completely taken with her."

"What?"

"They got together at the Christmas party. I guess it was a mutual thing. Now I understand why Daniel was not at your mother's party, and why Loren said she would explain later."

"You are not serious, are you?"

"That's what she just told me."

"That's incredible!"

"Well, it's not that incredible. He is very good-looking and extremely nice, so I'm not surprised that she liked him. As for Loren, she is beautiful beyond belief and I can completely understand how Paul could fall for her." She pressed her lips together, remembering the shock she had gone through learning about Sebastian's immortality and the way Gabrielle had taken the news about Troy. If this turned out to be serious, Arielle was pretty sure Paul would be in for the shock of his life. She chuckled at the thought.

Sebastian looked at her surprised. "What now?"

"I would like to be there when she breaks the news to him," she said, now laughing out loud. Sebastian smiled too, remembering.

"Oh, boy," she said, shaking her head. "This is getting to be like the *Peyton Place* of the immortals," she giggled.

"What is *Peyton Place*?" he asked.

"Oh, it's an old film, and I think I'll make sure we watch it together one of these days," she said, giggling again. He cocked his head in amusement. Arielle closed her eyes again and thought about the six of them being together in St. Jean de Luz. How wonderful it would be. The only thing that could ruin their trip would be Annabel and Arielle was determined not to let Annabel upset her again. She pressed her lips thinking again of how hateful Annabel was. *But Sebastian is mine, and I won't give him up no matter what it takes,* she thought.

She opened her eyes and saw that he was sitting on the bed next to her, watching her carefully.

"You are pressing your lips together," he said. "You only do that when you are worried about something."

"How do you know that?"

"Arielle, I know a lot of things about you."

"No, you don't."

"I'll bet I do."

She sighed and closed her eyes again. She was planning to tell Gabrielle and Eva about her dreadful gift on the trip and was hoping they would understand why she had kept it a secret from them for so long. She fervently hoped they would remain her best friends after her revelation; she couldn't bear the thought of losing them.

Later in the day, when Sebastian got out of bed and walked into the shower, Arielle waited for him to finish because she knew what would happen if she followed him in there. She smiled to herself and walked into the family room. She sat down at the piano and looked through the music, choosing a couple of melodies to help soothe her emotions. Playing the piano always helped her regain her focus when she was feeling stressed. As she was playing she completely lost track of the time, fully absorbed in the music. When she finished, she kept her fingers on the keys for a short time as if to absorb the calm that she had achieved while playing. She looked out at the stormy waters and noticed that they had no effect on her at all. She felt calm and content.

*Well, I guess it's time to go and take a shower. Sebastian must be finished by now,* she thought. She slowly rose to her feet and turned away from the piano. She was startled to see Sebastian leaning against the doorframe, his hair wet, a bath towel wrapped around his waist. He looked like a model posing for a shoot. His eyes were closed, and his face looked tranquil.

"Hey. How long have you been standing there?" she asked.

"Oh, for quite a while."

"You could have said something…"

"I didn't want you to stop. I love listening to you play. And Mendelssohn's 'Venetian Gondola' is one of my favorite pieces."

"Yes, I know that," she said. Reaching up, she cupped his jaw and traced the curve of his bottom lip with the tip of her thumb.

"Mmmm," he moaned. "It was beautiful…*you* are beautiful."

"Tell me that you love me," she said and moved even closer. His arms snaked around her, molding her body against his.

"That piano has to be the best piece of furniture in this whole house. It makes you happy, and I love just to hear you play."

She reached up on her tiptoes and touched his lips softly.

"That's not good enough," he whispered.

His lips were partly open, and she could smell his delicious scent, which always completely unbalanced her. She sighed with excitement as their lips met in a wild kiss.

"Can you play?" she asked, as she pulled back from him, breathless.

"A little."

"Let me hear you play something."

"That is your piano."

"Please play something for me?" she pleaded as she took his hand and pulled him towards the piano.

He sat down, paused for a moment, and then his hands moved

across the keys with ease. He didn't use any music, he just played. The music was so beautiful that she was overwhelmed; she couldn't believe how talented he was. When the melody was over, he stood up and walked toward her.

"Oh. My. God. How can you sit and listen to me play when you are such a master?"

"You say that because you love me," he said. His hand cupped the back of her neck, and he tangled his fingers in her hair as he tilted her face up and his lips came down on hers with a stormy passion.

Arielle shut her eyes and sagged against him. She couldn't seem to control either her equilibrium or her thoughts. She was lost in Sebastian's arms as pleasure spiraled in and settled deep in her very core.

Finally, she opened her eyes and their gaze locked. She pulled back from the kiss and cleared her throat. "Sebastian, be serious. You are amazing," she stammered.

"This piano is still for you to play and me to listen. You promised. So we'll not talk about this anymore."

She paused and reluctantly pulled away from his embrace. "I'm going to take a shower, and I'll be right back." Then, a loud shriek escaped her as he moved with his high velocity speed and lifted her into his arms.

"Well, here, let me help you," he chuckled.

"I thought you just took a shower," she said as he walked into the shower with her and closed the door.

"I like to be extra clean," he laughed, and let her down slowly. His arms enveloped her and held her against him with fervor. She loved him so much, and she couldn't help the wild desire that swept over her every time he was near. How could she feel this way every time they touched?

Arielle had never dreamed that her life would turn out this way. She understood he was not like any other man. Still, the depth and intensity of her feelings for him were just unbelievable. She was sure that she would die if she couldn't have him in her life.

Sebastian pulled her tighter against him and, bending down he took her mouth and crushed her lips beneath his, moaning painfully. His muscles were aching with unfathomed desire. Their encounter went deeper than mere seduction or simple indulgence; it was a scorching inferno born of intense love and passion for each other. Arielle held on to Sebastian breathlessly, unwilling to move a single inch away from him.

"Isn't it better taking a shower with me, baby?" he murmured, brushing his lips across her jaw. She moaned and nodded, incapable of uttering a single word. She heard him chuckle and, pressing his lips on her forehead; he let her go. He pulled the shower door open and started to walk out. Arielle opened her eyes, a happy smile on her face.

"I guess we're done here?" she finally said flirtatiously. He stopped mid step and turned around.

"Did you want to go another round?" he asked playfully. He reached and pulled her back in his arms. "Because if you are, I'm ready." His lips were curved up into that amazing smile, and leaning in she took his mouth and savored a hot kiss. His lips parted, her tongue found her way into the warmth of his mouth, and the kiss deepened. Arielle moaned, and Sebastian groaned, heat rising rapidly. "I thought I was indestructible, but you are going to kill me," he mumbled as he pushed the shower door closed once again.

Sebastian stepped out of the shower first, and she followed. She didn't have anywhere to go, so there was no need to hurry and get dressed. But she did need to think about their upcoming trip and what she was going to pack.

"You are drifting again," he said.

"I was just thinking about you."

"That's a good thing," he said happily. He took a book and walked off toward the family room, still wrapped in just his bath towel. She followed him, eyes filled with awe as a light shiver coursed through her muscles. She smiled wide and shook her head in disbelief.

Arielle decided to phone Eva and Gabrielle to talk about their trip to St. Jean de Luz. They couldn't get over the fact that Sebastian was giving them such a generous gift. They went on and on about how wonderful he was, and of course, Arielle felt the same. They talked about their wardrobes and little details about what they would need to bring. "The weather is so beautiful in the south of France," Arielle said. "It's nothing like Brighton weather." She told them they would need mostly summer clothes.

The night before the trip Arielle had terrible nightmares about Annabel. Once again, she could see the wild look of hatred in her eyes and could hear her repeating over and over again. "Sebastian' will never belong to another woman. Stay away from him I am warning you before it is too late." She woke up in a cold sweat, shivering with fear. She looked over at Sebastian. He was sleeping peacefully, looking like an angel. She moved a little closer to him, and he instinctively encircled her in his arms without waking up. She closed her eyes and drifted off to sleep, only to have the same dream again. This time, she stayed awake for several hours, in a complete panic, wondering what it all meant.

She didn't get to sleep until early in the morning, so she was very tired when the time came to get ready to go to the airport. While Sebastian drove, she kept her eyes closed, trying to get some rest. Sebastian reached over and stroked her cheek with the back of his hand.

"Is there something wrong, baby?"

Arielle felt his gaze on her face. "No, I'm just a little tired. I didn't get much sleep last night."

"Why is that?"

"Bad dreams," she replied and shivered, wrapping her arms around herself protectively.

"Oh, let me guess, Annabel?" Taking his eyes off the road for a quick second, his gaze swept over her face inquisitively.

"Mmmhmm," Arielle said and nodded without opening her eyes. Sebastian's mouth flattened into a hard line, and he concealed an oath.

"Do you want to talk about it?"

"No, not really, I'll be okay."

Sebastian "humphed," and eyes narrowing, he turned to look at her once again. "Are you sure?" He sounded anxious.

Arielle's eyes sprung open at the sound of his voice, and she fixed her gaze on him. "Sebastian, I'll be all right. I'm just a bit tired from not sleeping. I'm sure I'll be able to sleep on the plane, and I'll be fine."

The airport signs came into view, and Sebastian reached for her hand. "Are you excited about the trip?" he asked, his voice full of concern. She turned to look at him.

"Sebastian, I'm just tired, but I'm also super excited about having a wonderful holiday with our friends," she answered, giving him a smile. But her inner discomfort was obvious to Sebastian. He leaned over and gave her a quick peck on the lips.

"I love you, Arielle. Please don't worry. I'll keep you safe," he said and smiled reassuringly.

She reached over and ran a finger across his lower lip as he drew in a deep breath. "I love you too. I'm not worried, I'm just tired," she said, and she stared out the window. But deep inside, her heart twisted, and a murmur of unease filled her thoughts. She swallowed her anxiety as every nerve cell in her brain was sending frantic signals of warning to her sensory cortex. She shivered. She was suddenly suffocating. She shut her eyes tight and reached for that last safe line in her mind to help her relax to allow more oxygen into her lungs. She shifted nervously and slowly she turned to look at Sebastian, only to find him watching her warily.

"Is it Annabel again?"

"Um...yes," she murmured and turned to stare out the window.

She was aware of the complex and dangerous life she had plunged into when she fell in love with an immortal. But she didn't want to change a thing, and she wasn't going to give him up, she couldn't give him up. He was now part of her life, the air she breathed. There was no world out there for her without Sebastian.

"Arielle, please look at me, baby," he pressed on.

She turned and their gazes locked. "You have to start trusting me," he said and reaching over he cupped her chin, holding her to his gaze. She nodded and tried to pull away, but he held her firmly narrowing his eyes at her.

"Trust me?"

"Yes," she replied.

"Then, stop worrying."

She nodded again, and he let go of her chin turning his attention on the road.

As the car pulled up to ticketing, she winced at the thought of

Annabel once again.

Sebastian held her door open and reaching inside he pulled her out of the car and into his arms. "I'm not going to let anything happen to you."

"I know," she replied, her voice unconvincing. She did trust him, but strangely enough, she could almost taste Annabel's fury. Stepping out of the car, she wondered, *was this going to be an amazing holiday or a nightmare from hell?*

**THE END**

Enjoy a sneak peek of the third book in the
*Immortal Rapture Series:*

# *Arielle Immortal Passion*

 **Chapter 1**

THEY ARRIVED IN ST. JEAN DE LUZ early in the afternoon. The weather was beautiful and warm, a distinct contrast from the weather in England. Arielle shivered with excitement knowing that this was the place where she and Sebastian had met and fallen in love, which made it forever magical. He wrapped his arms around her waist and pulled her towards the airport exit, where he had arranged for a limousine to pick them up.

The drive to the house was amazing. Arielle marveled as the car left the airport and headed into the countryside. The scenery was indescribable.

"How could you ever describe the beauty of this place to anyone?" she exclaimed as they drove.

There were acres of misty green fields with tall grass and colorful wildflowers popping up everywhere, creating a fascinating multicolored view. The trees were green, full, and open to the sky, absorbing the sunlight. The deep blue shade of the ocean was inviting, and many sailboats were drifting on the horizon. The sight of the white sand beaches filled Arielle's heart with tranquil contentment. Her heart thumped double-time as they passed the location where she had first set eyes on her dream come true, Sebastian. *I can't imagine my life without him now*, she thought.

Everyone commented on the beauty of the place. "It's paradise," Eva said, summing it up. Everyone agreed with her.

Arielle couldn't wait for them to see Sebastian's amazing house. The road traveled mostly along the beach, making it a peaceful and relaxing drive. As they drew nearer to the house, Arielle could see her friends' faces changing to looks of incredulous wonder. At the huge entrance at the edge of the property was a large sign stating that they were entering private property. The family name was written in beautiful script, "Résidence de Gaulle."

The property was covered with flowering rhododendron shrubs with white, lavender, and pink. The aroma from the jasmine was unbelievable. The azaleas were blooming profusely. They drove by a large pond where the reflection of the long grass and the trees surrounding that part of the property shimmered. Slowly, they pulled into the circular driveway in front of the house and stepped out of the car.

Gabrielle and Eva grabbed Arielle's hands in excitement. "What a magnificent house!" they exclaimed in unison, and all of the girls giggled in nervous excitement. Ian looked mesmerized. Troy, on the other hand, looked like all of this was very familiar to him. As they climbed the huge staircase toward the front door, Arielle had to admit the house looked glorious. *A thousand times better than I remembered,* she thought. With the walls covered in ivy, it looked quite amazing in the sunlight.

Everyone was speechless trying to absorb the magnificence of the place. Arielle smiled with pleasure as she took Sebastian's hand and pressed it. He was just preparing to put the key in the lock when the door swung wide open, and Mrs. Wilson stood in the opening, a happy smile painted her face.

"Sebastian, welcome home!"

"Elena, it's nice to see you. Let me introduce you to my fiancée, Miss Lloyd, and my friends, Troy, Gabrielle, Ian, and Eva. They will be staying with us for a few days."

"How wonderful. Welcome, welcome," she said cheerily. Stepping aside, she let them walk in. Arielle watched her quietly and smiled.

She was wondering if Mrs. Wilson remembered her from her visit to the house last summer.

Her thoughts were interrupted by Mrs. Wilson's kind voice.

"Haven't we met before, dear?" she asked, gazing at Arielle inquisitively.

"Yes, Mrs. Wilson, I was here last summer with my little cousin, and you gave us a tour of the house," Arielle replied, smiling shyly.

"Ahh, that's right, I remember now. I'm happy to see you again, and please call me Elena."

Inside the front hall, Sebastian introduced them to his butler, Mr. Struthers, and another housekeeper, Mrs. Lefevre.

As they went through the introductions, Arielle, and her friends—except Troy—were aware that they were stepping into an amazing world, a world with which they had very little experience. It was thrilling. Sebastian wrapped his arm around Arielle's waist and pulled her into the foyer. She laughed out loud when she heard all of her friends cry out in harmony.

"Wow! What a place." Ian let out a long whistle.

"If these walls could talk..." Eva said as she leaned closer to Ian.

"What do you mean?" Ian asked, turning back to look at her.

"Well, I'm sure we would have been told fascinating stories about this house, or should I say this castle. Somehow the word 'house' doesn't fit this spectacular place. I would love to get an evocative glimpse of the past."

Sebastian heard Eva's comments, and as he glanced back, Eva noticed the ghost of a smile touching his lips. Eva's eyebrows furrowed. "Well?" she asked, looking pointedly at Sebastian.

His smile became more evident. "It's true," he said. His gaze swept the surroundings. "This house has been through some horrid times, and has borne witness to some tumultuous events, such as during the Hundred Years War between France and England." His voice was firm, filled with pride. "There are a few estates similar to this one that are scattered around France and date back to the first century. They have huge landscapes, amazing gardens, stunning lakes, fountains, and awesome, unsurpassed views of the ocean. I have heard that they offer mystique and romance to the people that step inside these estates," he said. His mouth curved into an enigmatic smile. Silence filled the space between the friends as they stared intently at Sebastian, waiting for him to elaborate on his statement. However, he didn't. He just shook his head as if he had awakened some long, unheeded memory, and snaking his arms tighter around Arielle, he bent down and brushed his lips against her ear.

It was Gabrielle who broke the silence. "Was this house ever open to the public?"

Sebastian didn't reply at once, his jaw was set at a straight line. He seemed to be lost somewhere, in another place and time. Then he replied, his voice cautious, "It was, but that was a very long time ago."

Arielle noticed the way the words fell from his lips and the change in the tone of his voice. *What in the world is wrong with him?* Arielle thought. *There's nothing wrong with Gabby's question.* Looking up, their gaze locked.

"What is it, Sebastian?"

Sebastian seemed alarmed that she had been able to see into his troubled thoughts. "Nothing," he said quickly. Turning his gaze toward Gabrielle, he said, "It is my home now, and it's closed to the public."

Arielle made a mental note to probe into Sebastian's thoughts later on, in the privacy of their room. It was obvious that he didn't want to discuss it now any further. But again, she couldn't understand what the big deal was about a simple question such as whether the house had been open to the public.

"Is the place haunted?" Ian asked, looking around the huge foyer. "I've heard that most castles in France are haunted."

Sebastian scratched his chin thoughtfully and chuckled. "I've never seen any ghosts in this house. I don't think you need to worry about that. But then again, some mysteries are better kept than shared," he added, smiling mischievously.

Ian's, Eva's, and Gabrielle's eyes widened. Troy laughed out loud at their expressions. Sebastian joined in laughing.

"He's playing with you, Ian," Troy said. "The stories about ghosts are just stories to attract visitors."

"Of course, I knew that," Ian said and laughed along with his friends.

Gabrielle had moved to the window. She traced the panel with her fingertips. "I sure would love to hear the history behind this house," she said, glancing at Sebastian with a pleading look.

"Me too," Arielle whispered. They were all in agreement.

Sebastian gave Arielle a playful squeeze. He was happy to walk them through the house and share stories about each face and every portrait. Arielle and her friends were amazed at the amount of information and the details he provided. There were stories behind almost every piece of furniture and every piece of art.

"It's like listening to a CD from the History channel," she said delightedly.

Sebastian arched a brow. He bent down and pressed a soft kiss on her lips. He told them about the stones and other materials that his ancestors had shipped to St. Jean to create this massive, beautiful structure, as well as the names of famous masons and architects of the sixteenth and seventeenth centuries who had put themselves, body and soul into completing the work. He talked about the woodcarvers who spent thousands of hours carving the shapes and designs that decorated the window panels, doors, and ceilings; about the sculptors who created the beautiful statues in the house; and finally, the famous painters who painted the canvases that covered the walls.

"What about the tapestries? Were those purchased or made by the ladies who lived here?" Gabrielle asked.

"Some were purchased during trips to the Far East, and others were handmade in this house," Sebastian answered. "Some of them were made by my great-great-grandmother, Elizabeth Gaulle. She loved to create beautiful art. She made all the tapestries that are hanging in the halls upstairs. Her portrait is right here."

He walked slowly and stopped in front of the portrait of a lady. Her beauty was striking. The color of her eyes was a deep green, just like Sebastian's. Her lips were sensuous, and her hair was long and dark. The hair color made her pale face stand out like a statue of a goddess. Just below the portrait, a label read, "Elizabeth Gaulle."

"She is stunning," Arielle said, wonderment in her voice. "Her eyes are that amazing emerald green color, the same as yours."

"I have my mother's eyes, and she had her mother's eyes," he murmured softly so the others couldn't hear.

"I would love to see a portrait of your mother," Arielle whispered, casting a glance at their friends, who were engrossed in examining various portraits on the wall.

Sebastian clasped her hand and pulled her a few feet down the corridor, stopping in front of another portrait. Arielle was anxious to look at the face of the woman who had given birth to her gorgeous dream. She approached the painting and stared. She was a striking woman.

"She's lovely," Arielle said, smiling with pleasure. Reaching up, she ran the back of her hand down Sebastian's amazing face. He trapped her with his gaze, and drawing a taut breath, he nodded.

"Sebastian, she is gorgeous," Gabrielle and Eva said with one voice, coming up behind them.

Sebastian smiled and looked at the painting of his mother with pride. "I know," he said, a slight catch in his velvety voice. "This was my great grandmother," he added, knowing the questions that would arise from Eva and Ian if he told them the truth.

Arielle leaned closer to read the name below the portrait. It read, "Syele Gaulle."

"Syele," she whispered. "What a fascinating name!"

"That was my great-great-great-grandmother's name as well," Sebastian added and tightened the grip on her arm. Turning to face his friends, he smiled lightly. "Let's go upstairs. I will show you the bedrooms, and you can choose where you want to stay. They have all been prepared, and all the views are wonderful, so just make your choices, and take as much time as you like to freshen up. We'll meet—let's say in a couple of hours—down at the library if that is all right with you."

They climbed the huge staircase together, and suddenly Arielle was back in a familiar hallway. This was the very hallway that had sent waves of fright down her spine the last time she was here. But somehow, she didn't feel the same way now. She felt safe and warm walking next to Sebastian. As if he could hear her thoughts, he wrapped his arm around her and pulled her closer to his side.

All the bedrooms were spacious and decorated with exquisite taste. Gabrielle and Eva picked bedrooms with views of the cliffs and the beautiful ocean extending as far as the eye could see. Gabrielle looked at Arielle with a great big smile, her eyes bright with excitement.

Eva ran over and hugged Sebastian and Arielle, and the guys shook Sebastian's hand with pure delight. As Sebastian and Arielle walked away, they could hear them all chattering with exhilaration about the house and the location.

They walked down a long hallway and finally arrived at Sebastian's room, which was located at the west corner of the house. Arielle yelped as he scooped her up in his arms, as if she were completely weightless, and carried her into the bedroom. Her jaw dropped. She was stunned by the grandeur of the room. It was huge and decorated with impeccable taste. The furniture looked expensive and quite old. Arielle was sure that these were precious antiques. Sebastian's bed was massive. It featured a remarkable backboard carved with beautiful images of foliage, birds, and flowers that looked like rare orchids. The bed cover was magnificent. It was made of black silk with brown and cream designs that matched the backboard carvings. A huge pile of pillows was heaped on the bed. Sebastian set her down, and Arielle suddenly had a strange desire to run and jump on the bed. She was sure it would be soft and very inviting. She suppressed the desire, giggling at the thought, as she moved around the room, exploring.

Sebastian stood leaning against the doorframe, arms crossed over his chest, watching her.

"What's so funny?"

She glanced his way, and her lips curved up.

"The bed is huge. I'll need a ladder to get up there," she said, giggling again.

"That will not be necessary," he said, moving so fast that she almost gasped in shock. He picked her up and quickly set her in the middle of the bed. Arielle giggled with delight.

"That wasn't hard at all was it?" he said, laughing out loud.

Arielle loved listening to the sound of his laughter. "No, not for you, but what if I'm here alone?"

"Oh… trust me; you'll *never* be alone in this bed, baby," he said. He reached out and pulled her off the bed, and into his tight embrace. "Welcome home, sweetheart," he whispered and brushed his lips against hers.

His words startled Arielle. She had never believed that she could be the lady of a magnificent house like this one.

"You have got to be joking."

"About what?"

"This glorious house? Being my home?"

"As an immortal, you know that I can't tell a lie," he said and added, "Arielle, you'd best just get used to it. This is your new life."

He pulled her toward the sofa. "Now sit down," he said. "I have something to show you." He moved toward the closet and pulled out a large flat package. He set it in front of her and smiled.

"I love you, Arielle. I hope you love this as much as I do."

Arielle blinked, and he held her gaze. "What is it?" she asked.

"That would be telling," he chuckled.

"For me?" she whispered.

"Yes, for you. It's a gift, open it and see."

Her hands shook as she pulled the paper away, and her jaw dropped.

She looked at him astonished, and it took a long moment for her mind to wrap around the overwhelming sensation as tears welled up in her eyes, and her lips trembled. "Sebastian, this is so thoughtful," she said. "What have I ever done to deserve someone like you?" Powerful emotions surged through her body, and tears streamed down her face, but she didn't care to brush them away. She was speechless. Delight welled up in her like a long wave in the ocean that moves continuously without breaking.

The gift was a painting of the beach at St. Jean de Luz. What Arielle thought of as "their" cove was detailed down to the last grain of sand. A girl with long brown hair was sitting on a beach towel, just as she had been when they first met. On the bottom of the painting was the title, "Arielle."

Arielle brushed the tears from her face and tried to focus on the details of the painting, but she failed miserably, finally letting them fall freely. Surging up to her feet, she turned and placed the painting on the sofa carefully. Then, spinning around in one swift move, she flung herself into his arms in sheer bliss. Sebastian rocked back and chuckled, he steadied himself. Cupping her chin, he lifted her face up until their gazes were locked. His mouth came down on hers, and her lips parted, giving him access to the softness of her mouth. He kissed her hungrily. She slipped her fingers into his soft hair, molding into him.

He pulled back from the kiss, winded. "I guess you like it, then," he said, his voice low, a whisper.

"Yes! Yes! Yes! Yes! I love it! I've never seen anything so beautiful in my life—besides you, that is." Her gaze scanned his face and their eyes locked. He chuckled, and his lips hungrily returned to hers, driving his need to a maddening level. Her heart leaped to her throat and scalding heat washed over her like a tsunami. She was drowning in his wild passion. Sebastian felt her need, the tension of her muscles, and his nerves unraveled dangerously. She tried to break away, but his arms tightened around her like a steel cage. She surrendered to his powerful persuasion with a deep groan. Sebastian smiled inwardly, his body ready to explode with joy. She was his, and would be his for eternity.

When she finally broke away from his kiss, he eased her back, and she stumbled, trying to rein in her faculties.

Finding her voice, she looked up and met Sebastian's adoring gaze. The floor wavered beneath his feet as her sparkling sapphire eyes met his, enveloping him with a potent heat, and leaving his mind reeling utterly out of control. He hauled in a sharp breath. *I will never understand the effect she has on me. I'm completely and utterly bewitched,* he thought to himself and shook his head astounded. He tried hard to focus on her next question.

"When did you have this done? I've been with you most of the time." His lips curved slightly, and his hands reached for her. "Oh, I had this ordered some time ago. But it was delivered just last week."

Arielle ran her finger lightly across the frame and smiled, enchanted. She just couldn't get over the detail on the painting. It looked so real; she couldn't keep her eyes away from it.

"Can we take it to Brighton? I want to look at it every day."

"Sure. That was the plan," he said, and his lips curved into a full smile.

Arielle thought that this was the perfect moment to find out why Gabby's simple question about the house being open to the public had created such a troublesome look on Sebastian's face. As she watched him closely, without saying a word, he immediately narrowed his gaze. "What is it?" he asked, voice tense.

"Sebastian, why did you find it so hard to answer Gabby's question?"

"I'm not sure I follow you," he said, feigning ignorance.

"She asked you if the house was open to the public, and you seemed quite troubled by the question. Or at least uneasy."

Sebastian stiffened, but quickly he shrugged his shoulders, feigning nonchalance. "Oh, I'm sorry you thought I was uneasy. I just had nothing more to say." *Was I that obvious?* He thought. Arielle's next statement stunned him into a shocked state of disbelief.

"Yes, you were that obvious," Arielle said calmly as if she were answering his thought.

He took a sharp breath. A puzzled frown spread across his face. He studied her face, his eyes peering in her very soul. "Arielle, can you read my thoughts?" His eyes narrowed, and his breath caught in his throat, waiting for her answer.

His question lingered between them for a short moment. "Oh, God no!" she replied, appalled. "Why would you ever think that? Do you think I would ever hide something like that from you?"

Reaching around her neck, she unlocked her necklace and placed it in his hand. "Maybe you want to check for yourself," she said, her tone a bit short. *How could he doubt me?* She thought.

Sebastian gazed into the calm of Arielle's eyes and smiled, pleased to find out that she wasn't able to read his thoughts. For a moment, he lost himself in her eyes, but then quickly shook his head. His lips curved lightly. "I don't mind if you can read my thoughts," he said, "I only wondered why you didn't tell me."

"Well, I can't," she said, utterly frustrated. Taking her necklace back, she fastened it around her neck. "So, now that you know… maybe you can answer my question, and quit trying to change the subject."

Pulling her tightly into his embrace, he bent down and pressed a tender kiss on her lips. "Always in need of details," he chuckled.

Arielle shrugged her shoulders. "Yep, that's me," she said, stifling a giggle.

Swallowing, Sebastian closed his eyes and let the past slip right into his brain. Opening his eyes, he let his gaze move past Arielle and, smiling softly, he started to tell his story.

"My father had a precious letter opener that was given to him by my mother as a wedding gift. He kept it in his study, in his desk drawer. It was beautiful and very valuable. The handle was adorned with precious stones: rubies, sapphires, and emeralds. It was my father's most valued possession, not because of its worth, but because it was given to him by my mother."

His voice was underlined with emotion as he continued. "The house was open to the public centuries after my parents passed on, but the treasures remained in the house. I had hired one of the most reliable security companies in France. All their employees were active or retired members of the French Interpol. I felt pretty secure that nothing would be disturbed as long as these men were in charge of the house while people visited the grounds and walked through the house."

He took a deep breath and let out a deep sigh. "One day, I received a call from the head of the security office advising me that there had been a break in, and some of the most valuable items in my father's study had disappeared. When I arrived, I immediately closed the house to the public and went through the list of stolen items with security. The letter opener was one of the items missing. I don't think I have ever felt pain like that. This letter opener was the only thing that reminded me of my human side. It was a true symbol of the love between my parents, of their union." He stopped talking, lost in thought.

Arielle held back the tears as she listened to him speak. She took a deep breath and reaching up, she ran her fingertip down the side of his beautiful, sad face. "I'm so sorry for upsetting you with my dumb questions," she said, regretting her curiosity.

He reached for her and drew her into his embrace. "I've looked everywhere, but I haven't been able to find any of the items. But I have a feeling that I know who took them."

Her eyes shot up, "You know?"

"Yes," he said and dragged in a breath. "He's immortal, and he has a home not too far from here. I'll find him one day, and I'll deal with him in my own way," he added, his lips set into a straight line.

"His home is near your home?" Arielle asked, studying his face.

"Yes, his home is open to the public because he doesn't live there any longer. I was told by a few acquaintances that he was heard to be bragging about some of the items in his possession. Items. That. Belong.

To. Me!" he said, enunciating each word with a passion. Putting his finger under Arielle's chin, he lifted her face to his and pressed a soft kiss on her lips; he said, "And it is *our* home, not *my* home."

Arielle blinked and smiled tenderly. "Okay, our home," she murmured happily and kissed him back.

Then clasping her hand, he pulled her toward the bathroom. "Let's take a shower," he said seductively, and she shivered with anticipation.

They took a shower, freshened up, and went downstairs to meet the others, who were already there looking through the thousands of books on the shelves of the enormous library. They all turned around as Arielle and Sebastian came into the room.

"This is the most fascinating library I have ever seen," Ian exclaimed. "Some of these books go as far back as the twelfth century."

Sebastian's lips curved appreciatively. "Thanks, Ian, many members of my family have added books to this library, each according to their own preference. I'm sure there is a book in there to suit everyone's needs."

Ian's gaze swept the library one more time, and waving his arm in the air, he exclaimed once again, "Sebastian, this is a hell of a library, man."

Sebastian just smiled. "How would you all like to go horseback riding?" he asked.

"Well," said Gabrielle, "now you are talking."

Arielle and Eva burst out laughing, knowing Gabrielle's passion for horses.

"So, you're a rider?" Sebastian asked.

Gabrielle nodded instantly. "Yes, I love horses. I've been riding since I was six years old."

"That was not so long ago," said Troy as he pulled her into his arms.

"What are you suggesting?" Gabrielle said playfully as she reached up on her tippy toes and set her lips to Troy's passionately.

"Mmmm," Troy muttered eagerly. "You're just a baby," he said teasingly.

"A baby? I'm twenty years old," she said defiantly.

Troy pulled her back into his heated embrace once again, and covered her mouth with his, stopping her from arguing. They all chuckled.

"Do you all ride?" Sebastian asked, glancing at Ian, Eva, and Arielle.

"Absolutely," Ian replied. Sebastian's gaze next focused on Eva. Her lips were pressed in a straight line. Sebastian's eyebrows furrowed. Eva's thoughts were an open book to him, but he couldn't stop himself from asking anyway.

"Eva?"

She swallowed hard, and glancing at Ian she said hesitatingly, "I don't know how to ride, but I'm willing to learn if Ian will help me."

Ian's eyes lit up, and he pulled her into his arms. "I'll be right next to you, my love, don't worry. You'll do fine," he said with a convincing smile as he bent down and gave Eva a peck on the lips.

Sebastian turned his gaze toward Arielle and found himself staring into a passionate pair of sapphire eyes. His eyes widened, and she lowered her gaze, turning away from him. He had obviously hit a sore subject. He snaked his arm around her waist and pulled her around to face him. "Are you telling me there is something you don't do well?"

Arielle frowned. "This is something I don't do *at all*," she replied in a low voice. Sebastian shook his head to and fro, and a low chuckle escaped his beautiful lips.

"I'm amazed that I've finally found something that you can't do. But why is that?"

"I'm afraid of horses. Eva and I are more the books and music kind of girls. We left all the athletic activities to Gabrielle." The three girls exchanged meaningful glances, remembering that after each summer holiday, Gabrielle was the only one that came back with horseback riding stories.

Silence stretched. "What's going on?" Ian asked, breaking the quiet.

"Nothing," answered Eva, glancing briefly at Ian.

"Come on, let's all go," Sebastian said. He put his finger under Arielle's chin and lifted it to meet his gaze. "I'll help you and show you that horses are a lot of fun." She opened her mouth to say something, but she changed her mind, and her lips tightened. "Come on; there is nothing to be afraid of," he pressed on, and clasping her hand in his he pulled her towards the door as everyone followed.

In the garage, there were a few very nice cars available for their use. "Take whichever car you like, and follow us," Sebastian said. "The keys are in the ignition." They chose a pretty blue four-door Mercedes. Sebastian opened the passenger door to a snappy red sports car, and Arielle slipped in. He turned the music on and pulled out of the driveway and onto the country road, followed by their friends in the blue Mercedes.

They rode for a long while in silence. Arielle peeked at Sebastian from the corner of her eye, and she could see a grin teasing his mouth. He looked relaxed as he settled back contentedly against his seat, keeping his eyes on the road. She felt anxious, feeling the pressure of having to be part of something she considered difficult, unattainable. Despite her desire to please Sebastian, all she was thinking was she wanted to turn and go back. Horseback riding was Sebastian's sport, his true passion. Suddenly she was guarded, fear claiming her thoughts.

Sebastian felt her anxiety. "What's wrong?" he asked and squeezed her hand affectionately.

"Sebastian, I'm not sure about horseback riding. I'm scared of horses," she said, shifting in her seat uncomfortably.

"I'll be right next to you, my love. I will not let anything happen to you," he said and gave her a reassuring glance. "You might find that you enjoy it."

She stared at him for a long moment, assessing his words, and started to protest but decided against it. She just shrugged and pressed her hand against her pounding temple. "I am sure I will not," she muttered sulkily, her doubt palpable.

Sebastian smiled, and leaning over, he pressed a kiss on her cheek. "You might be surprised, you never know," he insisted. She didn't reply, just waved her hand indifferently.


When they arrived at the stables, a young man was sitting outside, leaning back in his chair against the wall. He jumped up when he saw Sebastian approaching. "Hello, Mr. Gaulle," Arielle heard him say, a bright smile on his face.

"Hello, Edward, how are you?"

"Just fine, sir. Are you going to do a little riding today?"

"Yes, can you please get six horses ready for us? Two very mild ones for the two young ladies over here," he added, pointing at Eva and Arielle with a teasing smile. Then he turned to Ian and Troy. "Let's change into riding gear while the girls get familiar with their horses."

They walked to a small house next to the stable. The girls waited outside for the horses and enjoyed the amazing view of the hills and the ocean. The fresh scent of hay and the crisp fragrance of the morning air made Gabrielle smile.

"Arielle, he must be very wealthy," Gabrielle said when the men were out of sight.

"I don't know. I've never asked," Arielle said truthfully.

Before long the guys came back outside, and the girls nearly swooned. They were outfitted from head to toe in the most elegant riding gear the girls had ever seen. They looked like they had just stepped out of the pages of a Gothic novel. They were tall, stunningly handsome, with smiles that would make any young woman's heart rate double. They were quite literally a breathtaking sight.

"Girls, your turn," Sebastian said. "Everything you need is in there. There are various sizes and colors you can choose from," he said to Gabrielle, knowing that she was an experienced horsewoman. Eva and Arielle had no idea what they would need, so they waited for Gabrielle to guide them. As she helped them dress, she also gave them a short lesson about each item, beginning with the riding helmet. "You need the helmet because there is always a risk when you are riding."

"Don't remind us, please, Gabby," Eva said.

"Next, we need boots," Gabrielle said. "These are great. They're paddock boots, specially designed to prevent your foot from getting caught in the stirrup if you're thrown from your horse." Arielle looked at Eva, who wasn't looking so good. "Next, the vest."

Arielle was fighting nausea as she listened to Gabby explain that the vest was designed to protect their vital organs if they fell. She wasn't sure that this was something she wanted to be doing today, and she knew that Eva was feeling the same. Gabrielle looked at both of them, at their grim expressions, and laughed out loud.

"The pants aren't essential, but they make the ride much more comfortable," she said. That was somewhat comforting until she added that they were designed to protect the lower leg from irritation or bruising due to rubbing against the stirrup straps.

"My God!" Arielle exclaimed in a voice full of anxiety. "Is there anything safe about being on a horse?"

"It's a lot of fun, but you need to be protected," Gabrielle said with a chuckle.

"I'm not sure I want to do this," Eva said.

"Oh, come on you guys, get over yourselves. We'll all be with you; nothing is going to happen." Gabrielle turned around and walked toward the door followed by Eva and Arielle.

"Oh boy, here we go," Arielle said quietly, glancing at Eva. Eva opened her mouth to say something, but she was interrupted by the sound of laughter. Both Eva and Arielle turned as one and found Gabrielle looking at them, hands on her hips, shaking her head at them. Finally, she threw her hands up in the air in an over-the-top movement. "You both look like you are going to the guillotine."

"You are not funny, Gabby," Arielle mumbled, glaring at her, utterly frustrated.

"Okay, okay, I'm sorry," Gabby said, walking back and standing in front of her two friends. "I was only joking. I truly believe that you'll enjoy it if you just give it a chance." She stared at both of them with a sincere look on her face, then turned and walked out the door. "Cowards," she said, loud enough for them to hear her and laughed again. And this time, she didn't stop. Turning back, she saw her friends watching her, stunned shock on their faces.

"Oh, my God!" she called out, throwing her hands once again up in the air. "I'm *joking!*" This time, they all laughed, and Gabby let out a sigh of relief.


The guys were standing by their horses, carrying on an inaudible conversation. But the girls could tell that whatever they were discussing was quite amusing because they were laughing ardently. As they approached their beaux, the three stopped and stared in awe at these three astounding specimens of male beauty.

Ian was the first one to look up and notice the girls. "Mmm-mmm, get a load of that," he said in admiration.

Troy and Sebastian whirled around and found themselves staring at three stunningly beautiful girls—*their* girls." Deep smiles curved their lips, and long, low whistles divulged their appreciation of the girls' beauty. Ian moved toward them slowly, and as he approached Eva, he reached for her. They stood for a moment gazing into each other's eyes. Then, Ian lowered his gaze and stepped much closer. Reaching out he pulled Eva into his arms. "You look amazing, but a little worried," he whispered, "Don't worry, I'll not leave your side, my love." Eva looked up at him and smiled nervously. Clasping her hand, he pulled her toward the horses.

Gabrielle was already standing by her horse, a big male beauty named Rêve de Minuit. With one hand she was holding the reins, and with the other she was petting the horse on his neck with soft sweeping strokes while whispering sweet nothings in his ear. *What in the world is she telling that horse?* Arielle thought and chuckled at the sight. Gabby looked as if she could feel the joy of her touch emanating from the horse. She noticed Sebastian and Troy exchanging glances. Finally, they both laughed out loud, at one point doubling over with laughter.

She couldn't hear what Gabby was saying, but of course, immortal ears could hear a pin fall in the hay.

Gabrielle looked up, startled, and saw Troy and Sebastian straightening up and winking at each other.

"What in bloody hell is wrong with you two?" she called out.

Troy waved his hand, dismissing her question, and with two long strides, she was in his arms and locked in a hot kiss.

Arielle had felt the heat of Sebastian's body before she saw him move. He was suddenly standing close to her. She looked up and their gazes locked. His arms snaked around her waist, and he pulled her closer. She wanted to ask about Gabby and what she had said to the horse, but his mouth came down on hers with toe curling passion, wiping away every thought she ever had. His tongue slipped inside the softness of her mouth and pleasure spread like fire. They lost themselves in the moment, forgetting where they were.

A soft cough made them stop and look around. Troy was busy with Gabby, and Ian with Eva but Edward was still standing close by, trying to look inconspicuous, but clearly uncomfortable with the displays of affection. Sebastian dropped his hands, and Arielle pulled away from his tight embrace. Sebastian cleared his throat, and clasping her hand, he pulled her toward her horse.

"Are you ready to do this?" he asked, grinning.

"I'm not so sure. But I'll try," she said honestly.

"Don't worry, baby. I'll be right next to you."

"Don't worry," she said, trying to mimic his calm voice, but she felt anything but confident.

A wide smile spread across Sebastian's face. "You look a bit pale, darling. Do you feel all right?" he asked, chuckling. Arielle now knew that he was playing with her, not understanding her very real fear.

"She's fine," Gabrielle said. "She's just scared."

"Oh, gee, thanks, Gabby." Arielle shot her friend a look of disapproval. Gabrielle just laughed. Arielle could see that in her mind she was thinking warmly of her and that she was excited to be on a horse again.

Sebastian's desire to kiss her increased. He cradled her face in his hands and bending down he captured her lips in a warm kiss. Pulling back from the kiss reluctantly, he smiled and pulled her to stand next to a very large horse.

"Look," he said. "Eva is already on the horse."

She looked up, surprised to see that he was right. Eva was sitting on the horse, but she was not looking as confident as the rest of them. Arielle could read her mind and what she saw in Eva's mind was nothing like the look on Eva's face. She was clearly scared to death but wanted to do this for Ian. Arielle looked up at Sebastian and pursed her lips together. His lips curved into a sensual smile.

"Come along!" he said and helped her get into the saddle.

Clutching at the horse's bridle, she drew in a deep breath. "Oh, God, here I go…" she said, in a low voice, but they all heard her and laughed out loud. She took a deep breath and shifted on the saddle uncomfortably. She was trembling, face ghostly white, but she was on the horse. *Well,* she thought to herself, *this isn't so bad. But of course, the horse hasn't moved yet.*

Sebastian handed her the reins and quickly showed her what she needed to do. He vaulted onto the horse with ease, and he looked glorious.

They all started to move forward slowly, and Arielle found out that the ride was not as bad as she had feared. Ian stayed close to Eva, and Sebastian close to Arielle. Troy and Gabrielle were very comfortable, and they rode a bit ahead.

"What is the horse's name?" Arielle asked when she dared to say anything.

"Whisper," Sebastian answered.

"Why, for heaven's sake, should I do that?" she asked, glancing at him, puzzled.

"Do what?"

"Why should I whisper?"

Sebastian tried but failed to suppress laughter that was slowly pulsating through his body. He finally succumbed and exploded into laughter, followed by Ian and Eva. When they finally stopped laughing, they found Arielle watching them all, speechless.

"What in bloody hell is so funny?" she finally asked crisply.

There was an abrupt silence, while Sebastian, Ian, and Eva exchanged amusing looks.

"Well, am I going to be privy to your joke?" she asked. She feigned indifference, but she was hurt.

Sebastian coughed to clear his voice and kept his lips from turning up into a smile.

"I'm sorry, baby, but this was quite funny. Whisper is the horse's name," he explained.

Arielle's eyes widened and her mouth shaped into an "Oh." She clapped her hand over her mouth and chuckled quietly.

"He and Shadow, Eva's horse, are very mild, wonderful horses. You will be fine. Trust me."

Arielle looked cautiously over at Eva. She wore a big smile on her face and looked good riding Shadow, right next to Ian.

Anyone who looked at Eva and Arielle would have seen two girls too scared to do anything *but* trust their horses. They started out at a slow trot and, little by little, Arielle started to relax the topline. The saddle was comfortable, and she began to feel a bit more secure.

She could see that her friends were all skilled in horsemanship methods. They had great command of their horses. Eva, too, looked as if she was doing well.

After a while, Arielle also began to relax and actually enjoy herself.

# *Note to Readers*

Thank you to my fans. It is the most rewarding and surreal experience to receive your wonderful feedback after reading my books. To the future readers, thank you for loving books and making my book your choice. This is the second novel in my *Immortal Rapture Series*. I hope you will enjoy it.

# ALSO BY LILIAN ROBERTS

*Arielle Immortal Awakening* (Paranormal Romance) Sebastian's and Arielle's love may be eternal, but they could be running out of time.

## Contact Information
My website: lilianroberts.com
My Twitter: @lilian3roberts
My Blog: lilianroberts.blogspot.com